The Vampire's Accidental Wife

Nocturne Falls, Book Eight

Kristen Painter

THE VAMPIRE'S ACCIDENTAL WIFE:
Nocturne Falls, Book Eight

ISBN: 978-1-941695-29-6

Published in the United States of America.

Welcome to Nocturne Falls, the town that celebrates Halloween 365 days a year. The tourists think it's all a show: the vampires, the werewolves, the witches, the occasional gargoyle flying through the sky. But the supernaturals populating the town know better.

Living in Nocturne Falls means being yourself. Fangs, fur, and all.

Las Vegas headliner and vampire Desdemona Valentine is one cool, collected diva on the outside. On the inside, she's petrified of falling in love after her last relationship nearly killed her…literally. Protecting her wounded heart makes for a lonely life, but she has her fame and fortune to keep her company. Who needs anything more?

Julian Ellingham does. One look at Desdemona on stage, and the vampire is smitten. She initially ignores him, but his relentless pursuit pays off when a wild night ends in a Vegas wedding. Finally, Julian has everything he wants while all Desdemona wants is…a divorce.

Julian sweet-talks Desdemona into letting him prove his love, but his time is running out. Especially after someone repeatedly tries to turn his bride to ash. When Desdemona flees Vegas for the spooky streets of Nocturne Falls and Julian's protection, he's more than willing to help out. But can he convince Desdemona to trust him, or will 'death do us part' become a reality?

Dedicated to my amazing mom.
Thanks for your support,
your proofreading, and the morning walks.
Love you.

SEPTEMBER

For the briefest of moments, Julian Ellingham awoke thinking tonight was going to be just like every other night of his life. But then he remembered the woman in the bed beside him, and he smiled.

Tonight was not *at all* like every other night of his life. Tonight was the start of something very new and very wonderful.

He rolled onto his side and propped his head in his hand.

There she was. The most beautiful creature he'd ever laid eyes on—and in his nearly four hundred years, he'd laid eyes (and other things) on more women than he could count.

Her gorgeous brown skin gleamed against the ivory bedsheets with the glow only a goddess of her magnitude could achieve. Because make no mistake, she *was* a goddess. A Caribbean goddess, made even more desirable by the fact that she was also a vampiress.

Although her desirability was pretty high already.

He loved the lilt of her voice, the way she cut her eyes at him when he did something she deemed questionable, the curves of her body, her wit and intelligence, and the tiny heart-shaped birthmark on the instep of her left foot. But those things were not to be outdone by the haughty tilt of her head that accompanied any suggestion she thought beneath her, the almost feline grace she possessed that caused men to watch her walk by, the brilliance and speed of her thought processes, and the way she constantly smelled of orange blossoms.

He was sick with love. Besotted. Giddy as a schoolboy. And he'd never been happier. Because not only was the great and glorious Desdemona Valentine in his bed, but as of last night's wild, but amazing, events, she was also now his wife.

The woman he'd been wooing for these many, many months had finally succumbed to his charms, but the evening's outcome had been beyond his wildest dreams.

It was pretty incredible what you could accomplish in Vegas at all hours of the night.

Granted, it hadn't been that late when they'd gotten the marriage license, but then they'd also started drinking rather early. Champagne and lots of it, because Desi was in the mood to celebrate, champagne was her favorite and when it came to spoiling her, there were no limits.

Then they'd found themselves in the Little White Chapel. Or the Chapel of Love. Or maybe it had been the Blue Suede Chapel? He couldn't really remember, but he knew they'd been in a chapel and he knew they'd gotten married, just like he knew they'd kept the party going long after they'd tied the knot.

Desi had imbibed quite a bit more than he had but, right up until the moment she'd passed out in his arms, she'd seemed pretty much in control of her faculties.

After that, he'd carried her back here to her condo in the Skye Towers and they'd crashed. Well, technically, she'd already been crashed. He'd just gotten her out of her dress, tucked her into bed, then tucked himself right in next to her.

The marriage had yet to be consummated, but taking care of her came first. That was what a husband did for his wife. Everything else could wait. Besides, they had centuries ahead of them.

He sighed in happiness.

As much as he wished she'd wake up, he also wanted to let her sleep. She might be just a touch hung over. He wasn't, but then, he'd had a fast metabolism even as a human, something becoming a vampire had only increased.

He slipped out of bed, careful not to disturb her, and went into the kitchen to see what she had in her fridge. A shelf of steaks, six liters of blood, and a case of good champagne. He laughed. A woman after his own heart, but then, that's why he'd married her.

He took out a pint of blood and poured himself some breakfast. He wasn't so fond of it cold, but warming it up would make noise.

For his beloved, he would suffer.

He downed his meal, then decided to pour a goblet for Desi. If she wasn't awake, he'd just leave it on her nightstand while he took a shower. And if she wasn't up by the time he got out, he'd wake her. Gently. She had to be up soon anyway. She had a show to do at nine p.m., and getting ready took an hour and a half.

After all these months, he knew her schedule better than he knew his own.

He would not be the reason his lovely bride was late for work, nor would he cause all those ticket holders to riot if the Vamp herself didn't show.

Vegas was known for its outrageous shows, and hers was no exception. Vamp was an extravaganza of music, magic, dancing, and special effects. Not surprisingly, the production had become the hottest ticket in town in the year it had been running. It was genius really, the kind of stuff Nocturne Falls had turned into an industry.

She was a vampire playing a vampire, and no one knew the truth, but her magic on stage was her magic in real life, and some of the special effects were just her inherent vampire abilities. There was a witch who worked on the show too, providing some of the other illusions, but Desi's true nature was the real star.

He walked back into the bedroom, leaving the lights off so as not to wake her, and sat in the chair at her dressing table, setting the glass there for a moment so he could just take her in and appreciate what a lucky man he was.

Watching her show was also how he'd fallen in love with her.

He'd gone to see it on a lark when he'd been in Vegas researching wedding chapels before opening one in Nocturne Falls, and the title of her show had intrigued him. He'd seen her stunning face on billboards and taxi advertisements, and had decided it was time to check her out in person. He'd gotten bored with the nightclub scene, anyway. Hanging out in the VIP section, surrounded by a new squad of beautiful young women every night, was fun for a while, but no human woman would ever really be enough for him.

He wanted a partner. An equal. And while his brother Hugh had successfully turned his human girlfriend into a vampire, Julian didn't want to attempt it. Turnings weren't always successful, and the thought of losing the woman he loved—and being the cause of it—would have been more than he could take.

So that fateful night in Vegas he'd gone to Vamp, expecting to see a pitiful imitation of his reality and hoping, at best, to be pulled out of his doldrums for a while. Instead, he'd been enthralled. He'd watched from the front row, mesmerized by Desdemona's beauty and magnetism for the entire seventy-five-minute performance.

By the end of it, he'd had a strong suspicion that Ms. Valentine was doing all her own stunts. The underwater routine, appearing at three different places in the theater within seconds, gracefully lifting her dancers overhead without any sign of effort…those were all feats that would be difficult for a human without some kind of technical assistance, but for a vampire? Small, easy tasks.

But the most telling of all her "special effects" was the glow in her eyes. How would any show producer know to add that unless they'd met a vampire, or the star of the show actually was one?

It all added up to a pressing desire to meet her. And so he did, using his vampire charm and speed to slip past security and into her dressing room before she returned to it.

She'd sensed him before she'd seen him, confirming everything he'd suspected.

"You're not the first," she'd said, slipping out of her jet-encrusted headdress.

He'd played dumb. "Not the first what?"

"Vampire to come see me." She'd drawn a black silk robe over her barely there outfit that was mostly rhinestones and leather.

"So you know what I am?"

She'd finally faced him. "Just like you know what I am."

He'd smiled and nodded. "I had to see for myself."

She'd looked bored, which amused him. "And now that you have, you can go." She'd gestured toward the door with one long, pointed, blood-red nail.

"Come to dinner with me," he'd countered.

"Why?"

"Why not?"

She'd proceeded to give him a dozen reasons and promised to keep going, so he'd acquiesced and left. The damage, however, had been done.

He wanted her. How could he not? She was a challenge, and that wasn't something he was used to, or willing to back down from. It was intoxicating. He sent her an extravagant bouquet of rare Juliet roses the next day and returned to his front-row seat at her show the next night.

She'd made brief eye contact with him, giving him hope.

He'd sent more flowers the following day with a note saying he hoped they could become better acquainted on his next visit to Vegas.

They hadn't. But he'd persisted. And over the course of the next several months, he'd made numerous trips.

He liked to think it was his charm that had finally gotten to her, but it was more likely that he'd worn her down with his persistence. He'd even changed his hours back to those more traditionally kept by vampires—evenings only— when he was in Vegas with her. He considered that a sacrifice since his family amulet allowed him to be in the sun whenever he liked.

Whatever the reason, she'd finally relented and gone to dinner with him.

Their friendship was a tenuous one. She didn't want a relationship, she made that clear. She liked her life just as it was.

He, on the other hand, wasn't especially fond of his unattached life. And there was something about her he couldn't get enough of.

Then last night had happened. She'd been deliriously happy after finding out that she was getting a television special on a cable network. It was incredible news, and she'd been desperate to celebrate. He'd been in the right place at the right time.

How right, he hadn't imagined until they'd found themselves standing in that chapel.

Even now, sitting in her bedroom, the truth felt surreal.

Married. He, Julian Ellingham, was married. And happy about it. He laughed softly. Who would have thought?

She stirred and rubbed a hand over her face, then yawned and pushed up on her elbows to look toward the windows.

"Good evening."

She jumped. "You."

"Yes, me. Sleep well?" He stood up and carried the goblet to her. "I brought you breakfast. I thought you could use it after last night."

She squinted up at him. "Last night? I don't remember much of it." She looked at the rumpled sheets on the other side of the bed. "Did we—"

"No. We were both very well behaved. Sadly."

Curiosity screwed up her face. "Then what did we do?"

"My darling Desi, we had quite an evening."

Her head agreed with him. She wasn't exactly hungover—that would take some doing for a vampire to achieve—but she also wasn't exactly a hundred percent. If partially hungover was a thing, that's where she was at. She sat up gingerly and took the goblet he was offering. That would help. "Apparently. Come on, what happened?"

His grin was downright annoying. Like he knew something she didn't. Which he did. But still. "Have a look at your hand."

She held out her right hand.

"No," he said. "The other one."

She set the goblet down and stretched that hand out.

Even in the dark, the enormous diamond was impossible to miss. She shrieked. "What the bloody hell is that?"

He laughed. "It's your engagement ring, darling."

"No." She choked back a gasp, trying to keep the panic at bay. "Look, I like you well enough, but I do not want to be engaged." She started to tug the beast of a diamond off her hand. It might be the most gorgeous thing she'd seen since Julian himself, but it was coming off. She refused to go down this road. Again.

"Lucky for you, then."

She stopped pulling at the ring. "Why? I'm confused. Are we not engaged?"

"Technically, no, we are not engaged."

She sighed in relief, her concerns evaporating. Julian did enjoy teasing her.

His smile grew impossibly bigger. "We're married."

Had her heart been beating, it would have stopped. "What?"

He frowned. "Do you really not remember any of last night?"

"I remember celebrating my television deal. And you ordering that magnum of champagne."

"More than one." He held up three fingers.

Her mouth fell open. No wonder her head hurt. "We drank three magnums of champagne?"

"I had half of one. The rest were all you." He shrugged one shoulder. "You seemed pretty happy about it last night, and you were holding up well enough, but…maybe I should have said something."

She shook her head, instantly regretting it. "It wouldn't have stopped me. You know that."

"I do." His smile returned. "It's one of the things I love about you."

She rubbed her temples as the throbbing intensified. She couldn't say those words back. Wouldn't. Because she refused to love anyone. It was one of her rules. And while she liked him tremendously, marriage was off the table. Another of her rules. How on earth had she agreed to such a thing?

He stood. "You need to leave for the show soon. Can I do anything for you? I will, you know. Whatever you need."

She nodded. "I know." He would, too. He was a kind, albeit persistent man. It made him easy to like. Too easy. He was also charming. And handsome. And a real pain in the neck. She lifted the goblet, drained it, then set it down. "Thank you, but I just need to shower and get moving."

He picked up the goblet. "I'll have a refill waiting. And it'll be warm. I didn't warm it up the first time because I didn't want to wake you."

She slid out of bed. She was in the same bra and underwear she'd had on last night, so apparently, they really hadn't consummated the marriage. Yet. Because she could see herself doing that part. Just not with the marriage attached to it.

Rules were rules. Especially when they meant surviving.

She glanced at the ring again. It was a stunner, but then, Julian never did anything by half measures. It was his blessing and his curse. She smiled at him, a little sick at how much she enjoyed his company. "I like you, Jules."

He smiled back. "Always nice to hear from one's wife."

She ignored that. "But I can't be married." She used her standard excuse, because the awful truth was no one's business but hers. "I'm not ready for that. My whole focus is my show and my career."

"I won't interfere, I promise."

She couldn't imagine that would be true. "But what kind of relationship would that be?" She tried to look appropriately disappointed, which wasn't that hard. "What happened between us last night was fueled by alcohol, not love."

"Maybe not on your end, although you had no problem professing your feelings last night."

Now that surprised her. "Well, okay, but it's not really how I feel now." She tugged the ring off and offered it to him. "Please, Jules. I can't accept this. It's too much, and keeping it would be unfair."

He retreated a step. "I don't want that back. You picked it out. It's yours."

"Julian, come on. This isn't some cheap little bauble. It must have cost a fortune." She held it up.

"Unless it's not real. Is this one of those fancy fakes they sell at the casinos?"

He jerked back. "I would never marry you with a fake. It's completely genuine."

Of course it was. Because he was the same way. Completely genuine. And utterly worthy of a woman who could give him everything he deserved. "Then, by all means, return it and get your money back."

"I don't want to. I love you, Desdemona. And you might not feel that way about me yet, but can you say that's not the path we were already on?"

She hesitated. It wasn't her path and never would be, but she didn't want to hurt him any more than she already had. "I...I don't really know."

"Well, I do. I've never felt this way about anyone in my life. And it's been a long life. I'm not giving up this easily."

She groaned. "I'm not saying I don't want to see you anymore. I just can't be married. To you or anyone."

His jaw tightened, and hurt shone in his eyes, making her feel awful. But leading him on would be worse. She liked him too much not to be honest with him.

"One year," he said.

"For what?"

"Stay married to me for one year. Nothing will

change between us. I'll come visit you once or twice a month, like I've been doing, and we'll let things continue to progress the way they have been. I'll make no other demands on you. And at the end of that year, if you still don't love me, we'll get divorced. I won't give you a second of grief about it. You'll never have to think about me again."

It made her sad to consider her life without Julian. He'd become a friend. One of the few she had, which was deliberate, but she also knew that love was a fleeting thing and how quickly it could become something else. Besides, her career was just taking off. Being someone's wife didn't fit into that picture at all. But what was a year? In a vampire's life, not much at all. "Nothing would change?"

"Nothing."

She doubted that, but Julian had never been anything but honest with her. "We live our lives exactly the way we have been."

"Exactly."

She thought about it, tried to play it out in her head. He'd probably get bored before that many months passed. Maybe decide the divorce was the right way to go on his own. "I guess I can do that." She held up the ring. "But I can't wear this. It's the size of a headlight. It'll never go unnoticed. Not to mention I'd have to get Sam one."

Her double, a lovely young woman named

Samantha Arnett, did all of Desi's daytime appearances. Sam could easily pass for Desi, because she was also a skinwalker, meaning she could mimic almost anyone. That made her the perfect double, and thanks to her, Desi's vampire side remained a secret. And Sam was paid handsomely for her work. But not so handsomely that Desi wanted to shell out whatever this ring had cost. Even a fake would be pricey in order to get the quality necessary to make it seem real.

Julian sighed. "Fine, no ring. Just keep it somewhere safe until you're ready to wear it."

She held it out to him. "You keep it. Then, if the day comes that I do want to wear it, you can put it on my finger." That day would never come, but that truth would only cause Julian to hurt more than he already did.

He frowned, but took the ring. "All right." He studied the diamond, mouth still bent in frustration. "You'd better get in the shower. The show must go on."

MAY

Julian stared out the windows of his penthouse in the Excelsior. He'd just gotten back from Vegas on the red-eye a few hours ago and had yet to sleep. The sun was up, and it promised the sort of day in Nocturne Falls that made you want to be outside, soaking it up. A gorgeous day, bright and sunny with a cloudless blue sky you could get lost in.

But all he could think about was how eight months had come and gone, and Desi's mind hadn't changed a bit. This last trip had been more of the same. No progress toward anything beyond a casual relationship. They were slowly learning more about each other, and becoming better friends, but that seemed to be where things stalled out.

Divorce loomed, and he was already heartbroken about it.

To make matters worse, not a soul knew he was married. No one in the town, none of his friends, and none of his family. It was better that way, but it meant he was going to suffer this misery alone while being forced to keep a happy face on in public.

Maybe that's what he deserved. This mess was rather of his own doing. But Desi had been as giddy about the idea of marriage as he had been that fateful night in Vegas.

That was truly the problem. It had been one night, fueled by champagne. He should have known it was the alcohol distorting her feelings. He was a fool for thinking otherwise.

And for being madly in love with a woman who didn't share his plans for the future.

Yes, this was all on his shoulders. He'd man up and deal with it, but he didn't know how he could get through this without it changing him.

His family would notice. They were so used to him being Julian the playboy, how could they not? But there was only one woman he wanted. The rest paled in comparison, and although he'd flirted and pretended to keep up the appearance that nothing had changed these past eight months, his heart belonged entirely to his wife.

He laughed bitterly. Did she ever think of him as her husband? He doubted it. Frankly, he wasn't sure she thought of him at all. Perhaps that was unkind. She probably did think of him now and then, but certainly not with the frequency with which she invaded his thoughts.

And apparently, he was a masochist, because he sincerely hoped they could remain friends. Not having her in his life at all might be a fate worse than divorce.

He rested his forehead against the glass.

Being in love was rather awful. At least when it was unrequited. His brothers seemed to be managing their love lives very successfully. But then, they had devoted partners who loved them back.

That was the key. And the one thing he didn't have.

He sighed and walked toward the bedroom. He needed a shower and then sleep. He was scheduled to be the VOD this evening. And being Vampire On Duty meant flirting and carousing with the female tourists. To be that "on," he had to sleep this sullenness away, or he might singlehandedly ruin the town's economy.

He laughed at that thought, instantly feeling a little better. But the fact that he was known as a playboy was rather ironic. Women loved him. They always had.

Just not the right one.

Months ago, Willa Iscove, the fae jeweler in

town, had helped him keep up his Casanova charade by making him a bespelled charm that allowed him to flirt and carouse with the women in town without them becoming suspicious when all he did at the end of the evening was wish them good night and send them on their way.

Thanks to her magic, the women left smiling and satisfied and under the impression that they'd had a much better time than they actually had.

Her charm had saved his reputation and helped him keep his marriage hidden. Could she also make him something that would mend his broken heart?

That was probably asking too much.

He tossed his travel-worn clothes into the hamper and walked into the bathroom. Just as he was about to crank on the shower, his phone rang. He'd never heard this particular ringtone actually come out of his phone before, but he knew instantly who the caller was because of the song.

As the opening lines of Whitney Houston's *Queen of the Night* echoed through the room, he snatched the phone off the dresser and hit answer. "Desi?"

"Jules?"

"Yes, darling, it's me. Shouldn't you be asleep right now? It's daylight there."

"Yes, but something's happened." She let out a ragged sigh. "I feel awful for calling you about this.

It's not fair of me at all, especially with everything that's going on between us, but I didn't know what else to do. And…I don't trust anyone else."

"What happened?"

"It's been, well, there was…" She swallowed.

She wasn't the kind of woman who was ever at a loss for words. Plus, she sounded panicky and off-kilter, something else he wasn't used to from her. It made the hair lift on the back of his neck, but for her sake, he kept his own voice light and jovial. "Hey, you can tell me anything, you know that. That's one of the privileges of being married, so you might as well use it while you can. What can I do for you?"

An odd little noise came out of her. "I know I don't have a lot of right to ask you for anything, but I don't know where else to turn. And I really don't want to disrupt your day, but I need your help."

"You're not interrupting anything." He was as stunned as if she'd said she loved him. For her to come to him like this was progress. At least, that's what it felt to him. Hope sprang to life. But then he focused on how miserable she sounded. "What do you need, Desi? What's going on?"

Silence answered him for a moment. "I think…I think someone might be trying to kill me."

"What the bloody hell?" Rage overtook him, and for a moment, the only word he could get out was, "Explain."

"Sam—Samantha. My double. You know who I mean."

He shoved a hand through his hair as he paced the bedroom. "Yes."

"She was in a car accident today. A hit and run. The driver rammed into her, then took off. She's got two fractured ribs and a broken leg."

He stopped pacing. "That's awful, but I don't think that's evidence someone's trying to kill you."

"There's more, but…I don't want to talk about it over the phone. Like I said, I trust you, but that's about it right now."

Her voice cracked on the last word, sending a shock wave through him. Desi was scared. That alone spurred him to action. The fact that she trusted him? Icing on the cake. "I'll be there as quickly as I can. Stay in your apartment. The Skye Towers is safe. You should be fine there."

"You're coming today?"

"Yes, absolutely."

"Oh, that's great, thank you. And I can't go anywhere anyway. At least until Sam's leg is healed, because everyone thinks she's me, and they'll expect me to be recovering. The show will be dark until Sam's better too. That's just how it has to work, because the press has reported I was the one in the accident. It'll be six weeks until I can work again, minimum, even though Sam will recover faster than that. Can't let anyone know the truth about either of us."

"I understand." Being constrained by human limitations for the sake of secrecy was the price of being a supernatural sometimes.

"I knew you would."

"Six weeks, six months, whatever, it'll be fine. It's not a good idea for you to return to work until this *problem* is solved anyway. If someone means you harm, I'm going to deal with it. Now stay put. I will be there as quickly as I can. I love you."

"Okay." Her voice was soft and full of relief. "Thank you, Jules."

"You're very welcome. See you soon. Try to get some sleep."

"I will." She hung up.

He did the same, then immediately called his brother Hugh.

"Hello, Julian."

"I need the jet."

"I'm fine, thank you."

Julian rolled his eyes. "Yes, hello, I hope you're all well, but this is an emergency. I need the jet."

"An emergency? What kind?"

He ground his back teeth together. His two older brothers never took him seriously. Granted, he'd sort of allowed that over the years, as it played into his persona and made his life pretty carefree, but now was not the time for a thousand questions.

"A friend is in trouble. Is anyone using it or not?"

"No, you can take it."

"Great, I'll explain more when I can. Have to run. Love to Delaney and George." He hung up and dialed the airfield where they kept the family plane, then the pilot they had on retainer, making all the necessary arrangements for his trip to Vegas.

With that handled, he dressed quickly, then packed an overnight bag just in case. He locked up and headed downstairs.

The doorman's brows shot up as Julian walked through the lobby. "Leaving us again so soon, Mr. Ellingham?"

Julian nodded. "Can't be helped, Freddy. Keep an eye on things. I won't be long."

"You got it, sir." The man tipped his head as Julian left.

He slid into his GranTurismo, thankful that the Maserati was capable of high speeds without effort, and took off, his only concern for the beautiful vampire awaiting him in Vegas.

Desi knew she should be dreaming by now. The sun was high in the sky, prickling her skin, and daysleep tugged hard, but she was too keyed up to let it take over. Normally, when she couldn't sleep during daytime hours, she'd stand in front of her UV-proof windows and pretend she was outside, but right now she didn't even want to go near them. Not even the ones that overlooked the enormous private balcony that was part of her Skye Towers condo. Being seen, however remote the possibility, just wasn't a good idea.

Instead, she was holed up in her room, sprawled on the bed watching movies, blinds closed. Except she wasn't really watching the movies so much as they were providing a background for her speeding thoughts. It was hard to concentrate on frivolous entertainment when someone was out to get you.

She tipped her head against the headboard and stared at the ceiling. She'd had stalkers before. A few overzealous fans, really. But nothing like this. Never anything where whoever was after her had repeatedly attempted to physically harm her. And as far as the person out to get her now knew, they *had* harmed her. They just didn't realize it was actually Sam who'd been the victim of the hit and run.

The fact that there had been actual violence freaked Desi out. The random crazed fan rarely did more than write a threatening note and, even then, those were isolated cases.

Until this one. And this one was hard to pin down. Whoever it was seemed to think she was a vampire but had also attacked her (Sam) in daylight. She wasn't sure what they thought about what she really was. Did they think she was a vampire who could daywalk? Was that what had gotten this person so upset? If only she could make sense of everything that had happened so far. Someone was definitely targeting her. But why? To what end?

But thinking about it over and over only stressed her out more. She could feel the tension knotting up her muscles and tightening around her head like a clamp.

She tried to focus on the movie, but still ended up checking her phone every couple of minutes.

The text she was looking for, the one telling her Julian had arrived, had yet to come. Where was he?

On his way, she knew that. But the waiting, combined with her out-of-control thoughts, was getting the best of her. Maybe she should go work out. A good run on the treadmill might do her some good and, since the Towers were home to all kinds of supernaturals, no one would blink when her speeds far exceeded the standard human's.

Except what if the person who was after her had a spy in the building? Or what if they lived here? She bit her lip. They seemed to think she was a vampire after all. They might be a supernatural too.

She put her hands on her head and groaned. "C'mon, Julian, I need you." But even as she said the words, she knew she didn't have a right to them. If she wasn't going to give him what he wanted, it was unfair of her to ask him for anything.

And yet, she was asking. She had no choice if she wanted to live. At least, that's how she felt.

But his impending arrival came with a brand-new set of thoughts. Like how he was in love with her and she couldn't reciprocate those feelings. She liked him very much. Trusted him implicitly, which was a true accomplishment for her and the reason she'd called him. But love…that was not in the cards for her. Not ever again. And especially not with another vampire. Plus, Julian deserved someone without all of her baggage.

Which meant she was knowingly using him. Because there'd been no question about whether he would help her. Julian would do anything for her. He'd told her that time and again.

Fortunately, today was the first day she'd ever needed anything from anyone in a very long time. She hated the feeling, because it came with memories best forgotten. Not that there had been anyone around to ask for help then.

She sighed and watched the couple on the screen. Whatever their petty problems were, it was nothing like what she was facing. No one was trying to kill them. And they weren't being forced to ask a favor from someone they shouldn't.

She hugged her knees to her chest. She and Jules would be divorced soon. She'd agreed to the year only because she'd thought that would be enough time for him to get tired of her and see that she wasn't the woman for him. So far, that hadn't worked, but the year wasn't over yet.

She hoped they could part friends. That would be nice. She'd grown used to him in her life, and as hard as it was to admit, it made her sad to think of him not being around.

But chances were, once the year was up and her mind remained unchanged, he'd want nothing to do with her. And she couldn't blame him a bit. She stretched her legs out and leaned into the nest of pillows that decorated her bed. Daysleep pulled at her, causing her lids to drift down.

Three loud knocks rang out from her door, causing her to jump. She'd fallen asleep. Panic overtook her for a moment as she shook off the tiredness. Then she realized it must be Julian. She grabbed her phone, slid off the bed and ran toward the front of the condo, then skidded to a stop in the hall. What if it wasn't?

She texted him. *Are you at my door?*

His reply came a second later. *Who else?* He'd added a winking emoji.

Relief swept her. She walked into the foyer and opened the door.

"Hello, love." He smiled at her. "Nice outfit. Maybe not the best for being incognito, though."

She glanced down at her leopard print leggings and hot pink cropped T-shirt with the words *Blink if you want me* printed on it. It wasn't much different than anything else she ever wore. And the outfit was tame compared to some of the things she sported—and didn't—on stage. She shrugged and smiled at him. "It's not like I'm going out, but I can change. I'm so glad you came. Thank you."

"You're welcome. And don't ever change." He walked in. "Did you sleep?"

"A little. It's hard."

"I understand. You must be stressed."

"I am. But a little less now." She hugged him. It wasn't her way—she wasn't a physical person—

but if there was anyone who deserved a hug, it was Julian.

He tensed for a moment in her embrace, then patted her on the back. "It's all going to be fine, you'll see."

She released him. "I hope so."

"Have faith, love." He kissed her cheek, then looked around. "Now, where are your bags? The car's waiting."

"Bags? What are you talking about?"

His brows pulled together. "You didn't pack?"

"For what?" She thought through the conversation they'd had. She didn't remember him saying anything about her leaving. "Are you trying to take me somewhere?"

"Yes." He stared at her like she'd lost her mind. "You called me to come out and get you, didn't you?"

They'd definitely had a miscommunication. "I called you because I think someone's threatening me. I wasn't trying to leave Vegas."

His brows lifted. "If you're in danger, you can't stay here."

"The Skye Towers is perfectly safe. But we do need to go out for a little bit as soon as it gets dark."

"Why? Where do you need to go?"

"To see Sam. I need to see how she's doing."

He crossed his arms. "That's the last place you should go."

"She's hurt because of me, and she's all alone in the hospital. I have to get over there as soon as I can."

"Send flowers, call her, but it's a bad idea for you to go anywhere near her. If someone really is after you and they figure out you and Sam are two different people, you could both be in deeper trouble than you were before."

"But I'm worried about her."

"I am too. What kind of supernatural did you say she was?"

"She's a skinwalker and very capable of taking care of herself. But…" Desi opened her mouth, then closed it again to think for a second. "She's still injured and vulnerable."

"A skinwalker." He nodded like he was thinking. "Now I remember. She can take on any form, then, correct?"

"Within limits. And being this injured, I'm not sure she can shift at all."

He frowned. "Then you're right about her being vulnerable. We can't leave her this way. This has to be dealt with." He took out his phone.

"What are you going to do?"

"Call in a favor." He dialed, then waited. "Van, hello, it's Julian Ellingham. Good, how are you? Excellent news. Yes, actually. Do you know anyone who could handle a security job for me in Vegas? I need someone trustworthy. This is a high priority."

He nodded a couple times. "Perfect. Immediately." He twisted the phone away. "What hospital is Sam in and what room?"

Desi told him, then he went back to the phone. "Las Vegas General, room 1905. Woman's name is Samantha Arnett. Very good. I owe you."

He said goodbye and hung up, tucking the phone back into his pocket. "Sam's about to have a new friend, a gargoyle by the name of Harlan who comes highly recommended from someone I trust. He'll stay with her until this is cleared up."

Desi raised her brows. "That's awesome, but I don't think Sam can afford that kind of protection, not that she should have to. This all happened to her because of me, so I'll take care of Harlan's bill. What's it going to cost me?"

"Nothing, it's handled."

That got her back up for reasons she refused to acknowledge. "No. I'll pay for it."

His eyes narrowed for a moment, then he nodded. "I'll let you know."

"Okay. Thank you." She had her own money. And this was her problem. "But it was kind of you to offer."

He didn't look like he totally understood, but she was all right with that. Her past had made it so.

He tipped his head. "Now, about getting you out of here. Is there any other reason you think you need to stay?"

She mulled it over. "I guess not."

"Good. Then you're coming back with me. You can stay with me while Sam recovers and we can figure out what's going on from a safe distance. Plus, it will give you some freedom. I doubt you'll be recognized like you are here."

"You want to leave just like that? Don't we need tickets? Or do you plan on driving?"

"No, I brought the jet."

"You have a jet?" He'd never mentioned that. But she understood. He'd kept key parts of his life back just like she had. She knew he had money, but not how much—not that his financials were any of her business. Just like she knew he was from Georgia, but beyond that, the most she'd gotten out of him was that he lived in a little town she'd probably think was boring. Right now, boring sounded okay, actually.

He nodded. "I do. And the only thing that needs to happen for us to get on it is for you to pack."

"You're serious about this. You want me to stay with you."

"I can get you a room elsewhere if you prefer, but I have plenty of space, and my building is secure."

His building. That was interesting. She'd always pictured him living in some big old creaky mansion. "No, I guess that's fine."

"You don't seem convinced."

"Well, like I said, I wasn't planning on going anywhere."

"Do you really think staying here is the safest plan? You won't be able to go out much if you do stay. Maybe not at all until Sam's out of the hospital, because that's where people think you are. And when Sam gets out, they'll at least expect to see you with a cast and crutches."

She sighed. "Ugh, yes, that's true. Okay, fine, let's go to your place. Where in Georgia do you live, exactly?"

"A lovely little town called Nocturne Falls. I can't think of a safer place for a vampire in hiding."

She had her doubts about that. "I'll go pack."

"I'll be on the balcony. It's a beautiful day."

She rolled her eyes as she walked past him. "Show off."

While Desi packed, Julian stood on the balcony and stared down at the city below. He didn't often see this view of the Strip during daylight hours. Without the gleam and glitter of its millions of lights, it looked rather…unmagical.

A breeze swept the grand outdoor space, stirring up remnants of Desi's orange blossom perfume and making him smile.

She was a proud person. Julian liked that about her, but hiring Harlan for twenty-four-hour protection wasn't going to be cheap. Maybe he'd split the bill with her. Without telling her. But no, that would mean there was a lie between them, and he couldn't have that. He sighed. She was a frustrating creature. Gorgeous, but frustrating.

He heard knocking on the glass behind him. He turned to see her waving him in.

He went inside. She hadn't changed other than

to put on sky-high black platform boots. Studs decorated the front of them. He laughed softly. "You are nothing if not practical, darling."

"I am who I am." She spread her arms wide. "And this is who I am."

Which was exactly what he loved about her.

Then she put her hands on her hips. "Plus, these Louboutins just came yesterday. You can't expect me to leave them behind."

"No, of course not. Although you might want to think about going a little more incognito until this whole mess blows over."

"Okay," she said, smiling. "I'll think about it."

He shook his head. There was a single Louis Vuitton duffel bag over her shoulder, along with her matching handbag. "That can't be all you packed. Where are the rest of your bags?"

"In the bedroom. I'll get them."

He laughed and headed for the bedroom. "Not in those heels. I'll handle the luggage. You go grab a coat. Evenings in the Georgia mountains can still be chilly in May."

"Okay." She sashayed off toward the foyer closet while he went to the bedroom.

Three enormous Louis Vuitton rolling bags awaited him. He sighed, but in his heart, he understood. He loved beautiful things himself, and often traveled with just as much. But for a quick getaway, this was a tad excessive.

But because he loved her and was happy to indulge her, he said nothing and wrangled them to the front of the condo, thankful his vampire strength made that a pretty easy feat.

When he rolled into the foyer, she was there waiting, wearing what he referred to as her Cookie Monster coat. The big fake fur jacket was bright blue and excessively fuzzy and one of Desi's favorites.

He brought the bags to a stop, unable to keep himself from teasing her a little. "I appreciate you packing quickly, but you know we're not going to a third-world country, right? If you forget something, you can buy it."

"I didn't forget anything."

He snorted and glanced at the luggage. "Clearly." He took his phone out to let the driver know they were headed down.

She hooked her thumb under the straps of her shoulder bag. "Don't you want to talk about what else has happened to me?"

"I do, but on the plane. Getting you somewhere safe is my main concern." He hoisted the bags again. "Did you call the lift yet?"

She nodded. "On its way."

They rode down in the elevator in silence, then got into the waiting car. The Skye Towers had the benefit of a drive-through lobby for the sake of its more sun-sensitive occupants, which made it very convenient for vampires. Especially those who might have a target on them.

The SUV he'd hired had UV-proof windows as well, a necessity since Desi didn't have anything to protect her from the sun like he did.

She'd never asked about the amulet he wore, or how he could withstand the sun, but sometimes he got the feeling she wanted to. He was glad she hadn't. He didn't want to lie to her, but the amulets were an Ellingham family secret and not something to be discussed.

Technically, he could have told her. She was his wife, but that was on paper only. If he thought she loved him back and that this marriage was more than an inconvenience to her, he'd not only tell her about the amulet, he'd ask Alice Bishop to make Desi one too. But that would require telling Alice about the marriage.

And his grandmother would have a fit if Julian got Alice to make an amulet for a woman who was about to be his ex-wife. The witch's powers were great but, in Elenora Ellingham's mind, not to be squandered.

He understood. If word got out about Alice's abilities, they'd be inundated with vampires trying to get an amulet for their own. His brother Sebastian had already dealt with a crazy ex trying to steal the secret of his daywalking ability.

No, this secret had to remain just that until Desi was truly his.

"You're quiet," she said, breaking the stillness of the car's vault-like interior.

He smiled. "Just thinking."

"About?"

He shook his head. "I wouldn't know where to start."

She smiled a little sadly. "I could tell you about what else my stalker has done."

"On the plane." He tipped his head toward the road. "We're almost there." The private airfield awaited them. The plane and crew were in a hangar so that Desi could remain out of the sun. He'd already told the driver where they were headed, so the man pulled right in, then jumped out to get their bags. Julian had left his in the back of the vehicle.

"Right into the hangar." She smiled. "You think of everything, Jules."

"I try."

Once they were in the sky, she seemed to relax. "This is a beautiful aircraft."

"Thank you. I had a small part in that. My brother Sebastian wanted something a little more utilitarian, but it's also his job to watch the funds, so what can you expect?" He laughed. "Not saying he's tight, but he might squeak a little when he walks. He is exceptional with money, but I do wish he'd lighten up."

She snorted. "I get the picture."

He shook his head. "Actually, he's loosened up considerably since Tessa's come into his life."

"Is that his wife?"

"Fiancée."

"And your other brother? Is he also engaged?"

"Married. Just had his first child some months back."

She smiled. "So you're an uncle?"

"I am, and damn good at it, I might add."

"I have no doubts." Her smile faded.

Enough small talk. "Tell me what happened. Tell me everything."

She nodded, her gaze growing distant with memories. "It started about a month ago. No, six weeks."

He did the math. "I've been to see you twice in that time. You didn't say anything."

"Because I didn't think it *was* anything. I have some…odd fans. I just figured this was more of that."

"Explain."

She folded her hands in her lap. "The bouquets of garlic came first. One a day for a week, each with a note that said things like, 'This show is going to kill you,' or 'This show will be the death of you.'"

Disbelief made his mouth drop open. "And you thought *that* was from a fan?"

"Yes. They don't know I'm really a vampire."

She shrugged. "I get things like that with these notes about how they want to protect me if a real vampire comes looking for me, how they worry that I'll make real vampires angry because I do such a good job of impersonating them."

"You have strange fans."

"Some of them, yes, but I have some amazing ones too. A lot of amazing ones, actually. And I love what I do. It lets me be me while paying the bills."

He could think of other ways for her to do that, like truly become his wife. He would spoil her silly. But this wasn't the time for that discussion. "What else happened?"

Her eyes narrowed. "Small, silver crucifixes started showing up everywhere. In my dressing room. In the mail. Found a couple on stage among the props. Even found one sewn into one of my costumes. Crazy."

"Did you still think that was just your fans?"

"I did. Until…" Fear showed in her eyes.

"Until what?"

She wrapped her arms around her body. "Someone replaced the lights in my dressing room with UV bulbs." She stared straight ahead. "Burned my left side so badly, Sam had to go on in my place that night."

He swore softly. "And you didn't tell me about that?"

She looked at him. "So you could worry? What good would it do? What could you have done?"

"A great deal. I could have set up a security team for you. I could have flown out and taken care of you. Anything would have been better than nothing." His hands were clenched. He took a moment to calm himself down, forcing himself to speak more softly. "I can't help but want to protect you."

"It's sweet, and I get it, but I knew you'd fly out the minute I said something. You proved that today. And I really didn't want to inconvenience you when—"

"You are *not* an inconvenience. Don't ever think that. You're my wife. You know what that means to me."

"I do. And…" She put her hand on his for a moment, lifting it away as soon as he'd made eye contact again. "Jules, if you want me to speak plainly, then the truth is, I didn't call you about all of this *because* we're married."

"What?"

She shook her head and looked away. "I know I agreed to the year, but it's colored everything I do now. I second-guess every action."

He smiled sadly, understanding. "You worry that I'll misinterpret any small kindness as you falling for me, is that it? That I'll read more into you being nice than is really there."

She stared at him, mouth pursed. But the answer was in her eyes.

He pushed back into his seat, wishing there was more space between them. He laughed, but the wound had been made. "Do I come off that desperate? I must look so pathetic in your eyes."

"Jules, that's not what I meant."

"No, no need to clarify. I understand completely." He kept his gaze straight ahead so she wouldn't see the pain of his heart being ripped in two. "When we arrive, I'll begin the paperwork for the divorce."

She was silent. "Thank you. But I don't think you're pathetic or desperate or any of those things." She looked pained. That bothered him, even though he was hurting too. "My inability to stay married is because of me, Julian. Not you. I just can't love anyone. I can't allow myself that luxury. And you deserve to be loved."

It was a curious statement from someone like her. "You think I deserve to be loved but you can't be that person?"

"Yes, that's right."

"How is it you think I should be loved?"

"With the same passion and intensity that you love. With your entire being. With your whole self. I've only had a taste of that part of you, and I know that you give yourself completely. You put on this show that you're the world's biggest playboy, but

when we're together, I see a very different man."
Her eyes seemed to shimmer with liquid. Like she
was on the verge of tears. An odd look for her, the
woman who didn't care enough to care at all.

And yet, she'd sussed him out.

She stared at the armrest between them. "I wish
things were different. I really do. But I'm not the
woman you want."

"That's for me to decide. You don't get to tell me
that what I want is wrong." He smiled, a thin,
tight-lipped bend of his mouth that barely
expressed what was happening inside him. Unable
to take any more, he got up, walked to the back of
the plane and found a new seat.

With her elbows propped on her knees, Desdemona let out an exhausted sigh and rested her head in her hands. She'd screwed things up royally. She'd thought telling Julian the truth about how she was feeling would be for the best, but then she'd seen the hurt in his eyes and realized how wrong that decision had been.

Even worse, Julian wasn't just playing at being married. He deeply, genuinely loved her. How that had happened, she wasn't sure. She considered herself pretty unlovable. Strived for that. Did her best to be superficial and cool, shutting down any emotion that grew too strong or too true.

But Julian apparently had seen through that or had some kind of immunity to her pretense. Which, of course he did, because he was amazing in every other way, so why not that too?

She squeezed her eyes shut. What a mess she'd

made of things. The pit of her stomach was in knots, and her heart, the thing she'd guarded so fiercely, ached at her own foolishness. Telling Julian the truth really wasn't the problem.

Not telling him the whole truth was.

But she wasn't going to do that. Couldn't. Didn't even want to think about it. The past should stay the past. It had to. It was the only way she could survive. She'd vowed that much after the man who'd tried to destroy her.

Alonso. The name slithered through her mind, causing her lip to curl in disgust. At least she knew he wasn't her stalker—if he was still alive. He wouldn't care enough to spend that kind of time and energy on her.

She shook herself, swallowing down the sour taste on her tongue. Dwelling on her past would kill her. Or turn her into a creature whose only thoughts were hatred and revenge, and that was no way to live.

And so she had to abide by the rule that made her life possible now. She would never allow herself to love again. The first time had almost cost her her life. She would never be that stupid a second time.

She twisted to peek through the space between the seats. Julian was sprawled on a couch on the right side of the aircraft, one arm bent over his face.

She doubted he was sleeping. Probably just

didn't want to talk to her anymore. But she really needed to talk to him. She turned back around and pressed her fingers to her temples for a long moment, working up some courage. Then she got up and made her way back to him, where she kneeled beside the couch. She put her hand lightly on his arm. "Are you sleeping?"

His answer came after a long sigh. "No."

She took her hand away. "You don't have to look at me. I just have to say a few things. I know I hurt you, Jules. I'm very sorry for that. It truly wasn't my intention."

He didn't move for almost a minute, and she thought he'd decided to ignore her until he turned away. "Don't worry about it."

She frowned. How could she not? But he clearly didn't want to talk about it. "Okay. Sorry."

"It's forgotten. Get some sleep."

She stood. Sleep probably wasn't going to be possible now. Just like there was no way he was going to forget what either of them had said.

This was going to be the longest six weeks of her life. Scratch that. The second longest. After what she'd endured at the hands of her ex, she would survive this just fine.

She walked back to her seat and settled in. She had lived through the impossible. These next few weeks would be a vacation. A crappy, miserable vacation, but still easily tolerated given the circumstances.

All she had to do was figure out how to become friends with Julian again while not making him think there was any chance for the future or making him feel like she was taking advantage of his kindness. Easy, right?

She grimaced. She knew going to Julian's was the best way to stay safe and figure things out, but right now she couldn't help but feel like she should have stayed in Vegas after all.

The growl of the jet's landing gear descending woke Julian. He was a little surprised he'd slept, but then it had been nearly forty hours since his last shut-eye, so it was understandable. And being heartsick wasn't worth staying awake for anyway.

He sat up and rubbed his eyes. Desi was still in her seat. Just seeing the back of her and those wild caramel and honey curls that he longed to run his fingers through made him hurt all over again.

He had to get past this, or the next month would be a downward spiral into darkness. How was he going to cohabitate with a woman he loved more than life but who didn't reciprocate his feelings? And it seemed, never would?

There was always Elenora's. But moving in with his grandmother, no matter how temporary, seemed like vacating the second level of hell for the ninth. No, that option had to be off the table. Unless something unbelievably worse occurred. And really, how was that even possible now? He loved a woman who'd just thanked him for offering to dissolve their marriage a few months early. They were clearly already at the bottom of the relationship barrel.

He could move in with either of his brothers, but being at Sebastian's meant seeing his brother and Tessa in a sickeningly happy relationship. It also meant listening to wedding-planning talk. So, no.

Being at Hugh's meant being subjected to a lot of the same happy couple business, but at least there he could spend time with his adorable nephew, George. But sadly, George now represented something Julian might never have. A family of his own.

He rolled his eyes, a little sick of how pathetic his life had become. No wonder Desi wasn't interested. What woman would be? He had to snap out of this. Somehow. He sighed, steeled himself for whatever came next, and headed back to his seat for landing. He sat down, strapped in and offered Desi a quick smile, trying to find some level of normalcy between them again. "Did you sleep?"

She shrugged. "A little. Too keyed up, I guess. You?"

It seemed obvious that he had, but he said, "Yes, the same," anyway. He left it at that. He searched for something else to say, but the tension that had been there before he'd fallen asleep remained. Didn't feel like it was going away any time soon, either.

This wasn't a genie that could be put back in the bottle.

Twilight bruised the sky purple as they landed, matching the way he felt. He was glad for the cover of darkness. Even with a vampire's heightened senses, it gave him the sensation of being hidden. And if he'd had the choice, that's what he would have done.

But he was VOD this evening, which meant getting Desi settled in, then leaving her alone. In his house. He didn't care about her snooping—didn't think she cared enough to bother. But it seemed odd to leave her there to judge his home without being able to defend it. Why he felt that way, he wasn't sure. Maybe because she'd ended things so summarily. Like no aspect of his life would be given a chance to win her over. Not him, or his home.

He frowned at his own ridiculous thoughts. She probably didn't care one way or the other where he lived or what the place looked like. Or how he was feeling. No doubt her thoughts were occupied with finding out who was after her and who'd hurt Sam.

He found enough empathy to offer her a genuine smile and some kind words. She was in a bad situation, after all. "You'll be safe at my place. Promise."

She nodded. "I'm sure you're right. No one knows I'm here, after all."

They landed and transferred the bags to his Maserati, which meant cramming some of her luggage into the backseat. More silence settled around them as he drove away from the airfield. She turned toward the window and leaned back. He thought she'd fallen asleep until they entered the town limits.

She lifted her head. "What kind of place is this?"

"Nocturne Falls is a tourist hotspot. The town celebrates Halloween year-round. There's trick-or-treating throughout the business district every Friday and characters that walk around constantly interacting with visitors. Except they're not really characters, they're real supernaturals."

She glanced at him. "Are you serious? How do humans not figure it out?"

"A very powerful witch, who works for my family, put a spell on the town's water, which is almost impossible to avoid drinking. The spell prevents the truth from coming out. Tourists either forget what they've seen or think it's all smoke and mirrors."

"That's amazing—wait, your family employs a powerful witch? That makes it sound like your family's in charge."

He shrugged. "My family turned the town into what it is today. Nocturne Falls exists because we wanted a place where we could live with some semblance of normalcy."

She leaned back in her seat. "So your family *is* in charge."

"To some extent."

"How about that."

He watched her out of the corner of his eye, wondering if this information would change anything. There was no way he would have been able to keep it a secret from her, not with her staying in his home. "It's no big deal."

"No, of course not. You just own a town, is all." She laughed. "Julian, that's pretty impressive. Even more so that this place has been specifically designed to give safe harbor to supernaturals." She went back to looking out the window. "This town must be loaded with supes. What kinds live here?"

"All kinds." Main Street was almost behind them now. The Excelsior wasn't too much farther.

"And they all get along?"

"Pretty well, yes."

"That's amazing."

"That's Nocturne Falls."

As Main Street disappeared behind them, she turned to him. "Why didn't you tell me about this?"

"I…" He shook his head. "We've never told

each other much about ourselves." Especially not their pasts. "And I didn't want you to think I was using my involvement in this town to impress you."

She tipped her head back and forth. "You're right, we haven't shared a lot. And I might have thought you were trying to impress me with this place. It is pretty impressive. But I might not have believed you, either."

He narrowed his eyes. "Why not?"

She smirked. "Come on, Jules. You have to know the kind of vibe you give off."

He turned into the Excelsior's parking lot. "Enlighten me."

"Rich playboy who doesn't work, lives to party, loves pretty women and fancy things, and never had a care in his life."

He parked, switched the car off, then faced her. "I guess that's who I was to some extent. But I do work. Not as much as my family realizes or acknowledges, perhaps, but I'm very involved in this town."

"What do you mean that's who you were? Aren't you still that person?"

"Not exactly." Not since she'd shown up in his life. At least not when it came to loving pretty women. There was only one woman he wanted. The one who didn't want him. He sighed. "Come on. Let's get you settled."

He unloaded her bags and set them on the pavement, then locked the car. She insisted on rolling one, plopping her duffel bag on top and starting for the lobby before he could argue.

He caught up to her and opened the door. Lou was on shift now. He nodded to the doorman. "Lou, this is my dear friend, Miss—" He glanced at Desi, unsure what to call her. Using Valentine might give her away.

"Clarke," she supplied.

"Miss Clarke." She'd answered so quickly, he wondered if it was an alias she used often. "She's going to be staying with me for a while. Treat her like you would me. All privileges."

Lou nodded back. "You got it, Mr. Ellingham." Then he tipped his hat at Desi. "Nice to meet you, Miss Clarke. You need anything, just ask."

"Thank you, I will."

Julian got them on the penthouse elevator, which sat to the left of the main bank, but he waited until the doors closed before he spoke. "We should have figured out the alias thing ahead of time."

"Clarke isn't an alias. It was my birth name." She laughed. "You didn't think it was actually Valentine, did you?"

"No, but then, who knows with a vampire?"

She glanced at him. "What was your surname at birth?"

Was she really interested or just being polite? It was hard to know. "Ellingham. We never changed it, just moved around. Until we settled here."

"Interesting. I feel like I've had a thousand names since I gave Clarke up." Her gaze went to a distant place, memories taking her away from him for a moment.

The lift stopped and they got out.

"Home, sweet home. Well, the foyer, anyway." He rolled her bags to the door, then left them to punch in the entry code to the penthouse.

"This is already nothing like what I imagined." She looked around.

He tried to see it through her eyes. Mostly he wondered what she'd think of his cobalt blue glass statue of Diana, the Roman goddess of the hunt. Even during his apartment's recent makeover, he'd kept that piece. Something about it just filled him with joy.

He knew his tastes were rather eclectic, but he'd already spent lifetimes living in the stuffy grandeur favored by many British nobility, and while that might be fine for the rest of his family, he was his own man. He liked modern things mixed with a few choice pieces from the past. "What were you expecting?"

Her gaze seemed fixed on the goddess. "Not this. Something a little more…traditional."

"You mean boring."

"No, I never thought you'd be boring. But many of our kind seem to surround themselves with things that remind them of their true youth. You know what I mean."

He nodded. "I do. My brothers' houses are very much like that." He almost said something about his grandmother's mansion, but caught himself. No need to spill everything. "Come inside, I'll show you around."

He let her go in first, then followed with the rest of the luggage. She hadn't gone far. She was standing in the interior foyer, mouth open.

"What do you think?"

She shook her head slowly and just said, "Wow."

Desi had imagined Julian's home would have one of two styles. It would either be all dark wood, heavy leather, and pricey antiques, a nostalgic look favored by many older, wealthier vampires, or she guessed he might go in the other direction, very modern and sparse with lots of expensive contemporary art. A kind of forced look that she'd seen some vampires adopt as a way of hiding their true age. As if living in an environment like that counteracted how many centuries they'd actually existed.

And for Julian, either extreme would serve as a perfect bachelor pad with the ability to impress.

She'd never expected the sort of serene luxury before her now. It was neither modern nor traditional, but the most stunning mix of both. An enormous mercury glass mirror sat atop a blond wood sideboard. Cream and white floors and walls were accented with bronze fixtures and black accessories and trim. There were touches of marble, pale white-washed wood, gray velvet, and lots of surprising patterns like brocade and herringbone.

She stopped gawking to face him. "This place is completely lux. It's gorgeous."

"You seem surprised."

"I am. And I feel like I owe you an apology for thinking it would be something so much more ordinary. You had an outstanding decorator."

"I did it myself."

She knew her face showed her disbelief. "For real?"

He nodded, looking pleased, which he had a right to. "Yes. I just redid it last year. Thought it was time for a change. I must confess, I was inspired by a few of the places I saw in Vegas."

She snorted. "Vegas wishes it looked like this. Well done, Jules."

"Thank you. I hope you like your room just as well." He led her down the hall, rolling her bags in, then stepping aside. "Will this do?"

"Absolutely. This is beautiful." And it was. It looked a lot like the rest of the penthouse that she'd seen, but the bedroom had a little more wood and a thick, tufted ivory rug that gave it a very cozy feeling despite its size. "I could live here."

"Good, because you're pretty much going to be."

She nodded. "I guess so." She took one of the rolling bags from him. "I should unpack and let you get on with your life."

"About that." He kept his hand on the handle of the second bag. "I have to work this evening."

She laughed. "Good one."

"No, I do. I'm the VOD tonight. The Vampire On Duty." He checked his watch. "And I should get going. I'm already going to be a little late."

She gave him a better look. "You're serious."

"Yep. I'll be home by one a.m. at the latest, but if you need anything, just call. Or ask Lou downstairs. Like he said, he'll be happy to help. There's satellite television, all the movie channels, pay-per-view, or if you want something more active, there's a pool and gym downstairs, too."

He was leaving her. She had no right to be bothered by that, but she was. Not bothered, exactly, but…bummed. Which was another emotion that wasn't hers to own when it came to Julian. She made herself smile even though she'd imagined them hanging out. "That sounds great. I'll be fine."

"Good. If you're hungry, raid the fridge or order out. Again, Lou can help you with that. If you need something a little more substantial, check the wine cooler. There's plenty of O positive, so don't be shy."

"Oh, nice, the good stuff." She ran her tongue over her fangs. "I could eat."

"Make yourself at home. I have to change. You need anything else?"

She looked around. It was so much nicer than her place. "Nope, I'm good."

He started to leave.

"Um, say goodbye before you go?"

A curious expression crossed his face. "Sure."

"Okay, great." He left, and she went to work unpacking and hanging up her things. She'd definitely brought too much stuff, but she'd been in a rush and had no real idea what she'd need. Still, four wigs were probably excessive. As were the cocktail dresses, high heels, purses, and three jewelry rolls. Especially since it appeared she'd be spending most of her time in this penthouse. At least she'd packed leggings and T-shirts. And a couple bikinis.

Maybe a swim would do her good. Help her unwind a bit. Then she'd order a steak from wherever Lou the doorman suggested and watch some movies. She hadn't had a night in since she didn't know when. Her evenings mainly consisted of entertaining a packed house of tourists.

She hung the last dress, then sat on the bed to take in the room a little more. It really was a gorgeous space. She already felt more relaxed than she had in Vegas. Maybe this forced vacation wouldn't be so awful.

If only Sam hadn't been caught up in it all. Desi

felt wretched about that. She pulled out her phone and was about to send a quick text to the woman when Julian walked back in.

"I'm headed out now, so—"

"Oh. My." Desi's brows shot up at the sight of his black leather pants, flouncy white shirt and black cape. A tangle of silver bracelets decorated each wrist, and she was pretty sure she detected some eyeliner that hadn't been there before. And possibly glitter. He somehow managed to look hot and ridiculous at the same time. But hot was winning. "Is that seriously what you're wearing?"

He spread his arms out. "Yes. What's wrong with it?"

"Nothing if you're in a local theater production of *The Lost Boys.*"

He rolled his eyes. "I'm supposed to look like a regular guy playing a vampire."

"Hmm. In that case, I think you nailed it." His willingness to be so silly for the sake of his family's business was kind of endearing. She wiggled a finger at him. "Do you get paid for dressing up like this?"

"In a way. I'm on a small salary. We all are, for the sake of the corporation." He shrugged. "The town is how we make our living, so we each do our part."

She held her hands up. "No judgment. It's kind of sweet." And sexier than she was going to tell him.

"Thanks. Are you going to be okay here by yourself?"

"I'm a grown woman. And nearly two hundred years old. I can handle a quiet night in. Kind of looking forward to it, actually."

"All right. I should go."

She waved her fingers at him. "Have a good evening."

"You too." He left.

She flopped back on the bed and stared up at the ceiling. It would have been nice if he'd stayed. He was exceptional at cuddling, something she knew from a one-time experience. It had only happened once. Because she'd enjoyed it so much, she'd vowed never to let it happen again. That path led to more intimate moments, and intimate moments often led to love. With Julian, there was no doubt in her mind that going to bed with him would involve her heart.

But tonight, after the day she'd had and the realization that someone meant to do her harm, she thought about relenting. About the cuddling, not the full monty. A little snuggling on the couch during a movie would be heavenly.

But also probably disastrous. Especially if she was going to keep some distance between them. Which she was, because as much as she liked Julian, she knew how quickly men could change. How love could turn to hate without warning.

She sat up and pulled off her boots, putting them neatly into their individual shoe bags and stowing them in the closet with all the others. She stood there for a moment, looking at everything she'd unpacked. She really had gone overboard. Not that she'd ever admit that to Julian.

But her past had turned her into this person. Her need to have things and have them around her was something she'd long ago stopped trying to control. She had the money—not Julian's level of money, clearly, but enough that she was very comfortable. So why not give in to that desire to never go without again? Why not indulge herself after the hell Alonso had caused her to endure?

It was ironic, really, considering why he'd done what he'd done to her. She laughed bitterly and shook her head. That was enough reminiscing.

She walked through the penthouse, turning lights on and having a look around. Didn't take long to find Julian's bedroom. It was the entire right side of the penthouse, and it was just as beautiful as the rest of his home, although not quite as sparse.

His dresser held a grouping of framed photos. The one in the center stuck out to her. A baby photo. The child was a chubby little thing with a shock of dark hair and sparkling eyes. He wore a button-down shirt with a little sweater vest and a plaid bowtie. The whole thing was so sweet it made her fangs ache. The sterling silver frame's plaque was engraved with the name George.

Julian said his brother and sister-in-law had recently had a child. This had to be him. And he obviously held a place of importance in Julian's life to have earned such a spot on the dresser. There was another picture, of an elegant older woman. She wore the kind of jewels that spoke of family money and had the kind of carriage that only good breeding and nobility achieved.

Another photo was a group shot, all the men in tuxedos and the women in evening gowns at some kind of event. In it, Julian seemed to be unaccompanied, whereas the other men all had dates. The older woman was at the center of the photo.

Family. Had to be. He'd spoken of his two brothers. This must be them. They were a handsome lot, but Julian was flawlessly beautiful. That kind of effortless magnificence combined with his kind eyes and warm smile set him apart from his brothers.

She studied the picture a second longer, then moved on to his closet. She couldn't help herself. He was not quite the clothes horse she was, but he enjoyed designer goods as much as she did.

She flipped on the light and peeked inside. The closet was more than a walk-in. It could have been a guest room. Everything was organized by color and style. There was a wall of shoes behind glass doors. Rotating tie holders. A long row of suits in shades from black to white and everything in between. A rainbow of shirts.

And a small section of what must be his work clothes. A few more capes, ruffled shirts, frock coats, a top hat…all the trimmings for a vampire disguised as a human pretending to be a vampire. She ran her fingers over the fabrics. Silk, velvet, wool, cashmere. Even his dress-up clothes were high quality.

She turned to the center island and its drawers. She hesitated. This was trespassing. It was one thing to wander through his house, it was another to open drawers and snoop.

But then, technically, she was his wife. That changed things, didn't it? Maybe a little, but it was still snooping. She recognized the uncoolness of her actions, but was too weak to stop herself. She wanted to know more about him.

She pulled the top drawer open. Velvet-lined, it held rows of expensive watches all displayed on matching velvet stands.

The next drawer had cuff links, tuxedo studs, and tie clips. And a small velvet box that she recognized instantly. Interesting that the ring wasn't in a safe somewhere. She shut that drawer quickly and opened the one below it.

The third drawer held sunglasses.

She stared at them as a little longing grew up in her heart. She hadn't needed to shade her eyes from the sun in a long time. They wouldn't be much protection anyway, unless they could cover her entire body.

She took a pair out and tried them on, glancing at herself in one of the full-length mirrors. Sunglasses weren't a common accessory for vampires. Sure, they could still be worn at night for added concealment, but depending on where you were, that could actually make you stand out more.

Sunglasses were generally for people who went out in the sun. People who weren't vampires.

She put them back in the same spot and shut the drawer. How Julian needed them, she had no idea. She knew he could daywalk. He hadn't kept that from her. But how that was possible remained a mystery.

It was one of those subject they'd left alone. At least, she hadn't asked and he hadn't offered. Maybe something had happened at his turning. Somehow he'd been able to hold on to that part of his humanity. Didn't seem possible, and she'd never heard of it happening to any other vampire, but how else could it be explained? Magic? Maybe. He had said his family employed a powerful witch.

Whatever made it possible, it wasn't Desi's

business. If he wanted to share, he would. If he didn't, no big deal.

She turned off the closet light and went out to the living room to watch a movie. The remote for the television was a tablet, and the touch screen made everything easy. She got the movie queued up, then went into the kitchen to dig around for something to snack on.

She opened the pantry and grinned. Apparently, Julian liked sweets. And not just any sweets, but soft, chewy ones. In fact, an entire pantry shelf was dedicated to them. There were industrial-sized buckets of gummy bears and Swedish Fish, bags of fruit slices, tubs of licorice of all sorts, and boxes of smaller individual packets of gummy cola bottles, Sour Patch Kids, and slightly gross gummy worms. There were some others she didn't recognize because the writing was all in Japanese, plus a few more packages of cherry and strawberry licorice twists. The man liked his candy.

She laughed as she looked at them all, then realized they might not be his. He'd said the town did trick-or-treating every Friday night. Maybe all this candy had something to do with that…he could be standing on the street right now, handing some of it out.

Regardless, it was cute to think that he was either stocking all this candy for the tourist kids who stopped to see him when he was on duty, or he had a sweet tooth that was stuck in fourth grade. Slick, lady-killer Julian had a definite soft spot for youthful indulgences.

How could she not like a guy like that?

He'd said to make herself at home, and with all this sugary goodness in front of her, the steak no longer held any appeal. She grabbed a bag of gummy cola bottles, a bottle of water from the fridge and went back to the movie.

An hour and forty-five minutes later, the movie was over, and she was bored. She sent a quick text to Sam, but there was no response. Desi imagined the poor woman was probably sedated and sleeping.

She went over to the windows to take in the view. It wasn't the Strip, but it was very pretty. In the distance, the lights of Main Street cast a soft glow on the night sky. Julian was down there somewhere. No doubt having a ball being the center of attention. She understood how fun that was, and in that way, they were very much alike. She could imagine how the female tourists reacted to him in that getup. He was already ridiculously good-looking, but in that costume, he was the vampire hero personified. Would he be flirting back? Yes. After all, it was part of the job.

How many selfies would he be in tonight? Her eyes narrowed as she pictured all that smiling and laughing and touching and—she frowned. She was jealous.

Wow. Where had that come from? She laughed. She wasn't jealous. That was just plain silly. If anything, she was just bummed to be missing out on the fun going on down there. That was all.

She knew how freeing it was to be your true self, even though she only got to do that on stage. But to walk the streets without a care that someone might think you were a vampire? Amazing. Even more so to think that in this town, it was encouraged.

She huffed out a breath. Why should she stay in when she could go out there and see for herself? It was perfectly safe. People here weren't likely to recognize a star from the Vegas stage, no matter how well known she was in that town. And no one knew she was here. Whoever was after her in Vegas thought she was laid up in the hospital with a broken leg.

Plus, she had brought all those wigs with her. She could change her look enough that not even Julian would recognize her.

Smiling, she headed back to her room to get dressed. Tonight wasn't going to be nearly so quiet as she'd thought.

Maybe the women were extra clingy this evening, but Julian felt like he hadn't had three minutes without one wrapped around him, holding out her phone for her friends to take a picture. If he had to pretend to bite one more neck, he might actually snap and do it.

He sighed. Internally. Because externally he was smiling and happy and flirting like it was his job, which it was.

He *wouldn't* be biting anyone. He'd think about it an awful lot, but his fangs would not touch skin. That was rule number one for being the VOD. Fangs were never to touch skin because fangs were sharp and blood would most definitely be drawn. And that could cause lawsuits. Worse, younger vampires might not be able to control themselves around real, warm, available human throats.

So. No fangs on skin. No matter how tempting it might be.

"Say plasma!" The woman currently embracing him smiled as her friend took the picture. She let go of Julian immediately to reach for her phone. "Let me see. Oh, that is definitely going on Instagram." She waved at Julian. "Thanks, you're the best vampire I've seen all night."

"You're very kind," he answered. He ought to be the best, considering he had been practicing for nearly four hundred years.

But his crankiness had nothing to do with the tourists and everything to do with the luscious vampiress in his penthouse. He'd much rather be with her than on this street, even if she didn't feel about him the way he felt about her.

That part sucked. No pun intended. But they were going to be spending a lot of time together, and there was always the possibility that she might fall for him, something he knew he should let go of, but just couldn't.

Or maybe he was just an optimistic lovesick fool. That was probably more likely.

The smiling and the flirting and the picture taking kept up at a pretty steady pace for the next hour or so, then he got a short reprieve as the crowd tapered off. He took the opportunity to check his phone. He hadn't felt it vibrate, but he wanted to make sure he hadn't missed

Desi trying to get a hold of him.

He hadn't. He put the phone away and looked up to see Hugh and Delaney coming toward him, pushing a pram. He grinned. Seeing George was always a treat. "Hello there, you handsome thing."

Hugh smiled. "Hello to you too."

Delaney laughed and Julian rolled his eyes. "You know very well I wasn't talking to you." He peered into the pram. "How's my darling nephew?"

"A little fussy," Delaney answered. "That's why we decided to take a walk. Helps settle him down."

Julian reached toward him but looked at Delaney. "May I?"

"Sure." She pressed her foot down on the pram's brake.

Julian lifted George into his arms. He smelled like powder and whatever that scent was that seemed to surround all babies. Julian gave George's fat cheek a big kiss. "Hello, Georgie, you handsome devil. How are you, little man?"

George put his hand on Julian's cheek and cooed.

"Why thank you," Julian said. "I think you're quite the looker too."

Delaney shook her head. "Why don't you three boys hang out while I run into the ice cream shop for a second?"

Hugh laughed. "I knew you had an ulterior motive for coming out tonight."

She gave him a coy look. "I don't have any idea what you mean. Want a scoop?"

"No, I'm fine. You go ahead."

"Julian?"

"Not while I'm on duty, thanks."

"Okay, but you're missing out. I heard the flavor of the month is chocolate bourbon toffee crunch." She waved over her shoulder as she headed into I Scream.

Hugh took the brake off the pram, moved it to the side, then locked it down again before moving closer to Julian. "Everything all right?"

"Sure, why wouldn't it be?"

He shrugged. "You sounded a little on edge when you called about the jet. And now you're back home already. I expected to find Greyson doing VOD tonight."

"Nope." Julian bounced George on his hip, making him laugh. "It's my shift, I'm working it."

"So I see." Hugh went silent a moment. "And I guess you're not going to tell me what you were doing in Las Vegas? Again?"

Julian peered at his brother over the top of George's head. "How do you know I was in Vegas?"

"Flight manifest."

Julian sighed. It was impossible to keep anything private in a small town or a large family. "Personal business."

Hugh nodded. "If you want to talk—"

"I don't." Julian forced himself to lighten up. Hugh wasn't the enemy here. "But thank you for the offer."

Delaney came back out carrying a large paper cup overflowing with ice cream, sprinkles, hot fudge and whipped cream. She pointed her spoon at the men. "Nocturne Falls should have an ice cream festival this summer."

"Not a bad idea," Julian said. He gave George another kiss, then put him back in the pram.

"I'm glad you think so," she said. "Get on that, will you?" She winked at him.

Julian smiled. "I'll see what I can do, but it's already May."

"August, then?"

"Maybe."

"Fabulous. I'd love to try my hand at a couple of flavors. Right now, I'm thinking peach cobbler with a brown sugar rum swirl. Doesn't that sound yummy?"

"Darling," Hugh said as he checked that George was secure. "Don't you think you have enough irons in the fire already with your shop and George?"

"Probably, but honey, *ice cream*. Besides, Julian will help with Georgie, won't you, Jules?"

"I'd love to." Just maybe not while Desi was in town. Tourists were milling around, trying to catch his eye, a sure sign they wanted pictures. "I should get back to work."

Hugh took hold of the pram and knocked the brake off. "Have a good night. Let's do lunch this week."

That sounded like another attempt to talk, but Julian just nodded. "Great. I'll call you." Which he wouldn't until he had things with Desi figured out a little more. Although, if she was going to keep normal vampire hours, his days would be free. In Nocturne Falls, he adhered to human hours. In Vegas, with Desi, where he had no other responsibilities than her, he slept through the days like she did. "Have a good night."

As the happy little family left, Julian went back into VOD mode, but the small crowd waiting on him was taken care of in half an hour. Then he was alone again with his thoughts.

"Quite the enterprise you have here," a husky female voice said.

The statement turned him around. He squinted at the woman in front of him. Her face was familiar, but the sleek brown hair and bangs were throwing him off. And there was something different about the eyes. "Pardon?"

She laughed, and he recognized the sound instantly.

"Desi? What are you doing here? And why are you talking like that?"

"Just trying to fool you." She shrugged, back to her normal voice. "I got bored."

"How did you get into town?"

"I called a Ryde." She grinned at him. "How do you like my new look?"

The skintight jeans and tan leather jacket were surprisingly tame compared to what she'd been wearing earlier. The high-heeled leopard boots should have been a giveaway, however. "I like it very much." She was beautiful no matter what she had on. "The hair threw me. And your eyes are different."

She leaned in and as the wind shifted, he caught a whiff of her orange blossom perfume. "It's a wig and colored contacts. Plus some different makeup. I used to do it in Vegas once in a while when I wanted to go out and be left alone. I'm too well known for that to work there anymore. But here? Like a charm."

"Now I know why your suitcases were so full."

"I like to have all my tools with me at all times." She nudged him. "You sure keep busy, don't you?"

"As VOD? Yes." He narrowed his eyes. "How long have you been watching me?"

"Long enough to see you work that last crowd." Her eyes took on an odd light. "The ladies certainly love you."

"They love the idea of me. It's why they come here. To mingle with the creatures they know aren't real."

She pursed her lips and touched one of the flounces on his shirt. "If only they knew."

"They'd probably stop coming."

Her expression turned sly. "You'd better keep up the flirting, then. It's good for the bottom line."

"It's also part of the job description. Keeping the tourists happy."

She smiled. "Technically, I'm a tourist. Are you going to keep me happy?"

He laughed. "That is my intention. What would you like?"

"A tour of this crazy town." She looked around. "This place is really something. When do you get off again?"

"Not until midnight or so. I'll come straight home and get you, and we can walk around."

"Will anything still be open? Some of the shops are already closed."

"A few bars."

She sighed. "That's not much of a tour."

"Tomorrow, then. As soon as it's dark."

"I guess. But I'm bored now."

"I'm sure you are, and I'd rather be with you, but a job is a job." He smiled gently. "Until this thing is figured out, you need to be somewhere safe. Or at the very least, not alone."

"Jules, no one knows I'm here, and secondly, you didn't even recognize me. I'm perfectly safe."

"Maybe. But you're still alone. I don't like that.

I'd rather you wait until I can go with you."

She seemed to be considering that. "Tomorrow night, then?"

"If you agree to go back to the penthouse now."

She huffed out a breath. "Fine. Is there at least a club we could go to? Somewhere to dance? Get some drinks? Hang in the VIP section?"

"This isn't Vegas, but yes, we do have one club like that. Insomnia. And if you get that Ryde driver back here now, I'll take you tomorrow night after our tour." That should be safe enough. Insomnia was only for supernaturals, and if her stalker was a human, they'd never get in on their own. And if her stalker was a supernatural, Julian would be there to protect her, along with a host of other supernaturals. No one would get to Desi while they were both in that club.

"Okay, calling now." She pulled out her phone. "Speaking of calling, I sent Sam a big get well soon bouquet, but I didn't sign my name. Just put D on the card. She'll know."

He frowned. "How did you pay?"

"Credit card. How else?"

"I don't think that's a good idea. If they're tracking you—"

"By my credit card? That's illegal."

"So is stalking someone, but hasn't made a difference, has it? Look, I'll get you some cash, but no more using any of your cards. We can't risk it."

"I don't want your money. But you might have a point about the credit card thing."

He made a face. He knew she had issues with anything she considered charity. "You can pay me back."

"You're sure?"

He nodded, a little distracted as two giggly women came up to him. The tall one waved her phone at him. "Can we get a picture when you're done?"

He put on his best smile, showing off his fangs. They giggled some more. "Absolutely!"

Desi held up her phone to show him the Ryde app. "Driver's a minute away. See you later, I guess."

"Sorry," he said. "I know this isn't easy on you."

She shrugged. "I'll live."

"That is the plan."

She snorted. "True. See you later."

She headed for the curb, waving to the silver SUV that must have been the Ryde. Julian waited until she was in the vehicle before taking the picture with the waiting tourists.

Not even one night and Desi was bored. Keeping her safe might be harder than he'd imagined.

The Ryde driver glanced back at Desdemona. "The Excelsior, correct?"

"Yes, thank you." She was going back to Julian's penthouse, all right.

But she wasn't staying there. The night was young, Julian wasn't getting off until at least midnight, and she was bored.

Plus, he'd let slip that there was a club in town worth visiting. That was all the motivation she needed.

She stopped at the desk in the lobby and put on some charm. "Hi there, Lou."

"Hello, Miss Clarke. How can I help you?"

"Call me Desi. All my friends do."

"Okay, Miss Desi."

She smiled. "Since Julian's working, he told me about a club I can go dancing at. Insomnia. Do you know it?"

He nodded. "Yes, ma'am. It's a supernaturals-only club and very popular with the locals and tourists alike. And like I said, only supernaturals, so you can be yourself." He laughed. "Even more than you can be in town."

"Speaking of being yourself…" She gave him a quick once-over. He had the thick build of a retired football player. "I'm sure you already know what I am, but I can't quite figure out what you are. If you don't mind sharing?"

"Don't mind at all." He stood up a little straighter. "Ogre on my father's side, uncertain amounts of sasquatch on my mother's side."

No wonder he was such a big guy. She smiled enthusiastically. "Only half ogre, then? You certainly got all the best traits of that particular race, didn't you? I feel so safe knowing you're guarding this entrance." It wasn't a lie. Ogres made incredible bodyguards. They were like flesh-and-blood tanks. Nothing stopped them. Throw the sasquatch into the mix and there was a good chance Lou was also untrackable.

He preened. "I do my best."

"So, Lou, have you been to Insomnia?"

"I have."

"What do you think of it?"

"The wife and I don't get many date nights now that we have the twins, but it's a good evening out if we can get a sitter. Very fancy."

He tipped his head. "Would you like to go there?"

"I would, very much. What's the cover charge?"

He grinned. "For a guest of Mr. Ellingham's? Nothing. Just give me a moment."

He picked up the phone and dialed. "This is Lou Kovac at the Excelsior. A guest of Julian Ellingham's would like to come to the club this evening. Yes." He covered the mouthpiece with his wide hand. "Are you bringing anyone with you?"

She shook her head. "Just me."

He went back to the conversation. "Just Miss Desi Clarke. Thank you." He hung up. "You're on the list."

"Perfect! You are a doll. Thank you, Lou. I assume the club has a dress code?"

He frowned. "No jeans, sorry. It's kind of dressy."

"No worries, I'm headed up to change anyway." She gave him a little wave. "See you in a bit."

She hopped on the penthouse elevator and went straight up to Julian's apartment. She'd left the door open since she didn't know the code for the keypad, but no one was getting past Lou anyway.

In the guest room, she flung wide the closet doors and studied what she'd brought, now thankful for her inability to pack light. She decided on a short, sequined mini-dress. Her new black platform boots would be perfect with the dress's dramatic rainbow stripes.

She changed, then added darker evening makeup. She glanced at the wigs she'd brought, but the one she had on was working so she left it. A couple of bracelets, some big earrings, her black satin micro crossbody bag, and she was out the door.

When she got to the lobby, she approached Lou again. "I realize I never asked you how to get to the club. I need the address for the Ryde driver."

"You look very nice, Miss Desi. You're going to fit right in."

"Thank you." It was a shame Julian wouldn't get to see her like this. She did look pretty amazing.

He smiled. "And I can handle the transportation for you. The Excelsior has a Ryde account, and we're happy to assist our residents when they need it." He leaned in. "It's a special account that only sends us supernatural drivers."

"Perfect!" Even the Skye Towers didn't do that.

He got his phone out, pulled up the app and tapped in the info. "Okay, there's a car on the way. Less than three minutes. Your driver is Trevor, and he's an avian shifter. Owl, I believe."

"Excellent. I'm going to wait outside and enjoy the air. You've been a tremendous help. I'll be sure to let Julian know."

He seemed pleased about that. "Happy to help, Miss Desi. You have a good evening."

The Ryde driver showed up right on time, and

about fifteen minutes later, they were pulling into the parking lot of what looked like an abandoned factory. Caldwell Manufacturing was painted on the side of the brick building, but the letters were badly faded.

She peered out the window. "Are you sure this is it?"

"Absolutely. This is the industrial part of town, and not much goes on here anymore, but that's why they put the club here." He looked around, head swiveling with the unnerving flexibility of his animal form. "Lots of cars. Should be a decent crowd inside."

She checked out the parking lot. There was a Jaguar next to them. In the rows, she spotted Mercedes, Alfa Romeo, BMW, a Bentley, a couple of Corvettes, a Ferrari and even a Rolls. High-end cars like that wouldn't just be sitting here for no reason, but the abandoned look of the building was giving her second thoughts. "Let me go have a look inside and decide if I want to stay before you go, okay?"

"You got it. I'll sit here until you give me a sign."

"Great." She hopped out, a little uneasy but also curious. Lou wouldn't have sent her here unless this was a good place. And Julian certainly wouldn't have mentioned it. She walked cautiously to a large, rusted steel door on the side of the building. She listened hard. If there was a club here, shouldn't she hear music? Or at least the dull thump of the bass?

But silence greeted her. She glanced back at the car. The driver nodded like it was all right. She examined the steel door again. Yes, it was rusty, but the handle had a little shine to it. Like it was used regularly.

She grabbed ahold and pulled.

Inside, rows of worktables and machinery filled the vast warehouse. She stepped in, but kept the door open. The odors of dust and grease complemented the absolute stillness of the place. It seemed like no one had been here for ages. And yet, that door handle had definitely been used.

"Can I help you?"

She shrieked, then laughed as she realized the voice had come from across the room. A large bear of man in a suit stood beside a freight elevator. A doorman, maybe? She hoped so. Because the alternative was he was just some weirdo hanging out in an abandoned warehouse with a bunch of crazy expensive cars in the parking lot. "I'm looking for Insomnia."

The man nodded. "You've found it."

Her brows lifted. "You're sure?"

"Yes, ma'am. Been working here for three years."

"All right, then." How about that. She sighed in relief as she turned to the driver and gave him a thumbs-up. The driver took off, and she walked toward the doorman. "I'm Miss Clarke. Lou from the Excelsior called?"

The man nodded. "Nice to have you with us this evening, Miss Clarke. I'm Chet. Always a pleasure to make the acquaintance of a beautiful woman."

She smiled. "Aren't you a charmer?"

He shrugged, looking a little sheepish. "My mother just raised me right."

She laughed. "I'll say so."

He punched a code into a very modern keypad next to the elevator. The buttons glowed blue, and the soft turning of gears hummed through the warehouse.

The doors opened. He reached in and pushed another button, then nodded at her. "Have a good evening."

"Thank you, Chet." She stepped on. The Basement button was lit up. Interesting. The club was below street level. That had to be why she hadn't heard anything. The doors closed and down she went.

When the doors slid open again, she smiled, more than pleasantly surprised. "Now *this* is more like it."

She strolled out, head held high and feeling very much at home. Not in a million years would she have guessed that a place like this existed in the cunning little tourist destination of Nocturne Falls.

She stood still for a moment and took it in. The joint was legit. Dark and gorgeous. Just like her. She laughed to herself as she walked toward the bar, letting the thump of bass wash through her and set her pace. The vibe was industrial, which she loved, and sleek in that kind of clean, modern way, but still plush and luxurious. The leather seating helped with that, as did the water features and the soft drapery that set off the VIP section.

Had Julian had a hand in decorating this place too? If so, he'd done an outstanding job. She imagined if he were with her, they'd be headed right up to that VIP area, but seeing as how she was on her own, she'd have to settle for coach.

She strolled to the bar and found an available seat. A bartender approached her immediately, a beautiful Asian woman with glowing purple streaks in her hair and the aura of magic about her. A witch maybe.

The woman set a black cocktail napkin down in front of Desi. "Welcome to Insomnia. What's your poison?"

"Champagne. The best you have by the glass."

"Excellent. I'll be right back."

Desi twisted to watch the crowd. If everyone here was a supernatural, Nocturne Falls had a very diverse community. She spotted shifters of all kinds, some vampires, a few nymphs, a good number of witches, and a few people she couldn't quite place. Clearly, being yourself was welcome here, because most seemed to be in full or half forms, eyes glowing and fangs showing.

She realized she was still in locked-down human mode. She relaxed and let her true nature hang out a little more. She ran her tongue over her fangs. It was nice. And not something she could do in Vegas unless she was on stage.

"Here you are."

Desi twisted back around to see a tall flute of champagne waiting for her. "Thank you."

"I'm Elmira, and I'm happy to take care of you this evening. Would you like to start a tab?"

"Put it on Julian Ellingham's account." She was curious if that would work, but after the ease with which Lou had set things up, it was worth a shot. Besides, Julian didn't want her using her credit cards so what choice did she have? She'd make sure to get a receipt and pay him back.

Elmira hesitated.

Desi pointed back toward the elevator. "You can call Chet if you need to confirm that I'm Julian's guest. He spoke with Lou at the Excelsior about it earlier."

"I probably should." The woman smiled a little nervously. "It's not that I don't believe you, but I don't want to get in trouble with my boss, either."

Desi sipped her champagne. It was *very* good. "I understand."

Elmira darted off. Desi spun in her chair again to people-watch. It was one of her favorite things to do, and while it was mildly entertaining in Vegas, where she liked to play a little game of Spot the Supernatural, in this club, it was a lot more fun because it was about trying to figure out what each person was, and what they were up to.

The couple at the far end of the bar seemed utterly bored with each other. Maybe a first date that wasn't working out?

The five or so women grouped around one of the high tables were celebrating something. A birthday perhaps, since no one was wearing anything that might indicate she was a bride to be, but they all had drinks and were doing a lot of laughing.

There were men and women who were clearly on the prowl, some who looked like they were here to drink, a few more who'd yet to leave the dance floor.

But the area that interested Desi the most was the VIP section. Soft, billowy curtains sectioned the raised area off, but all of the curtains were drawn back. After all, what was the point of being a VIP if no one could see you?

Smoked mirrors covered the back walls of that area, reminding her of a small club in Vegas she'd once frequented. A place called Club Ninety-Six. They were known for their exclusivity and celebrity clientele. Until it was revealed that their mirrored walls were actually two-way and the owner of the club had been videotaping—and attempting to blackmail—the stars who went there.

Made her wonder about Insomnia. And who owned it.

"Miss Clarke?"

Desi turned to see Elmira had returned. "Yes?"

"I confirmed with Chet." She smiled broadly. "I put your drink on Mr. Ellingham's account."

"Excellent." She drained the last of her champagne. "And just in time for round two."

Elmira nodded and picked up the empty flute. "I'll be right back."

"Excuse me?"

The soft female voice came from behind Desi. She turned to see who it belonged to. A pretty redhead stood there. And behind the pretty redhead stood a serious-looking man with dark hair and piercing black eyes that even his glasses couldn't hide. He was frowning. She was smiling.

They didn't look very stalkery, so Desi couldn't imagine what this was about. "Yes?"

"I'm sorry to bother you," the redhead said. "But aren't you Desdemona Valentine?"

Desi hadn't expected to be recognized. Not here and not in her wig. She studied them a little closer as a new sense of panic rose up in her. The woman had a guileless smile and the man just looked bored. More importantly, Desi's gut said they were just fans. Or at least the woman was. And Desi wasn't one to disappoint her fans. Not with the television special coming up. She put on her best photo-op smile. "I am."

The woman nudged the man. "See, I told you."

Desi laughed. "I must say, I am very surprised to be recognized."

The man leaned forward. "And you probably want to be left alone. Sorry to have bothered you."

"No bother." She stuck her hand out. "You have me at a disadvantage, I'm afraid."

His frown stuck firm, but he shook her hand. "Cole Van Zant. And this is my fiancée, Pandora Williams."

"I saw you in Vegas," Pandora chimed in. "Well, I didn't see your show. I saw your billboards. And my friend lives in the same building as you."

"Your friend?" Desi held on to her smile, but small cracks were forming in her confidence. Being recognized was one thing, having someone know where she lived was another. Especially when she didn't know who was after her. "What's her name?"

"He's a he. Ivan Tsvetkov. He's an MMA fighter. Well, he was. He's retired now."

Desi shook her head. "I don't know him, sorry." She wasn't much for socializing outside of her very small group of friends. Her trust issues ran deeper than those that came with being famous. Another one of Alonso's little gifts.

"Well, it's no big deal," Pandora said. "Like I said, he's retired now. He lives here in Nocturne Falls with his fiancée. Oh!" Her expression brightened. "His fiancée's from Vegas too. Monalisa Devlin. Do you know her?"

Behind her, Cole shook his head. "Pandora, Las Vegas is a big city filled with thousands of people Miss Valentine doesn't know."

"Yeah, I guess you're right." Pandora shrugged. "I just thought maybe…you know."

But Desi was too shocked to answer. Monalisa Devlin was a name she recognized. Because Monalisa's father, Padraig Devlin, was a very powerful, very dangerous man. If there was a supernatural in Las Vegas who didn't know who he was, it was only because they hadn't been there very long.

He controlled a lot of what went on in Vegas, at least when it came to all things supernatural.

Desi found her voice. "Monalisa is engaged to an MMA fighter? How on earth did her father allow that?"

"Well," Pandora said. "It happened like this…"

Quarter after midnight. Julian had never gotten home so quickly after a shift, but then, he hadn't stopped at Howler's for a drink and hadn't met up with any eligible young ladies in a bid to keep his playboy reputation firmly in place.

No, tonight it was straight home to the little wife. He grinned. Was that what married life was like? Even if Desi wasn't interested in playing house, it amused him.

Greyson Garrett, one of the vampires in town who also worked at the VOD job, called as Julian was walking through the lobby of the Excelsior. He gave Lou a nod as he answered the phone. "Greyson, what can I do for you?"

"I might be a little late tomorrow night. I'll do my best not to be, but Lucien needs me for an errand."

Julian walked onto the penthouse lift. "No

worries. Is the old man all right?" Lucien was one of the most elusive and mysterious residents of Nocturne Falls. No one knew much about him, but Julian had been instrumental in helping the retired reaper settle here. He'd also helped the man set up Insomnia. They'd even brainstormed the name together. It was meant to be ironic seeing as how Lucien's former job was about permanent sleep.

"He's…" Greyson sighed. "Lucien."

"Understood. Take whatever time you need." The lift stopped and the doors opened.

"Much appreciated."

Julian hung up, walked through the foyer and into his apartment. "Honey, I'm home."

He laughed despite knowing Desi wouldn't be responding with the same sort of enthusiasm. Life was pointless if you couldn't enjoy yourself, and he refused to be completely destroyed by her rejection. At least not in front of her. He could save that for after she went back to Las Vegas.

"Join me in a drink?" he called out as he went to the bar to pour himself a bourbon. She still hadn't responded by the time he'd swallowed the first sip. It wasn't like her to ignore him completely.

He left the glass on the counter and went in search of her. Maybe she was on the phone with Sam. Or maybe she'd fallen asleep. Most daysleepers kept to a pretty rigid schedule, but she'd been through a lot. If she'd crashed, he'd let her be, even if it might potentially throw off her routine.

Her bedroom was dark. He peeked in and whispered, "Desi?"

But he didn't need vampire vision to see she wasn't there.

He scoured the rest of the penthouse without finding her. Just the scent of her perfume. Concern took hold of him. He picked up the phone and dialed the front desk.

Lou answered on the first ring. "Evening, Mr. Ellingham. How can I—"

"Did Miss Clarke come home?"

"Yes, but then she went out again. That's the last time I saw her."

The concern turned into something darker. She'd left a second time. Alone. He closed his eyes and tried not to let anger take over. "Do you have any idea where she went?"

"Absolutely. Insomnia. She said you'd told her to go there since you were working. I called her a Ryde."

He swore under his breath. "Thank you." Then hung up. She must still be there. He was going after her, but he was not about to stroll into that club looking like this. He ditched the jewelry, scrubbed the eyeliner off, then changed quickly into a white shirt and charcoal suit.

He was in his Maserati and headed to Insomnia

ten minutes later. Lou had looked a little worried as Julian had walked out, but he didn't have time to explain to Lou what was going on or to give him a crash course in everything he needed to know about Desi.

Not even Julian knew everything he needed to about her. But one thing was for sure: her decision to go out without him when someone might be trying to kill her wasn't the best idea she'd ever had.

On the drive over, he did what he could to talk himself down. He was angry. And worried. There wasn't much to be done about that. But he tried to see things from her side. She thought she was safe in Nocturne Falls, which she probably was, but until they knew more, there was no guarantee.

She was used to a fast-paced life lived primarily in the spotlight of fame. He understood that too. He'd lived it with her when he'd been in Vegas. It was nothing for her to head out after a show and spend the rest of the evening being adored and fawned over in the VIP section of whatever club she chose.

She was Las Vegas royalty. And she was treated as such wherever she went. No doubt a quiet evening home alone wasn't up to her entertainment standards.

He cooled down a little. She'd probably stayed home as long as she'd been able, but he could imagine what too much thinking had done to her. Probably spun her up. And without him there to calm her down…she'd needed an out.

So that's exactly what she'd done. Left to find a situation she was familiar with. Insomnia made perfect sense.

The anger mellowed into frustration, but the concern remained as he parked. He had to take better care of her. He never should have gone to work, regardless of what his brothers would have thought. He shook his head. No more being VOD while she was here. Hugh and Sebastian would just have to get over it. Between Greyson and some of the other vamps who subbed in, he'd get the shifts handled and that would be that.

Maybe Remy Lafitte could cover a few. The deputy might be too busy working for the sheriff's department, but it never hurt to ask.

Julian strode into Caldwell Manufacturing like he owned the place. He didn't, but he spent enough time here. "Evening, Chet. Elevator, please."

The bear-shifter nodded and hit the call button. "Yes, sir." He stood at attention. "How are you this evening?"

"Good. Soon to be better. I hope."

Chet smiled. "Meeting up with your lady friend?"

That implied she was still in the club. That was good. "You saw her?"

Chet nodded as the elevator opened. "I did. Very pretty. Nice too."

Julian snorted and walked on, then pushed the Basement button. "Just don't marry her," he muttered as the doors closed.

"What was that?" Chet called out.

But Julian was already on his way down. When the doors opened, he strode out, scanning the club for her. It didn't take long to find her.

In true Desdemona Valentine style, she was enthroned in the VIP section with a squad of people around her and plenty of ice-filled buckets holding her favorite champagne within easy reach. She was on full display to the rest of the club. An easy target.

Irritation blocked the edges of his vision, allowing him to see only her. She was as vulnerable as a newborn rabbit in an open field. He climbed the steps to the VIP lounge.

The party was in full swing and the crowd around her included a good number of people he recognized, Pandora Williams and her fiancé Cole Van Zant among them. He took some comfort in that.

Desi was mid-story when she caught sight of him. Her animated gestures stilled, and she let out a happy shriek. "Julian!"

"Desdemona." He nodded and smiled, even though that was the last facial expression he felt like making.

Pandora waved. "Hi Julian."

"Pandora." He raised his brows at Desi. "Could we have a word? Privately?"

She smiled coyly. "Of course, darling." She stood. "If you would all excuse me…" She walked around the cocktail table to stand in front of him.

He took her elbow and led her off to a spot in the reserved lounge that was vacant. His anger was back, and there wasn't time to talk himself out of it. "What the hell do you think you're doing?"

Her eyes rounded.

He'd never spoken to her like that. Regret filled him instantly. He sighed. "I'm sorry, Desi. That came out wrong."

She crossed her arms. "I'll say."

"I got concerned when I came home and you weren't there. Especially since we have no idea who's been harassing you. Then I walk in here and you're holding court like the Queen of Versailles and all I can think about is what a vulnerable position you've put yourself in." He scrubbed a hand over his face. He'd gone too long with too little sleep.

"I'm not vulnerable. I'm in a supes-only club." She lifted her chin. "It's not like just anybody can walk in here. No one knows me in this town anyway. Except for Pandora, but she only recognized me because she was in Vegas recently."

"And you just proved my point. If she recognized

you, who else might?" The irritation came back. "And can I remind you that we still don't know if your stalker is supernatural or human?"

She almost rolled her eyes, but caught herself as if thinking better of it. "Pandora being in Vegas was a random thing. A one off."

"And yet the number of people who know you're here has now grown by leaps and bounds since you invited everyone in the club to join you for champagne in the VIP lounge."

Her eyes narrowed. "It's not *everyone*."

He glanced over his shoulder. "Yes, you're right. The DJ is still in his booth."

She gave him a smug smile. "I don't think I'm in any danger here, even with all these new friends I've made." She shrugged. "Look, I might have overreacted. Maybe Sam's hit and run was just that—a hit and run. And maybe the rest of it was just what I thought—overzealous, creepy fans."

"So you're ready to go back to Vegas?"

"I'm—" She glanced down. "Hold that thought. My phone's buzzing." She pulled it out of the little black bag at her hip and checked the screen.

Her expression went blank. Then slightly horrified.

"What is it?" His phone was buzzing too. He pulled it free from his jacket pocket.

She glanced up at him. "Sam. She just got flowers and—"

"Hang on." The screen showed Harlan calling. "I need to take this. It's Harlan."

Desi nodded, clutching her phone to her body like it might try to get away.

Julian answered. "What's going on?"

"Sam just got a flower delivery. Black roses. And the card says, 'Next time, I'll finish the job.' She's pretty shaken up."

Julian breathed out a curse. "I'm sure. Did you see who delivered them?"

"A woman from Desert Blooms. It's a local place, completely on the up and up. And she didn't know anything about the order other than it was part of her hospital delivery."

"Can you dig deeper? See if they'll give up whoever placed the order?"

"I'll do my best."

"Protecting Sam comes first."

"Understood."

Julian hung up. All of Desi's bravado was gone. "I guess you know what the message on the flowers said."

She nodded, the wind very much out of her sails. "I don't feel so safe anymore."

Desi sat cross-legged on her bed, wearing a pair of leggings and an oversized tee she usually reserved for spa days. Her wig was off, the French braid that had been restraining her natural hair undone, and her face scrubbed clean. She stared blankly at the wall. Her mind was on Sam. And whoever was tormenting her.

Julian walked in with a steaming mug in his hands and held it out to her. "Here. Drink this."

"What is it?"

"Tea. Specifically, my grandmother's proprietary blend that she has shipped in from the UK. She thinks it cures everything. I disagree, but I thought it might help."

"Thanks." She took it and cupped the mug between her hands. The heat felt good.

He stood at the foot of the bed. "You okay?"

She shook her head, then sighed. "I'm worried about Sam."

"That's understandable."

"I'm also freaked out about everything else. I almost had myself convinced it was all in my head. That I was being paranoid."

"That note proves you're not."

She glanced up. "I owe you an apology. I'm sorry for doing such a dumb thing tonight. I just…I don't know what I was thinking."

He took a seat in the chair across from her. "You don't need to explain or apologize. And Sam's in good hands."

She sipped the tea. It was good. And deliciously sweet, like he'd added a big dollop of honey. The warmth traveled through her, making her feel comforted and cared for. Just like Julian. He was such a good man. "If you say she is, then I believe you."

"Good." He'd changed into loose, black cotton pants and a matching T-shirt. He looked like an ad for designer lounge wear. Sexy and sophisticated without trying. Of course, he'd looked hot in his suit, too. "You up to talking?"

"About what's going on?" She nodded. "I can't stop thinking about it, so why not?"

"Okay." He steepled his fingers on the arms of the chair. "Any thoughts on who might be behind all this?"

"Not immediately. And I've done a lot of

thinking about it, trust me."

"Who are your enemies?"

"I…I don't know." She frowned into the tea. "I always thought people liked me."

"And they do. They adore you. But clearly someone doesn't." He thought for a moment. "How have the negotiations with the studio been for the television deal?"

"Good. And done. There was compromise on both sides, and ultimately, I'm very happy with the final deal, as is my attorney." She shook her head. "I can't imagine anyone on their side would want to do anything like this to me."

He sighed. "Me either. Could this be a jilted lover?"

She laughed. "I think you know the answer to that. And if you don't, no. I haven't been with anyone in a long time."

He nodded. "I know how you resisted me. Who else, then? One of your friends?"

"I don't have many of those." It was just easier not to get close. "Do you think it could be another performer who's jealous?"

"Maybe. That seems like a big risk on their part, though. Getting found out would ruin their career. Is there someone specific you're thinking of?"

"No. All the performers in the show seem like really good people. Just thinking out loud and trying to make some sense of this." She mulled the possibilities a little more. "What if it is a fan? One who's gone over the edge?"

He narrowed his eyes like he was thinking. "It absolutely could be. But that's like trying to find the proverbial needle in a hay stack."

She put the tea on the nightstand and scooted forward. "Maybe not. I could ask the ticket office to run a list of people who've seen the show repeatedly in the last six months."

"That's a great idea. You know that I'm going to show up on that list."

She smiled. "Yes, but you're not out to kill me." She winked at him. "Not yet anyway."

He laughed softly, then leaned forward. "If this is a crazed fan, they've been interested in you since before the garlic bouquets started showing up. You should tell them to run the list for at least six months before the first bouquet arrived."

"Okay, I will. I'll send an email before I go to bed. It'll probably take them a day to get the info together. Any other ideas until then?"

His eyes narrowed. "Any chance you have the notes from the bouquets and the silver crosses?"

"It's all in my carry-on bag in a big envelope. I thought you might want to see that stuff."

"Good. I do. I'm going to take it into the sheriff's department tomorrow. Our sheriff is a werewolf. Great nose. Maybe he can pick up a scent from them, tell us if we're dealing with a human or not."

"I never would have thought to do that. Thank you." She got off the bed and dug the big envelope out. She offered it to him. "I really appreciate everything you're doing for me."

He took the envelope. "That's what friends do."

"Except I know your feelings for me go beyond friends. I'm sorry things can't be different between us."

He smiled sadly. "Me too."

Before she could say anything else, he got to his feet. "I'm exhausted. You must be too." He kissed the top of her head. "Sunrise is only a few hours away. Get some sleep. I'll most likely be gone when you wake up in the afternoon, but please, don't leave the house until I get back tomorrow."

"I won't." She smiled. "I can't, remember? Not if the sun's out."

He chuckled. "Right. Sorry."

She reached out and squeezed his hand. "Thanks again."

"Of course. Good night."

"Night." She watched him leave, then stood there a little longer, thinking about how fortunate she was to have a man like Julian in her life. He wasn't just a good man, he was a patient man. For all her rejection of him, he still treated her like she was worth his time and effort. And he didn't even know her reasons for rejecting him. For the first time in a long time, she was actually considering what it might be like to fall in love again.

But she couldn't entertain that thought without also remembering the consequences of such foolishness. Julian wasn't Alonso, but he was a man who put great value on things. His home and car and closet were proof of that. And as much as he professed to love her, Alonso had done the same.

No, being friends was as far as this relationship was going to go.

She shut her bedroom door, then pulled out her tablet to email the show's director about the ticket sales. After hitting send, she changed into a nightie, tied her hair into a scarf, and climbed into bed. Julian's choice of sheets was impressive. The cotton felt like silk.

She propped herself up with the pillows and turned on the television in search of something to help her escape her thoughts.

A documentary on Nefertiti seemed like just the thing. She sipped her tea and tried to disappear into ancient Egypt, but her mind kept returning to Julian and all the possibilities he represented.

Did she dare attempt love again? Could she handle it? Could she risk losing her heart again? Or worse?

After all, the first time she'd given her heart away the cost had nearly been her life.

Julian slept until nine, which was late for him, but he'd gotten so little sleep the last two days it was no wonder he'd slept in a little. Fortunately, the older a vampire got, the less sleep they needed, unless they were injured or ill. And despite what Julian's brothers thought about him, he was often up early. Normally, he'd get a workout in at the gym downstairs before anything else, but he had too much to do today. Helping Desi trumped his own needs at the moment.

That was how a marriage worked, and those were the rules he was going to abide by until the marriage no longer existed.

He showered and dressed, taking care to put on the shirt Didi had given him for Christmas. He'd never purposely call Elenora Ellingham that particular epithet to her face, but the pet name he and his brothers had given to their grandmother on account of her having once been a dowager duchess always made him smile.

Mostly because he knew how grumpy it would make her.

With Desi's envelope tucked into the leather messenger bag hanging off his shoulder, he swung by her bedroom on his way out. Her door was closed, but he could hear the television playing softly.

He hadn't expected her to be up so soon. He lifted his hand to knock, but then realized she could very well have left it on last night. If he knocked, it might wake her. Vampires slept very deeply in daysleep, but with all that was going on in her life, he didn't want to risk disturbing her. Instead, he eased the door open and peeked in.

She was curled in the silk coverlet and as still as stone, a sure sign she was in the cradle of daysleep.

Good. She needed to rest. He went in and turned the television off, then picked up the empty mug on her nightstand to carry it to the kitchen.

He paused at her bedside to take her in.

Somehow, she was even more beautiful asleep. He studied her for a moment longer, then grasped why that was. In sleep, her walls were down. Desi always had an air about her as if she was forever on the defensive. As if she'd been hurt and expected someone to do it again at any moment. Like it was a foregone conclusion.

That made him sad for her. And angry that someone had scarred her that badly.

A curl had escaped the silk scarf she'd tied her hair up in. He brushed the tendril off her cheek. "Love you," he whispered.

She didn't move, didn't stir. He was glad for that. She wouldn't have wanted to hear his sentimental drivel anyway.

He went to the sheriff's department first. Well, technically second after a quick, but necessary, detour for supplies.

"Why, Julian Ellingham, as I live and breathe," Birdie Caruthers exclaimed when he walked in. "What a nice surprise."

"Birdie, you get more beautiful every time I see you." He put the box he'd carried in on the counter. He knew Birdie well enough to know the three ways to properly grease her wheels. Flattery. Gossip. And sugar.

Her eyes widened. "Are those from the new doughnut place in town?"

"Yep. Zombie Donuts. Everyone's raving about them, so I thought, why not bring Birdie something that's almost as sweet as she is?"

She grinned and waved a hand at him. "Oh, you."

"And they're still warm." The zombie smiled up from the box. His decaying grin sat just above the slogan that read *better than brains*. Julian leaned in. "Did you hear that the owner might actually be a necromancer?"

"I did! Haven't met him yet, though, so jury's still out on that one. Maybe at the next chamber of commerce meeting." She opened the box and took a doughnut out, a lavender-iced monstrosity with green sugar crystals glistening on top like alien mold.

Her gaze shifted from the pastry to him and took on a shrewd gleam. "What can I do for you this morning? I know you're not here just to bring me doughnuts. Although both you and the sweets are always welcome."

He smiled. "I *wanted* to see you. But I also need to see Hank."

She tipped her head toward her nephew's office. "He's in. I'll buzz him."

She took a bite of the doughnut, then punched a button on the phone. "Hank. Julian Ellingham is on his way in."

The words were a little muffled by doughnut, but Hank seemed to understand. Or at least the grunt that came back in response sounded like he had.

"Go ahead," she said to Julian.

"Thank you."

She lifted her doughnut at him. "Thank *you*."

Julian went into Hank's office, not quite sure what to expect. He never was. Hank Merrow was a gruff sort. No-nonsense and short on words, but still a damn fine sheriff who'd always been there when the family and the town had needed him. "Morning, Sheriff."

"Ellingham." Hank nodded at the chairs across from his desk. A stack of paperwork sat in front of him. The top file was open. Hank saw Julian look at it. Hank closed the file. "What can I do for you?"

Julian took a seat. "I need your help."

"Uh huh."

Obviously, that was obvious. Julian restrained

his urge to roll his eyes at himself. Instead, he pulled out the envelope Desi had given him last night. "This is an odd request, but can you tell me if the scents on these determine if they originated with a human or a supernatural?"

Hank's eyes narrowed. "I'm not a bloodhound."

"I realize that, but I'm trying to protect a friend of mine, and whoever sent these is causing her some serious grief. In fact, they just threatened her life *again*."

Hank's brows lifted. He held out his hand.

Julian handed the package over.

Hank opened it, dumped the contents out, then picked up one of the cards from the bouquets. He held it to his nose, closed his eyes and inhaled. His nose wrinkled and he opened his eyes. "Garlic."

Julian nodded. "It was attached to a bunch of the stuff."

He closed his eyes again, his mouth opening slightly like he was trying to taste the air. Abruptly, he put the card down and looked at Julian. "Human *and* supernatural."

"What about the crosses?"

Hank frowned. "I'm not sniffing silver."

"Oh, right. Werewolf and all that." Julian sighed. "So both, eh? Doesn't do much to narrow it down. Any thoughts on what kind of supernatural?"

"Vampire. Best I can do."

"Still no help, because Desi touched them and that's what she is." Julian was disappointed. He wasn't any closer to figuring out who was behind this. "I appreciate the try, though."

Hank dropped the card back into the envelope, then held it out to Julian. He glanced down at the crosses. "You'll have to get those."

Julian stood and took the envelope. He scooped the crosses up, putting them away himself. He wasn't quite ready to let the conversation end, however. "Anything else you might have picked up? Even something that might not seem like anything."

"Perfume. Like flowers."

Julian shook his head. "That's Desi too most likely. She wears a scent like orange blossoms all the time."

Hank's eyes went down to slits. "What's going on exactly?"

Julian took his seat again and leaned back. "A very good friend of mine is being harassed, but like I said, we don't know by whom. She's staying at my house right now as things have gotten a little unsafe for her at home. I figured while she was here, we could get to the bottom of things."

Hank nodded slowly, like he was thinking. "Any trouble while she's been here?"

"Not so far, but she hasn't been as quiet as I'd like about her visit, so the possibility exists there

113

could be some in the future. Depends on how closely her stalker is watching her."

Hank tapped a finger on the desk. "And she's a vampire."

"Yes."

"I could spare Remy if you need extra security."

There was a thought Julian hadn't had. "I was actually thinking I might need him to pick up my VOD shifts, but Desi might like having another vampire around. Might make her feel safer. I know I'd appreciate it."

Hank nodded. "I'll send him over when he gets in tonight. You want him in uniform?"

"Plain clothes. For now." Keeping Remy's law officer status under wraps might give them an edge if Desi's stalker did show up. "Very kind of you."

"Happy to help."

Then Julian remembered his manners. "How's the little one?"

For the first time, Hank smiled. "Good. Feisty like her mama."

The family had sent gifts when the baby had been born, but Julian had been too wrapped up in wooing Desi to pay much attention to the birth. "What's her name again?"

"Hannah Rose." Hank whipped out his phone and showed Julian a picture. It was of Ivy, his wife, holding the baby. Hannah Rose was a precious little thing with bright blue eyes and chubby cheeks.

"You're going to have the boys lined up for miles with that one."

Hank turned the phone around to look at the picture himself. He nodded and smiled. "Yep."

"You'll have to get her and George together for a play date soon."

"Ivy and Delaney already have one planned."

"Of course they do." Julian stood and gestured toward the door. "I'll see myself out. Thanks again."

"Keep me posted if you need anything."

"Will do. Have a good one." Julian left, closing the office door behind him.

Birdie was sitting at the reception desk with a fresh cup of coffee next to her and a new doughnut in her hand. This time it looked like a jelly-filled one, based on the pink squiggles of icing meant to represent a brain. "Get what you need?"

"Enough. For now."

Birdie lifted the doughnut. "Come back any time."

Next on Julian's to-do list was an unannounced visit to his grandmother. Elenora Ellingham's estate sat up past the winery, in the hills of Nocturne Falls. It was a vast piece of land, which meant her closest neighbors weren't that close at all. Just the way she liked it.

He motored down the long drive and pulled to a stop outside the enormous double doors. The house would have been perfectly suited for the English countryside, which was exactly what Elenora had intended.

She never let on as though she missed the old days when they'd been nobility in England, but then, his grandmother could be rather closed-mouthed about a lot of things, the past being just one of them.

He got out, straightened his clothes and put on the sport coat he'd brought along for this visit. If there was anything Didi liked, it was proper attire. He hoped that balanced out the fact that he hadn't called before stopping by, something she might be less appreciative of.

But calling ahead would have meant this visit would have become something so much more. Most likely a fancy lunch, served in the dining room or possibly the solarium (although that was usually reserved for tea). And either way, it would have been, at minimum, a two-hour affair.

He wanted a quick chat. In and out. Nothing more. And while he was counting on his presence being enough to put her in an indulgent mood, he was smart enough to know that might not work.

If it didn't, he would have to play his ace. Which he did *not* want to do.

He went up to the door and banged the knocker three times.

The always dour Alice Bishop answered. "Julian."

His first instinct was to ask if she was currently sucking on a lemon. He shoved that aside and went with charm instead. "Alice, how nice to see you. Is that a new blouse?"

It wasn't.

She glanced down at her top, then tapered her eyes at him. "Your grandmother is in the garden."

"Perfect. I'll just pop through to the back, then."

Alice didn't move.

He broadened his smile. It was nice that Alice was so protective of Elenora, but it could be a real bother too. He was family, after all. "If you could just—"

She exhaled loudly through her nose. "I'll go tell her you're here."

"No need." Julian wasn't interested in being announced. He used his vampire speed to race ahead of the stubborn old witch and through the house, skidding to a stop at the French doors that looked onto the garden.

He adjusted his clothes once more, then opened the doors and strolled out onto the patio and down the steps into the carefully cultivated garden that was his grandmother's pride and joy. She was in the roses, doing whatever needed to be done to roses at this time in May.

She straightened and turned at the sound of the door, her gardening snips in one hand. "Julian." She smiled when she spotted him. "How are you, my darling?"

"Better now that I'm here with you." He leaned in and kissed her cheek. She smelled of something fresh and floral, the garden itself maybe. Whatever it was, it wasn't violets. That was a good sign. She wore a violet scent when she was feeling obstinate. "Lovely day, isn't it?"

Elenora was about to answer when Alice walked out onto the patio and said, "Julian's here." Then she saw him, frowned, and went back inside.

Elenora shook her head. "Why do you torment Alice so?"

"I wasn't tormenting her. I was just eager to see you." He gave her his best innocent look. "Is it my fault if she's slow?"

"Julie, you're a rotten child."

"I know." He wasn't fond of the nickname Julie, but he allowed it with Elenora, knowing it was one of her endearments for him. "But you still love me, don't you, Grandmamma?"

"Terribly." She gave him a stern look. "I do wish you would have called. I could have had Frauke make us lunch."

Frauke was Elenora's cook, and while the woman's food was excellent, it also tended to be rich. He would have needed a nap afterward. "We will do that soon, I promise. But I only had a minute today. I'm on my way to see Sebastian to go over some financials on the wedding chapel." Not true, but a good excuse.

She nodded. "How is that venture going?"

"Very well." It actually wasn't a bad idea to see Sebastian. Maybe he ought to so his words wouldn't be a lie. Elenora was the type to check up on such a thing.

"Still flying off to Vegas every chance you get?"

"If I was, would I be here?"

She pursed her mouth as if they both knew that wasn't an answer, but she wasn't going to push it.

"What can I do for you today, then? I'm sure you're not just here to say hello."

"Am I that transparent?"

She went back to her roses. "My darling, you are practically made of glass."

He sighed. "I could use a favor."

She smiled as she snipped something. "Out with it."

Which was exactly how he planned to proceed. Elenora could only take so much buttering up. Birdie she was not. "I am in desperate need of another amulet."

Her snippers stopped mid-snip. "You can't be serious. Have you lost yours? No, of course not or you wouldn't be here."

Damn it. That would have been an excellent excuse. Why hadn't he thought of that? But he couldn't pretend that was true when he was standing outside in the middle of the day. "No, I just need another, and I'd like not to have to explain myself."

She laughed and went back to work. "Yes, I'm sure that's exactly what you'd like. The answer is no, but then I suspect you already knew that."

"Grandmamma, I don't ask for much. Please. An amulet would be a tremendous help to me right now." If he could get one for Desi, it would make their lives so much easier. But the best part was she'd be safer. If her stalker knew she was a vampire, the quickest way to do her harm would be to get her outside while the sun was up. With an amulet of her own, she'd be protected.

Elenora slanted her eyes at him. "You know better, Julian. The amulets are a family secret. Lending one out to a *friend* is unacceptable."

"This is a special case."

She frowned. "Who is she?"

He frowned right back. He'd known it would come to this. "Someone I care very much about. And she's in trouble. I'm trying to help her because, frankly, she has no one else. And it's my responsibility."

Elenora looked at him directly. "Have you gotten someone pregnant? Because that's a very different—"

"No." Desi had yet to even let him in her bed. Save for the wild night when they'd gotten married, and all they'd done then was sleep off all the champagne they'd drunk.

"Too bad," Elenora sniffed. "I'd love another grandbaby."

"Giving me this amulet could lead to that." Or not. But it couldn't hurt to let Didi think it was a possibility.

She looked down her nose at him in that disapproving way of hers. "Get married, show me you're serious, and then come talk to me about an amulet. I'm not going to waste Alice's powers on—"

He groaned. "I am already married." He hadn't wanted to share that, but he knew how stubborn Elenora could be.

Her jaw dropped. Then she snapped it shut and went back to her flowers. "You're just saying that so I'll have Alice make up an amulet for you."

He sighed. "Part of me wishes I was. But the truth is, I *am* married. I have been for nearly eight months."

"Eight months?" She was clearly aghast. "Do your brothers know about this? Why have you been keeping this from me?"

"Grandmamma, no one knows. You're the first person I've told and I'd appreciate it if you could keep it that way." The thought of what his brothers would say, especially when they found out his wife couldn't wait to divorce him, wasn't something he wanted to deal with. Not even a little bit.

She reached out and cupped his cheek, concern in her eyes. "You're upset about this marriage. Why? Marriage should make you happy. You look miserable."

He shook his head and tried to look away, but her hand held him fast. "She doesn't love me the way I love her."

Elenora sighed. She took her hand from his face and started gathering up her things. "Come. We're going into the house to talk."

He was torn. Discussing the details of his

marriage would be painful, but also, maybe, a way to unburden himself a bit. He'd had no one to talk to about it. His grandmother was the last person he'd choose, but at least she was family.

They settled into her drawing room, the double doors firmly shut, although Julian had no doubt that Alice would find her way to the other side of those doors very soon. If she wasn't out there already.

Didn't matter. Elenora kept no secrets from the old witch, so Alice would know everything eventually.

His grandmother stared at him from her settee. "Start at the beginning."

He did, telling her everything, how he'd fallen in love with Desi, how their wild night had turned to marriage, and how their marriage had become a one-year waiting game the morning after.

Then he explained about Desi being threatened and how he hoped to help her with that, finishing with his trip to the sheriff's office that morning. Then he shrugged. "That's it. Now you know the whole thing."

Her gaze never wavered. "You love her?"

His heart clenched and his throat constricted. "Sadly, I do."

"How much?"

"So much it hurts. So much that when this divorce is final, I may go away for a while because I won't be able to stand seeing Hugh and Sebastian so happy with their partners."

She folded her hands in her lap. "And you think this amulet would help you…win her over?"

"A gift of that magnitude? It couldn't hurt." He shifted in his seat. "But more importantly, it will allow her some more freedom and keep her safe. If the person behind all this madness knows she's a vampire, the amulet will protect her by taking away Desi's one weakness—her vulnerability to the sun."

Elenora nodded. "I agree with all that. But what if she decides to stay with you strictly because of the amulet? Do you really want a woman who would use you just so she can warm her face in the sun once again?"

He swallowed. "I want to say no. But the thought of having her around even if…" He shook his head. "No, you're right. That would be no relationship at all. I don't think she'd do that, though. Desi isn't that kind of woman. She says and does exactly what she wants."

Elenora thought about that. "I can respect that."

He leaned forward and put his head in his hands. "But I want her, Grandmamma. I love her and I feel foolish for it, but I can't stop myself from feeling this way either." He groaned. It wasn't his style to share so much, but it was nice to confide in someone after keeping these secrets to himself for so long.

She came to sit beside him, putting her arm around him. "My poor boy. I hate to see you hurting." She patted his back. "I will give you the amulet."

Shock straightened his spine. "You will?"

She nodded. "On one condition."

That was very Elenora, but he wouldn't complain. The fact that she was willing to give him an amulet was huge. "Anything, just name it."

"You will bring this woman here. I want to meet her. Have dinner with her. Get to know her. I need to see for myself what kind of woman has stolen my sweet Julie's heart."

He took a deep, unnecessary breath. This would either be a good idea or a terrible one. He had a feeling it was going to be terrible, but there'd be no living with Didi now that she knew he was involved. Letting her meet Desi was his only hope for relief. "All right. When?"

"Tomorrow night." She stood. "Now, I must go talk to Frauke and plan the menu."

He got to his feet. "Thank you."

She looked down her nose at him. "Don't thank me yet."

He laughed, feeling lighter already. "Too late."

Desdemona blinked up at the ceiling. For a moment, she couldn't recall where she was. Then it all came back to her. This was Julian's place.

She sat up, pushing the covers away. The television was off, but she knew she'd fallen asleep with it on. She glanced at the door. Still shut.

Didn't mean Jules hadn't come in. She checked the nightstand. Her cup of tea was gone. She shook her head. He must have checked in on her. It was sweet, but then, the man was exceptionally good at making her feel taken care of. And unlike most people, he wasn't doing it because he wanted anything from her. Other than for her to love him back, which she'd told him on the plane she couldn't allow herself to do.

She got out of bed and padded into the bathroom for a long hot shower. It wasn't quite twilight yet. The sun's presence was a tangible thing. Like a wasp crawling on her skin. Only much more deadly.

She lingered in the shower, letting the steaming water wash away the remnants of daysleep. Julian never seemed to suffer from that. Or from the pull of it, either. Whatever his secret, the advantage it gave him was huge.

Forty-five minutes later, she was showered, had done her makeup and fixed her hair. She did her hair right away actually, running some conditioning oil through it, then finger-combing the curls into place to dry while she did her makeup.

Evening had settled fully, and the itch of the sun was gone, but she had no idea what the night would bring. That made choosing an outfit a touch tricky. She stood in front of her closet in her little silk robe, finally opting for skinny jeans, a slinky, off the shoulder black top and purple ankle boots. She could always change if need be.

Dressed and ready, she was about to head out when she heard a voice that wasn't Julian's coming from the living room. She paused at the bedroom door.

Someone else was in the penthouse. Julian was too, she could sense him. Then he joined in the conversation, his voice carrying through the hall. This new person was obviously a friend. One of his brothers maybe? But that thought didn't make her feel any less apprehensive.

She walked out to see who was in the penthouse, stopping at the end of the hall.

Julian stood as soon as he saw her. "Hello, love. Did you sleep well?"

The other man stood, too, his back to her.

She smiled at Julian. "I did." She glanced at the man, who'd turned to face her. He was handsome enough. A little too roguish for her taste. He bore no resemblance to Julian, so most likely not family. She joined them in the living room. "Who's your friend?"

"This is Remy, he's a deputy with the sheriff's department, and he's basically on loan to us for extra security."

Remy smiled and extended his hand. He had a healthy set of fangs on display. "Pleasure to meet you, ma'am."

The accent was familiar. It took her back to some unpleasant memories, but she was an expert in compartmentalizing that sort of thing. She smiled right back. "Nice to meet you too. You must be from Louisiana by the sound of that accent. It's very nice of you to offer your time this way."

He nodded, his grin growing. "Yes, ma'am, I am a Louisiana boy and happy to help another vampire in need." He tipped his head toward Jules. "I got the lowdown on your situation from Julian. Sorry to hear about your troubles."

"Thank you." She moved closer to Julian. Remy

might be friendly, but he was still an unknown. "Are you a daywalker too?"

Remy laughed in an *awe shucks* kind of way. "No, ma'am. I'm strictly a nightshift vamp myself."

"I'm not one, either, so we have that in common." It would be nice to have another layer of protection. And it would take some of the weight off Julian's shoulders. It would even allow them a little distance, which she thought at first might be a good thing, but the more she let that process, the less it seemed that way.

"Remy will be on call," Julian said. "We'll get his number programmed into your phone, and if for any reason you want to go out and I can't go with you, he'll accompany you."

She nodded. "Sounds good." Sounded just okay, actually. She didn't want to go out with anyone but Julian. Even in a platonic way. "Have you done any kind of security work like this before, Remy?"

"Not exactly, ma'am, but I think I can handle it."

"I'm sure you can but, please, you have to call me Desi." She smiled. "Ma'am makes me feel a thousand years old and I'm not quite there yet."

He grinned. "You got it."

She looked at Julian. "What's the plan for tonight?"

"What do you feel like? Still want to go out and see the town?"

"I'd love to. I think we can skip Insomnia,

though. Just a little tour of the town. Maybe grab something to eat? If you're not working. If you are, I'm sure Remy can go with me." Her smile felt a bit forced as those last words came out. She tried to brighten her expression. She didn't want Jules to think she was ungrateful for all the effort he was going to for her. She wasn't. She just wanted to spend some time with him.

"I'm free tonight, but I think Remy should go with us anyway. Harlan called earlier. The shop won't give him the info on who sent them, which means we're no closer to finding out who's doing this." Julian glanced at the other vampire. "Because of that, I'd like you to trail us and make sure no one else is doing the same. Just until we know the coast is clear."

Remy rubbed his hands together. "No problem."

Desi frowned. "You really think I could be in danger here?"

"I'm just being cautious."

"Okay." That made her want to keep Julian close even more.

"Still want to go out?" he asked.

"Yes." She wasn't canceling an evening with him on account of speculation.

"Great," Julian said. "I'll go grab my keys and we'll head into town."

He left. Desi smiled at Remy. After all, it wasn't his fault he wasn't Julian. "Where in Louisiana are you from?"

"New Orleans. But things are a little hot for me there right now. You know how it is when all your friends start to notice you're not aging. Anyway, I had to get away for a while." His gaze took on a melancholy bent. "At least until those who know me are...not around anymore."

She nodded. That hadn't exactly happened to her yet, because she'd moved around a lot and rarely let anyone get close to her, but she knew it was a possibility. It was a distinct downside to being a vampire. Especially if you hoped to settle somewhere. "Did you have family there?"

"I did. The Lafittes have a long history in that town."

She went still. "What did you say your last name was?"

"Lafitte." He grinned. "My granddaddy was Jean Lafitte, the famous—"

She gasped as the name slid razor-edged into her belly like a hot dagger. Her nerves went haywire, pinging small alarms throughout her body and making her tremble. "I-I know who he is."

Julian walked back out jingling his keys. "All right, let's head down to the—"

"No." She swallowed down the rank taste on her tongue and backed away. She flattened her hands against her stomach. "I don't feel like going out anymore."

Julian frowned. "What's wrong?"

She stared at Remy and shook her head. Memories took over and words became harder. She took another step back. "You need to leave."

Remy looked shocked. "I am deeply sorry that I said something to offend you. It wasn't my intent, I swear."

Julian glared at him. "What the hell happened? I was barely out of the room."

Remy shrugged. "I got no idea."

"Desi, what's going on?" Julian gave her his full attention. "You look like you've seen a ghost."

She retreated farther, wringing her hands together. The memories were overwhelming her. In a moment, she would crack. She could feel it coming. A low whine began to drown out all other sounds. Her temperature rose until she wanted to tear her clothes off. Then the stink of the ocean filled her nose. That wretched, low-tide, dead-fish smell that no amount of rain could wash away.

"Remy, go," Julian said. "I'll talk to you later."

A wall stopped her from going any farther. She stood there for a moment with her back against it, then she went down, crumpling into a heap. She wrapped her arms around her knees and started sucking in air in deep gulps. She didn't need it, but she couldn't stop herself either, just like she couldn't keep herself from rocking back and forth. The past owned her again, stripping her control away. It was a feeling she'd been fighting for centuries.

A door opened and closed, and then strong arms surrounded her.

"Desi, sweetheart, what's wrong? I think you're having a panic attack."

Julian. She knew it was him, but Alonso filled her head. Alonso and his lies. His betrayal. She let out a broken, raspy whisper. "Never again."

Julian pulled her onto his lap and held her against his chest. "No, never again. Whatever it was, I'll protect you."

He petted her hair and whispered soft reassurances.

She wept a few quiet tears. They stung like sea water on an open wound. She put her head on his shoulder and let out one last sob as she struggled to push the past down.

She had no idea how long they sat like that, but Julian never once moved. He just let her be.

Her whole body ached, but finally the worst had subsided. She lifted her head but couldn't make herself look at Julian. "I'm sorry."

"I don't know what you're apologizing for."

She wiped at her eyes. "For making a scene. You know what I'm talking about."

"You had a panic attack. You don't need to apologize for that."

She slid off his lap to sit beside him, both of

them with their backs to the wall. Thighs touching. That was good. She needed contact with something in the here and now. Something that wasn't a memory. "I'm sure Remy thinks otherwise."

"What Remy thinks doesn't matter to me." He looked over at her. "You do. You okay now? What do you need? Anything. Just tell me."

She smiled. How could she not? "I'm better." She was too. Mostly. "Thanks."

"You hungry? I could order food in. Or go out and bring something back. Whatever you want."

She glanced over at him, meeting his gaze. She stared at him for a long moment, trying to see through his smoky brown eyes and into his head. He wasn't always the easiest man to figure out. "You're not going to ask me what just happened?"

"I know what happened. You had a panic attack."

"But you're not going to ask me why?"

"Do you want to tell me?"

She looked away. That was a hard question. Julian was about the best friend she had, and even if she couldn't be married to him, she did want him to be part of her life. Understanding her past might help keep him around after the divorce was finalized. At least it would help him understand why she wouldn't allow herself to love anyone.

But at the same time, she'd done everything in her power to make sure her history stayed just that.

History. She didn't like to think about it, for obvious reasons, and talking about it would only be worse.

He patted her leg. "How about I order us some pizza? One of the great benefits to being a vampire is being able to eat all the junk food you like." He pushed to his feet. "And there's a place in town that does pizza that's so good it ought to be illegal."

"Julian…"

"Yes?"

She put her head down and found the last remaining shred of her courage. "I was…married once before."

Julian had heard and understood what she'd said, but it took a moment for the words to register. Married. She'd *been* married. *Been* was good. It meant not currently. But with vampires, that wasn't always how it worked. Sebastian was an example of that. "Are you still? I mean, besides to me."

She shook her head. She was staring at the floor, looking for all the world like a lost child. Her walls were down, destroyed by the panic attack, maybe, and she was the most vulnerable he'd ever seen her. "Pretty sure the statute of limitations has run out on that. If he's still alive. Which...I don't know."

His mind raced to a thousand different scenarios, but he kept quiet and let her talk. This was her story. And it was hers to tell as she saw fit. But more than that, she was finally sharing something from her past with him and that was new territory for them.

She glanced up at him, said nothing, and went back to studying the floor. "I loved him to the point that I thought I would die of it." Her voice was low and devoid of emotion. Almost monotone. Like that was the only way she could cope with sharing this much. "Fool that I was. First loves should be outlawed."

Except that she was his. But Julian continued holding his tongue.

"He was my..." She swallowed, and a few hard seconds ticked by, and this time when she spoke, there was pain in her words. "My life."

Julian sat down beside her again, facing her.

Her fists clenched, and she started shaking. Maybe with the effort it was taking to tell him this. "My heart."

He'd never seen her like this. Desi wasn't one to show this kind of raw emotion. At least she'd never done it around him. "Was he the one who turned you?"

"Yes."

That explained so much. Being turned was a bonding experience unlike anything else. Elenora had turned him and, in doing so, saved him from the plague that was killing all those around them. He owed his life twice to his grandmother. It was something he could never repay, and for that reason alone, he knew if the time ever came, he would lay down his life for her. "The bond that a turning creates is a powerful thing."

"Yes." She lifted her head. Liquid rimmed her lower lids. "I felt like he had given a part of himself to me. Like I owed him my life. In one way, I did."

Julian nodded. "I understand that. I feel that way toward my grandmother. She's my sire, and that bond sometimes feels stronger than our family ties."

Desi sat back, wiping her face. "His name was Alonso." A sobbing laugh tore from her throat. "I haven't spoken that name out loud in over a hundred years."

Julian brushed a tear off her cheek with the pad of his thumb. "You don't have to tell me about him if you don't want to."

"He made me who I am."

"That's what sires do, don't they? It's what makes them such a part of us."

"No," she said. "I don't mean by turning me into a vampire." Her eyes glowed with the magic of their kind. It was a sign of strong emotion, and right now, hers read as anger. "He destroyed me. Or at least my ability to love. He's the reason that you and I are never going to be more than friends, so I figure I owe you this much."

The muscles in the back of Julian's neck tensed up. This was the man who'd hurt her. The man who'd caused her to live her life on the defensive. "I'm listening."

"He was a privateer."

"A pirate." Julian understood her reaction to Remy now. "That explains why the name Lafitte had such an ill effect on you."

"I knew Jean Lafitte." She leaned back and tipped her head against the wall. Despite the daysleep she'd had, she looked exhausted. "He was nice to me. But I have no love for pirates. Not after Alonso."

She blew out a long breath. Like she was trying to rid herself of the memories that had been stirred up. She glanced toward the kitchen. "I could really use a drink."

"Water? I'll get it."

"No, something more substantial."

He understood. He gave her leg a squeeze. "You need to feed. I'll be right back."

He got up and went into the kitchen. His phone buzzed as he reached into the wine cooler and took out some O positive. He checked the screen. Remy.

He answered, already knowing the call was going to have to be quick, but Remy was a good man and deserved some reassurance. "Hello."

"Julian, I know what happened. I know *her*. Desi. She was Mary Clarke when I met her. I couldn't have been more than seven or eight, but you don't forget a woman that beautiful. She wasn't as polished back then, but it was her. I know it was."

"You're right."

He cursed in French. "She came to see my grandfather. She was with a pirate by the name of Alonso Mora. Alonso worked for my grandfather and his brother, Pierre, helping them with their smuggling operations. But my grandfather cut ties with him soon after that visit. The man was heartless. If the rumors of what he did to Mary Clarke are true, she has the right to hate every pirate ever born."

Julian took a moment to compose himself so that the anger coursing through him wouldn't spill out and further upset Desi. He cleared his throat, trying to loosen it enough to speak. "So I'm finding out."

The words sounded calm, but his mind was churning. What the hell had that pirate done to her to leave such lasting scars? How after all this time did he still have the power to send this strong woman into a panic attack?

Julian took a glass down and filled it. "Anything else you care to share?"

"I'll talk to my grandfather. See if he can give me any more information on the man."

"Perfect." If there was any chance this Alonso was also Desi's stalker, Julian would gladly end him.

"I'll be in touch as soon as I know something." He hung up.

Julian tucked the phone away and took the glass to Desi. "Here, drink this. It'll help."

She took it and drained it, then closed her eyes for a moment. When she opened them, she got to her feet. "I'm sorry for unloading all this on you."

"Desi, I love you. Don't apologize for sharing this with me." Although he still didn't know what this man had done to her. "There is nothing I wouldn't do for you. I'm happy you feel close enough to me to share it. And if I can help you bear this burden in some way, then so be it. I'm here for you in whatever capacity you need me to be."

She smiled weakly. "That kind of love will destroy you."

He shook his head, angst-ridden that her outlook on life was this shadowed. "Not if you love the right person."

She turned away, then walked the glass back to the kitchen. "I'm not that person, Julian. Because I can't love you back. Alonso took that ability from me."

Julian wanted to meet Alonso. And introduce him to the sun. "But we're friends, aren't we?"

She rinsed the glass and put it in the dishwasher. "Yes. In fact, you're my closest friend." She looked wistful. "I don't have a lot of friends. On purpose. But you sort of…"

"Forced my way in?"

She laughed. "A little. But I don't regret it." Her

smile faded. "I also hope I don't lose you after the divorce is final. But if it's too difficult for you to stay friends with me, I want you to know that I won't have any hard feelings toward you at all."

"Speaking of the divorce…I haven't started the process yet like I said I would." He sighed. "I was focused on finding out who was after you and it slipped my mind."

"That's okay. Finding out who's stalking me is more important. Especially with Sam being caught up in all this." She bit her lip. "Do you think we'll be able to stay in touch when this is all over?"

He hesitated, thinking about what it would be like to be just friends with the woman he loved so desperately. "I wish I could tell you it's all going to be fine, but I can't say that yet. And I don't want to lie to you just to make you feel better."

Her smile came back. A little sadder, but it returned. "I'm okay with that. I like your honesty. And whatever happens, I'll understand."

"Do you want to talk some more?"

She barely gave that a second of thought. "Not really. I've had about all of the past that I can take right now."

"You want to go out?"

"Very much."

"Where to? Dancing at Insomnia?" Although he didn't much feel like that, he would do anything she wanted. "There's a very nice French bistro in town if you're hungry and want something more intimate and upscale."

She tipped her head at him. "I want that pizza you were talking about."

"Okay, sounds good to me." He was happy to stay in with her, too. "I'll call and order. They're pretty quick with the delivery."

"No. I want to go there."

He stared at her. "The great Desdemona Valentine wants to go out for pizza? Have you ever done that in your life?"

"Not in a really long time. But I feel like it's exactly what I need right now."

"Then that's exactly what we're going to do." He glanced down at his suit. "But I might be a little overdressed."

She held out her hands. "How about me?"

"You're perfect." And he meant it, in every way.

She didn't actually remember the last time she'd gone out for pizza at a hole-in-the-wall sort of outfit. Or anywhere, really. She never did it in Vegas. It didn't fit her public persona. Desdemona Valentine was a caviar and champagne sort of diva.

Plus, the few friends she had were dancers in her show, and pizza wasn't exactly on their diets. Mostly because they were human. Julian was right that having a rapid metabolism was one of the great benefits of being a vampire.

The place he took her to was exactly what a local pizza place should be. Brick walls, red and white checked curtains, pictures of Italy and Italian celebrities, and a bustling open kitchen. But the aroma in Salvatore's was what really set the mood. It was a little smoky from the brick ovens, but it also carried the tang of garlic and the rich sweetness of the tomato sauce. Her mouth watered instantly.

The hostess, a pretty young woman with her hair slicked back into a ponytail and Georgia bulldog earnings dangling from her triple-pierced ears, greeted them as they approached the hostess stand. "Good evening. Two?"

"Yes, please," Julian answered.

She looked at her seating chart. "I think I have a table that just left. Let me go check if it's clean, and I'll be right back."

The restaurant was filled with humans, but Desi didn't mind it. Some vampires thought humans a lesser class, but she didn't. Not when they made her show in Vegas possible. Besides being her dancers, they were her audience, and she was incredibly grateful for their curiosity about her kind, even if they thought she was just a human playing a vampire.

Considering that, it was no wonder this town was so popular. Nocturne Falls catered to that same inquisitive nature and desire to be entertained. Where else could humans go to be so fully immersed in all things supernatural? Sure, there were a few other spots that dabbled in the paranormal side of things, but this place *owned* it. She smiled. The town was genius, really.

Julian leaned in. "Does the thought of pizza actually make you that happy?"

She laughed. "It does, but I was smiling for a different reason."

The hostess returned and picked up two menus. "Okay, right this way."

She led them to a small table in the back corner. It was out of the way, but had a great line of sight for people-watching. She put their menus at their places. "Tim's going to be your server. Enjoy your meal."

Desi gave Julian a look as they sat. "Did you call ahead and arrange this when I wasn't looking?"

His brows lifted. "Arrange what?"

"For us to get this cozy table back here. It's perfect. Is that the power of the Ellingham name?"

He shook his head. "My name had nothing to do with this. Just the right place at the right time."

"Huh. Well, good for us, then." She picked up her menu, then put it right back down. "I don't need to look. Order whatever you think is good."

He closed his menu too. "Anything you don't like on a pizza?"

"No anchovies, clams or seafood of any kind." That was a food category she could do without.

"How about spicy?"

"Jules, I'm from the islands. I can take the heat."

He grinned. "How hungry are you?"

"I'm…" She looked at his handsome face and sparkling eyes and thought about how willing he was to put her first. Part of her, a part she'd long thought ruined, ached for him in that moment. Ached to be close to him. To touch him. To kiss him. But those things had consequences. She smiled despite the war going on inside her. "Starving."

Tim the server came and got their drink orders. "I'll give y'all a few more minutes to look over the menus."

"I can tell you what we want now," Julian said.

"All right, what'll it be?"

"A large king and a large queen."

"You mean a slice of each?"

"No," Julian said. "One large pie each."

The kid picked up their menus. "Are there more people joining you?"

"Just us," Julian reassured him.

Tim gave him a thumbs-up. "Going for the leftovers. I like your style. I'll get that right in."

He left and Julian snorted. "Kid should be used to the way supernaturals eat by now, working in a town like this."

"Maybe he's new." She glanced back toward

their server, who was tapping their order in on a screen. "Are the larges really large?"

"They are. About twenty-four inches, I believe."

"That's a lot of pizza. But not a lot for people like us."

"Exactly."

Julian's hands were directly across from hers on the table. She moved hers to her lap to help resist the urge to touch him. "What kind did you get? What's a king and a queen?"

"A king is their version of a supreme and a queen is their white pie."

"Ooo, I love white pizza." Then she laughed. "I guess my fans would be disappointed to know that their vamp's favorite pizza is heavy on the garlic."

"Some myths are better left alone." He shifted in his seat. "It's one of my favorites too."

She put her hands back on the table. Inches from his. "Thanks for bringing me here. And for not pushing me to share more than I was ready."

"I'd do anything for you. You know that."

She nodded. "I do. I really do."

"Would you do anything for me?"

She gave him an odd look. That was a complicated question. "What are you after?"

He cleared his throat softly. "We've been invited to dinner at my grandmother's house. Tomorrow night."

She blinked at him. That sounded…serious.

Julian didn't expect her to answer instantly with a yes, but he also hadn't expected her to sit there looking at him like he'd suddenly developed a gaping head wound. After a long minute of silence from her, he frowned. "It's not that dreadful a request, is it?"

She shook herself like she'd been lost in thought. Maybe she had been. "No, I just…that's a lot to unpack, is all."

"In what way?"

Tim returned with their drinks, tall red plastic tumblers of Coke, two plates, and two sets of silverware wrapped in napkins. He put one of each in front of them. "Pies will be up shortly. Need anything else?"

"We're good," Julian answered. Except they weren't. He leaned in toward her as the server left. "You were saying?"

"Meeting your grandmother sounds pretty serious. And the fact that she's invited us to dinner implies that you told her about me, and if that's true, well, that's also serious. Did you tell her we were married?"

"First of all, it's not that serious. Yes, I told her about you. My grandmother would have found out sooner or later, and it was better if she found out from me. Trust me. So she would have wanted to meet you either way. She's sort of the silent ruling power in this town."

"That's reassuring."

He laughed. "Okay, that sounds worse than it is. And she's not always that silent. But she knows everything that goes on in this town, trust me. She'd never let it slide when she found out I had a woman staying with me."

Desi's eyes narrowed as she peeled the wrapper off her straw. "You didn't answer the last question."

He sighed. He couldn't lie to her. He wouldn't lie to her. "Yes, I told her we were married. Extenuating circumstances is all I can say about that. But look, it's going to be fine. It'll be a small, overly formal dinner for the three of us. Maybe four if her assistant joins us. But she's my grandmother—"

"And your sire," Desi whispered.

"Right. So what do you say?"

149

"Of course, I'll go."

Because she was obligated? With all Julian was doing for her, he wondered if that was her reasoning. Didn't matter, though. She'd agreed, and Didi would be satisfied, which meant his grandmother would get Alice to make Desi an amulet. "Thank you."

"It's a little nerve-racking, I have to say. About meeting her, I mean."

He nodded. "I understand. But you're a strong woman. Like her. You two will find you have a lot in common. And I'll be there with you, so if the conversation turns too personal, I'll redirect." He smiled broadly. "I'm the baby of the family, so I get away with a lot, being the favorite and all."

"Oh great, you're the favorite. No additional pressure at all."

"She's going to love you. I promise."

Desi snorted. "Yeah, I'm sure."

"What's that supposed to mean?"

"You're her favorite. How is any woman going to be good enough for you?" She fiddled with her paper napkin. "Especially one who already plans to divorce you." She glanced up. "Didn't tell her that part, did you?"

"Actually, I did. I figured she needed to know so as not to get her expectations up."

"Really?" Desi straightened. "And she still wanted to meet me?"

"Yep."

She sipped her soda. "Oddly, that takes a little of the pressure off."

Tim returned with another server in tow, each of them carrying a large pizza. Tim also had a metal contraption slung over one arm. He set that down first while balancing the pizza dish in the other hand. "This is our double-decker pizza stand. Without this, I don't know where we'd put the other pie."

He slid the king pizza onto the bottom rung, then the second server added the queen to the top. Tim stood back. "Good to go?"

"Good to go," Julian answered.

"All right. I'll be back to check on you in a bit."

Tim took off, leaving them and the pizzas alone.

Desi's eyes were wide. "That's a lot of pizza. And it smells amazing."

"Wait until you taste it." He picked up the serving spatula. "Which one do you want to start with?"

She held up her plate. "Let's not play games. One of each."

"That's my girl." He served her. The slices overlapped and draped over the plate at both ends.

He started with a single slice of the loaded king pie. He lifted it to his mouth, ready to take a bite, but Desi's low moan of pleasure stopped him.

He lowered the slice to see her better. Her eyes were closed in ecstasy.

She finished chewing, swallowed, and looked at him. "This is not like any pizza I've ever had before. It tastes exactly like what you think pizza should taste like, but never quite does." She looked around. "Is this place famous? Because it should be."

He nodded, unable to take his eyes off the way her tongue swiped across her bottom lip before she took a bite of the second slice. Then he realized she'd said something else. "What?"

"I said I don't know which I like better, the king or the queen."

"No, me either." He was mesmerized by her. Watching a woman like Desdemona eat pizza shouldn't be a revelatory experience, but it was. Maybe it was her vampire nature, or maybe it was her way of living life out loud, but she ate with such enjoyment that the simple meal seemed like a celebration.

He devoured his first slice, his appetite suddenly insatiable, then quickly moved on to his second in an attempt to catch up to her.

By the time Tim came to check on them, both pies were half gone. "Wow, you two are like pizza-eating professionals. I'll be right back with drink refills."

Desi smiled and shook her head as she reached for another slice.

"What?" Julian asked.

"I'm just having a good time. And I didn't expect that. I guess I kind of forgot how nice it is just to be a regular person."

"You mean a non-famous person?"

"Something like that." She took a sip of her soda. "What can we do after dinner?"

"Anything you want. Walk around, look in the shops, go for a drink, get some dessert, or if you're really feeling adventurous, there's bowling."

"Hah! I don't know if I'm quite there yet." She bit the point off her slice. "Do you have a movie theater?"

"No. You have to go to the next town over for that. It's not far, though."

She leaned in. "No movie theater?" She gave him a disapproving look. "You guys have this great town and yet your visitors have to leave if they want to see a movie? Think of the money they're spending in that other town. Who's in charge of business development?"

He snorted. "I am."

"Was there ever a theater here?"

"Yes, but it was closed long before we bought the town. That building was torn down to make room for the new fire station." He thought a little. "There is space for a theater near the lake. I've talked to my brothers about building there. A little outdoor retail area. The theater would be a nice anchor along with some restaurants and some shops."

"That sounds nice."

"It would be." He picked up his slice. "Thanks for the kick in the pants."

She laughed. "You're welcome. And I'm only asking fifteen percent of the profits."

"You're such a giver."

They bantered and ate and laughed and had such a good time that Julian momentarily forgot she wanted to divorce him as soon as possible. He almost didn't even care because things were so good between them, it felt like they'd always been this way, and might stay this way.

If it weren't for the undercurrent of reality and how soon their time would be over, he might have let himself fall completely into the fantasy that they were truly man and wife. But Desi had made it clear. This was a temporary, and indulgent, situation.

Tim brought the check. "Man, you guys ought to win an award for finishing off both of those pies."

Desi smiled up at him, dazzling him with a grin that made the kid redden. "Maybe we really are pizza-eating professionals."

He chuckled and stammered as he took Julian's credit card. "Yeah, well, you, uh, you should be. I'll, uh, be right back."

He left and Julian snickered. "Someone has a crush on you."

She smirked. "What can I say? I'm adorable."

"That's not the word I'd use."

"Oh? What then?" Her gaze tapered down, like he'd better choose his words carefully.

He leaned closer and took her hand. "Irresistible. Magnetic." He laced his fingers through hers. "Sexy."

Her eyes took on a soft glow, and she swallowed. "Oh." Then she slipped her hand from his and tucked both of them away on her lap. "That's sweet of you to say."

Had he just seen a glimmer of desire in her? For him? Something deep within him stirred. Hope, maybe. But he hadn't felt that particular emotion in so long he wasn't sure he could still identify it.

Tim returned with the check for Julian to sign and a plate of desserts. "Mr. Brunetti sent these cannoli and zeppoli for you, Mr. Ellingham, and said he's very pleased you dined with us this evening."

"Tell him that wasn't necessary, but very gracious of him and they look delicious."

"I will. Have a good night."

As Tim left, Desi's brows rose. "Well, look at you getting free dessert, Mr. My-Name-Had-Nothing-To-Do-With-It." She picked up one of the little fried dough balls. "I don't know what zeppoli are, but that won't stop me from eating one."

He took one for himself. "They're like Italian doughnuts." These were covered with powdered sugar, and from experience, he knew they'd have a hint of lemon.

"Mmm…" Desi answered, her lush mouth already sporting a dusting of sugar. "Boy, you sure know how to impress a girl."

He took a bite of the zeppoli, but his mouth was watering for a different reason. He wanted to kiss Desi more than anything in that moment. To take her in his arms and kiss her like there was no reason to stop.

But that would only upset her. She didn't love him. Couldn't love him. And was never going to reciprocate his feelings. So what was the point? It would be a self-serving action. And the last thing he wanted was to give her a reason to speed up the divorce.

"Anything important?"

Desi shook her head as she read the message on her phone. Her arm was hooked through Julian's so she let him lead while she walked beside him on autopilot. "Just Sam texting to say she got the flowers I sent."

"That's it? No new threats."

"Nope. She did mention how cute she thinks Harlan is." She laughed and put the phone away. "You may have started something there."

"He'd better be paying attention to keeping her safe and not just flirting."

She fluttered her lashes at him. "Isn't it possible to do both?"

He made a face. "Did you just bat your lashes at me?"

She shrugged. "It's all those carbs and that sugar. I feel like I'm drunk from it. I can't be held responsible for my actions right now."

"Oh, so I'm worth flirting with when you're intoxicated," he teased.

"That is how we ended up married." But he was right. When her guard was down, she had a tendency to forget her own rules. It was so easy to do around Julian. He was everything she'd want in a man. If she wanted a man. Which she didn't. "Speaking of sugar, I saw what was in your pantry. Is all that candy for you?"

"Maybe." He laughed. "Hey, we all have our addictions."

"You might need a twelve-step program."

Still laughing, he held tight to her arm. "I'm glad we came out tonight."

"Me, too. This is exactly what I needed. Especially since tomorrow night is going to be a lot more stressful."

He patted her arm. "I promise, if my grandmother makes you uncomfortable, I'll come up with an excuse and we'll leave early."

"Thanks." That was Julian. Always understanding. Always willing to put her needs first. Always ready with the right words or response. He was perfect. Too bad she wasn't, thanks to Alonso. She sighed, then forced herself to veer from that mental path. "What are you wearing to dinner?"

"A suit. My grandmother's a little old-fashioned.

She likes people to dress up." He glanced at her. "How about you?"

"I don't want you to think I'm caving to pressure, but I'll probably go with a little black dress."

His eyes widened. "Do you even own one of those? I thought everything in your wardrobe was neon or leopard."

"Hey, I'm wearing jeans."

"With bright purple boots."

She looked down. "Oh, yeah." She shrugged. "I have something suitable."

"I don't care if she likes what you have on or not. Wear what you want. Be you." He gave her a little nudge. "Never stop being you. It's what made me fall for you."

She slanted her eyes at him. He was staring at her mouth. She'd been around long enough to know what that meant.

He wanted to kiss her.

And why shouldn't he? He was her husband. He was in love with her. With all he was doing for her, the man deserved a little something for his troubles. There was a park up ahead in the center of the road. It divided Main Street. If she remembered correctly from the drive into town, there was a big fountain in the center.

She shifted direction toward it. "Let's go see the park."

"Sure."

They crossed the street and walked in.

"This is really pretty. I love this spot of green right in the center of town."

"Nocturne Falls has a lot of parks, but most of them are in the residential areas. This one is really for the tourists, and to give some of our locals who need the contact with nature a place to go while they're on break from the shops."

They strolled toward the fountain. There was no one around. Perfect.

She stopped and pulled away from Julian, then held out her hand. "Do you have a coin? I want to make a wish."

"I think I can manage that." He dug into his pocket and came out with a quarter. "Here you go."

"Thanks." She took it, turned toward the fountain, and tossed it in.

Julian stepped next to her. "What did you wish for?"

"If I tell you, it won't come true." She gathered her courage, hoping what she was about to do wasn't the dumbest decision she'd ever made. It was just going to be a show of her appreciation. That was all. "But I will tell you this. I don't know how to properly thank you for everything you've done for me, so while we're alone, I want to show you."

"But we're not—"

She put her hands on his forearms, leaned in, and kissed him, putting an end to whatever he'd been about to say.

He sucked in a breath as their mouths collided. His lips were soft and velvety, and the sweetness of the cannoli and zeppoli lingered. She knew she'd completely caught him off guard. She smiled against his mouth and was about to break contact, figuring she'd made her point, when he got over his shock.

And kissed her back.

His hands went to her hips and he bent into her, hungry for her in a way that shot dangerous spikes of desire through her. A low growl vibrated out of his throat and his hands gripped tighter. Possessively.

His fangs raked her lower lip, and the sensation sent a shiver of pleasure through her. He was an excellent kisser. So good she was powerless to stop the heat curling through her bones or the soft whimper that escaped her throat.

In response, he pulled her against him, and the solid planes of muscle beneath his clothing became instantly apparent. Her hands slid to his chest. More hard muscle. More undeniable maleness.

She'd held him at arm's length for so long that it had become easy to think of him as just a friend.

But the person kissing her right now was one

hundred percent man and one hundred percent vampire.

Her head spun as his tongue brushed hers. For a brief, blinding moment, she considered giving in to the deepest, darkest part of her that wanted to love again. Julian wouldn't hurt her, would he?

But she'd thought the same thing about Alonso and he'd tried to kill her.

She flattened her palms on Julian's chest and pushed away. His eyes were glowing like stars and his fangs gleamed in the park's streetlamps. If she was still human, she would have been very, very afraid. As a vampire, she understood that the creature in front of her was being driven by his emotions and what she was seeing was pure, unadulterated desire. "I shouldn't have…"

"But you did," Julian said.

"Because we're alone. And I wanted to say thank you."

He raked his hand through his hair. "We're not alone."

She blinked at him. "We're not?"

"I tried to tell you." He looked toward the fountain. "Nick?"

She followed his line of sight in time to see the gargoyle statue move.

She backed up. "What the hell?"

The gargoyle shrugged. "It's my job." Then he nodded at Julian. "Evening."

Julian frowned. "Keep this to yourself."

"You got it, boss. I didn't see a thing." He went still again. Ironically, like a statue.

Julian put his hand on the small of her back and got them moving forward. "We need to talk."

"I didn't know he was real."

"Not about that."

He didn't say another word until they were back in his car in the town parking lot. She wasn't ready to go home, but then, staying out with someone giving you the silent treatment wasn't exactly buckets of fun either.

She let out a long sigh before he started the car. "You want to tell me what I did wrong?"

He turned to her, leaning his arm on the steering wheel. "You kissed me."

"To say thank you for everything you're doing for me." She thought she'd made that clear.

He dropped his head. "Des, I am in love with you. I don't know how else to say it so that it sinks in." He lifted his head again, sadness bracketing his gaze. "You cannot kiss me like that. Not unless you've had some miraculous change of heart and you want to stay married. Or at the very least, stay involved. And I don't mean as friends."

He fell back into his seat and stared out the windshield at the parking lot. "I can't take it. I'm not some unemotional rock of a man. I was the baby of the family. I didn't have the responsibilities my brothers had, nor the need to school my emotions in front of others like them. They're great at hiding their emotions. Or maybe they just turn them off, I don't know, but I feel things very deeply."

His words stung. She'd hurt him. "I'm really sorry. I didn't mean to upset you. I just thought you deserved a kiss."

He barked out a short, hard laugh. "I do. From a woman who loves me."

"Ouch." She held her hands up. "I earned that."

He shook his head. "No, you didn't." He smiled, a little half smile that was clearly about making her feel better, because that's what Julian did. "Let's just put it behind us, okay?"

She nodded. "Okay." But that kiss of his wasn't something she'd soon forget. She could still feel his mouth on hers. The heat of it. The press of it. How hungry for more he'd been.

He shifted into drive, but hesitated before turning onto the street. "I don't know what Alonso did to you, but if he's still alive, he'd better hope our paths never cross."

Desi's kiss had brought life to Julian. Not the living, breathing kind of life he'd said goodbye to nearly four hundred years ago, but the kind that reminded him why humans spent their years chasing love with every fiber of their being. She'd set him on fire with longing. His bones ached with it.

His need for her had surpassed simple wanting. He'd become sick with it. The ache in his heart felt like a gaping hole.

One that would never be filled.

And yet somehow, he was going to have to hold himself together while she lived under his roof until it was safe for her to go back to Vegas.

He pulled into the parking lot of the Excelsior and paused in front of the lobby doors. "I'm sorry to drop you here, but I just remembered I was supposed to see my brother today and I didn't. If I don't go see him now, it'll just make things worse. I'll be back as soon as I can."

Her surprise registered for a moment, but quickly vanished. If that was because she understood what he was really saying was that he needed some time away from her, he was okay with that.

It was the truth, after all.

She nodded and got out. "See you later."

He watched her through the lobby's windows, waiting until she was in the elevator before he pulled away. He couldn't go to his brother's. Well, he could, but he couldn't bear Sebastian knowing how badly he'd screwed up his life. Sebastian already thought Julian's life was in serious need of help.

But he wished he could. If anyone understood unrequited love, it was Sebastian. He'd spent years pining for his ex-wife, who'd basically used him for his wallet, and all because of a long-ago promise to her dying father.

Now Sebastian was happily engaged to Tessa, a most amazing woman, and not just because she had the uncanny ability to make the grump of the family smile. (It was worth mentioning that, because of her, Sebastian also had a cat named Duncan living in his house. Something that basically counted as a miracle.) No, the chances he'd want to give Julian any advice besides move on were slim. There was no point in bothering him. He was probably asleep anyway, having adopted Tessa's more typical hours.

So Julian drove without any real destination in mind, his thoughts going round and round the problem of Desdemona, and his heart aching with the knowledge that she was never going to be his.

Somehow, he ended up at the lake. Maybe because of their conversation about the movie theater. He parked, got out and sat on the hood of his car. Probably a sacrilegious thing to do to a Maserati, but a car was just a thing, and things could be replaced.

He lay back and stared up at the stars.

His problem was that she refused to love him back because of whatever Alonso had done to her. That meant his real problem was Alonso. Without knowing what had happened between them, that problem was impossible to fix.

His phone vibrated. He thought about ignoring it, but only for a second. He checked the screen. Remy.

He answered. "Monsieur Lafitte. You have perfect timing."

"I take it that means you're not too busy to talk?"

"I can absolutely talk. Do you have something to tell me?"

"I do. If you want to hear it."

"Is it about Alonso?"

"It is. I talked to my grandfather—"

"Hang on a second. As much as I want to know what happened to Desi, this is clearly a deeply personal issue for her. It's her story to tell. You get my drift?"

"I do. I could tell you what happened to Alonso."

"That would be fine. I'd like to know. And I think Desi would too."

"After cutting ties with Mora, my grandfather found out that the man had been stealing from him too. He tracked him down in Barbados a year later and ran a stake through him. He said it was more for Mary—I mean, Desdemona—than for the stealing. That he couldn't live with himself without avenging her death."

"But Desdemona didn't die."

Remy laughed. "I told him that. He was pleased to hear it. But still felt he did the right thing."

"Thank you. I appreciate it."

"Anytime." Remy hung up.

Julian put his phone away. Alonso was dead. He'd have to find the right instant to tell Desi, a moment when she could process the information with whatever time she needed, but the knowledge that this man was never going to be an issue for her again ought to give Desi some closure on whatever had happened to her. He wondered if she'd ever tell him what that thing was. Would she eventually feel ready enough to share it? He hoped so.

Just like he hoped it happened sooner rather than later, because at some point, he imagined his new problem would be the emotional toll of loving Desi without her loving him back. The consequences of that worried him. He really didn't want to have his heart harden the way hers had.

Then a realization came to him. There was a way to prevent his complete destruction. But it would require a great deal of effort on his part. Not to mention some pain.

Could he manage it? Maybe. But if he didn't at least try, he'd be shattered by this.

Really, he had no other choice.

The delicious aroma of coffee awakened Desi. She opened her eyes. The sun was still up, but twilight was close. She could feel it. And they'd be leaving soon for dinner at Julian's grandmother's.

Julian.

He'd dropped her off last night, driven away, and when she'd gone to bed, unable to resist the pull of sleep any longer, he still hadn't returned.

She tossed the covers back and swung her feet to the floor. If there was coffee, he must have made it. She chewed on the inside of her cheek. Was that a good sign? He wouldn't have made coffee for them if he was in a bad mood. Of course, that assumed the coffee *was* for both of them and not just for him. Hmm. That would certainly determine where his mental state was at.

She drew on her short robe, untied the silk scarf from her hair and ran her fingers through her curls to loosen them. A quick glance in the mirror to check that she hadn't woken up on the hideous side of the bed, and she padded out to the kitchen.

Julian was there, his back to her, wearing nothing but silk pajama pants that hung low on his hips. The sight was enough to make her throat tighten in hunger. He was lean and hard (as she'd found out for herself last night). The muscles in his shoulders and back danced as he moved.

The man was beautiful in every way.

"Evening." She tried for a light tone, testing to see if he'd even respond.

He spun around, a big smile on his face that brought her instant relief. "Hello, beautiful. How'd you sleep?"

"Great." He was saying all the right things, but there was tension in the air between them. She could feel it.

"Coffee?" He held up the carafe. "We're due to my grandmother's in about an hour. I hope that's enough time for you to get ready."

"Coffee would be great, then I'll put it into high gear." She took a seat on one of the sleek counter stools as he turned to get a cup. There was no point in pretending what had happened…hadn't. So she dove in. "About last night…I wanted to say again that I'm sorry."

"I'm sorry too." He slid a mug and spoon toward her, then added a sugar bowl and a short pitcher of cream. "I shouldn't have just dumped you here and taken off. You threw me."

"You don't need to apologize."

"I do. For one thing, I lied about going to see my brother. That was just an excuse."

"I figured that."

"And for another, you're my guest, and it was rude. I let my feelings get the best of me and I'm sure it didn't make you feel very comfortable."

"I'm a big girl, I'll be fine." She added three spoonfuls of sugar and a splash of cream.

He sipped from his own mug. "Doesn't change that I acted inappropriately."

"Well, you're forgiven, but there's nothing to forgive." She gave the coffee a stir.

He smiled and shook his head. "Very kind of you. It won't happen again. I had a long think last night. Wasn't fun. But I realized that I've been a little childish about this whole thing." He shrugged. "So we got married. There's no point in me holding you hostage for four more months."

"You're not hold—"

"You're a grown woman. You just said so. You know your mind. And I'd rather us remain friends, than let things go south just because of some silly, self-imposed deadline."

She squinted at him. "What are you saying?"

"I'm saying I did what I should have done a long time ago. I called an attorney this morning before I turned in. The annulment papers will be drawn up by the end of the week. When you return home, it'll be as a single woman once again."

"That's…great." But a gloom settled over her. "You can just turn your feelings off that quickly?"

He stared into his coffee. "Last night was a real eye-opener. I'll just say that."

"Oh." The happiness she'd felt just a few moments ago had completely drained away. But she shouldn't be feeling that way. She should be thrilled. This was what she'd wanted. She fixed her expression into a smile and made the right words come out of her mouth. "That was nice of you. Thank you."

He nodded and tossed back the rest of his coffee. "I do have to ask you for one favor."

"Anything." She would have given him the world in that moment. Anything to make him stay.

"Would you be willing to wear your ring this evening? Seeing as how I told my grandmother we were married and all. If you don't show up with a ring, she'll give me such grief if she thinks I didn't get you one. She'd probably think that's why you were divorcing me." He laughed. "It would just make things easier. For me, anyway. Would you?"

She wanted to sob. She held her smile steady instead. "Absolutely."

"Thanks." He put his cup in the sink. "I'm off to get ready. See you back here in sixty?"

She nodded, face still frozen in a grin she didn't feel. "You got it."

He strode off.

Her smile died. She looked at her bare hand. All night long she was going to wear the beautiful reminder of how much he loved her. *Had* loved her. And all night long she'd think about how his emotions had shifted as quickly as a werewolf in heat.

She swallowed. On the surface, this proved what she'd believed about men since Alonso had betrayed her. That men could turn their feelings off and on as if they worked on a switch, but she'd done this to Julian. Pushed him to this with her refusal to love him. She had only herself to blame. And Alonso, damn him.

She cursed him and her past for the thousandth time, disappointed that her fight to get beyond what had happened to her raged on. She wanted to move ahead, to trust the future, but her fear always won.

If ever there was a man worth accepting, worth the struggle of overcoming, it was Julian. Too bad he'd already decided he'd waited long enough. And too bad that decision had come after she'd fallen in love with him.

Julian leaned his head against the shower wall and let the hot water beat on him. He had never felt worse than he had lying to Desi. But it was the right thing to do. In a twisted sort of way. He had to let her go in order to salvage what was left of his heart before it hardened like hers had.

And if she never told him what had really transpired between her and Alonso, that was fine. Maybe it wouldn't help him understand anything about her. Maybe it was just a crutch she used to keep herself from getting hurt again.

Good for her. At least one of them would come out of this unscathed.

He rinsed and got out. He'd have time to wallow in his misery when this was all said and done, which meant that starting tomorrow he was going to get to the bottom of whoever was harassing her so that she could return home as soon as possible.

How, he wasn't sure, but he'd figure something out. Maybe her people would get back to her with the ticket info. Maybe they already had. He needed to ask her about that.

He dried off and dressed in a simple suit, although he allowed himself a slightly bolder tie choice than his grandmother would probably approve of. He didn't care. He needed to make himself happy.

The last thing he did was take Desi's engagement

ring from the drawer in the island in his closet. It should have been in a safe.

No, it should have been on her finger.

He closed his eyes and sighed. Those kinds of thoughts weren't going to help him. Just like keeping the ring with the rest of his personal effects wasn't a healthy thing to do either. He opened the box and studied the brilliant, flashing stone. It was enormous and had cost a ransom, but he hadn't blinked at the price.

She was worth a thousand diamonds like this. No matter what happened between them, she'd still have a place in his heart, but one thing was for sure. This ring had to go somewhere else.

Maybe he'd take it to Willa and see if she could find a buyer for it. He snapped the box closed and tucked it in his pocket, then headed out to wait on Desi.

But she was already in the living room. "You got ready fast."

"Didn't want to be the reason we were late." She was in a sleek black dress. The hem was a giant ruffle that danced above her knees in the front and just below them in the back, showing off the dress's hot pink lining. Her high heels were also black, but covered in jet crystals. Her earrings, dangling below her riot of curls, looked to be made of the same. He imagined this was about as conservative as she got.

She held out her arms and did a slow twirl. "You like?"

"Stunning." As always. He put his hand to his broken heart. "Just one thing you're missing." He dug the box from his pocket and opened it.

Her smile wavered. Or had he imagined that? She stretched her hand out as she walked toward him. "Ah, yes. The ring."

He took it out of the box and slid it onto her finger, holding her hand a moment longer than necessary.

She laughed. "It's heavier than I remember."

"Well, you only had it on for a few hours. And most of those you were asleep for."

"True." She looked up as he looked at her. Their eyes met and the tension that had been present over coffee returned. Then she smiled. "So tonight I'm the good little wife, am I?"

"No need to lie, but…it would be nice if my grandmother could see that we are actually friends."

"Easy enough." She picked up the black clutch on the counter. "Because we are. Friends."

Was she reminding him or herself? He wasn't sure. But if there was tension between them, Elenora would pick it up like a hound dog after a rabbit. Sure, she knew that he and Desi were getting divorced and tension would be natural, but it would set off Elenora's uncontrollable urge to fix things. If she thought everything was going well between them, she'd be more likely to leave them alone. Maybe he could play off an uneasiness on Desi's stalker. That was a good reason for them both to be on edge.

He took his keys out of the glass dish on the foyer table. "Come on, I'll give you the Elenora Ellingham primer on the ride over. Everything you ever wanted to know about your soon-to-be ex's grandmamma. And probably some you didn't."

They headed down to the car and were soon tooling along. Julian told Desi a few funny stories about Elenora, mentioned some of his grandmother's pet peeves along with some of her favorite things, talked about the history with Alice and how her spell on the town's water supply kept the tourists in the dark, and finished up with all the charity work Elenora did. He hoped that provided some balance to Elenora's pricklier side.

He ended just as he pulled into Elenora's long drive. The estate was lit up, as it was every evening when she was expecting company, and even to his eyes it looked impressive.

Desi must have thought so too. She leaned forward to see out the windshield a little better. "Is this for real?"

"One hundred percent."

"You didn't mention your grandmother was a baller."

He laughed. "She is basically the OG of Nocturne Falls."

Desi squinted at him. "You're way too white to talk like that." Then she laughed too, and went back to looking at the house. "This is one legit crib. I can't wait to see the inside. You think she'll give me a tour? Or would that not be appropriate?"

"She'd love to show you the house. Just know it'll add at least half an hour to the evening."

Desi shrugged as he parked in front of the grand double doors. "Aren't we a little early anyway?"

"A little, yes." He smiled. What did it matter if they stayed longer? "So you should definitely ask her."

"Thanks. I will." She kept her gaze on him. "Are you nervous about tonight?"

"Not really." He was a little. Why, he wasn't sure. What did it matter if Elenora and Desi got along? They'd never see each other again after this. And frankly, getting an amulet for Desi was only going to be a temporary situation now that the divorce papers were being processed.

Nothing that happened tonight would make much difference in anyone's life. And yet, as he got out and walked around to open her door, he wanted everything to go smoothly in the most desperate way. As if Desi liking Elenora was going to change her feelings about him.

He was a fool, despite his decision to push his

feelings down and see Desi on her way. It was proving much, much harder than he'd anticipated.

He opened her door, helped her out, then offered her his arm. "Shall we?"

She took it. "Lead on."

He did, taking her up to the doors. He rapped the knocker three times. About thirty seconds later, Wentworth, Elenora's special occasion butler, answered the door. Elenora must really want to impress Desi if she'd brought Wentworth in.

"Good evening, Master Ellingham."

He was the perfect butler for Elenora. Tall, thin, and snooty. Julian wondered why she didn't keep him around full time. "Evening, Wentworth."

The man backed up, opening the door. "Your grandmother is expecting you. She's in the library."

"Thank you. We can find our way."

His mouth thinned to a narrow line that was almost a frown. "Very good, sir."

Julian shook his head as he escorted Desi deeper into the mansion. He snuck a glance at her. She was all smiles and big eyes. "Having fun already, hmm?"

She nodded. "Having a butler is pretty fancy. But in a house like this? Seems normal." She glanced at one of the enormous oil paintings in the hall, then her gaze drifted to the spectacular crystal chandelier overhead. "This place is incredible."

"Glad you like it." He paused at the library doors. "Ready?"

She stared at the doors a moment, then smoothed down the front of her dress. "Yes."

He opened the door. Elenora was on her chaise talking with Alice. "Hello, Grandmamma." He nodded to the old witch. "Alice. How are you both?"

Elenora rose, her gaze briefly touching him before moving on to Desi. "Very well." She held out her hand. "You must be Desdemona."

Desi shook Elenora's hand. "I am. It's an honor to meet you."

Elenora's eyes narrowed as she took Desi in. The ring did not go unnoticed. "And you, my dear. I hope it remains that way."

Desi shot Julian a look. He'd told her this wasn't going to be a cake walk. "Grandmamma, you're forgetting Alice."

"Ah, yes." Elenora turned. "This is Alice Bishop, my dear friend and assistant."

Desi nodded at her. "Nice to meet you, Alice."

Alice sniffed. "Mm-hmm."

That was Alice, Julian thought. Such a sparkling conversationalist. "We should have some wine," he suggested. "I know I could use a drink."

"Excellent idea. Wentworth?" Elenora called. She sighed. "Where is he?"

Then the sounds of the front door opening

filtered in, followed by a lot of chatter. Julian froze as he recognized the voices. He somehow kept from spewing the stream of curses dancing on the tip of his tongue, but he knew his anger was clear in his eyes. This was exactly what he hadn't wanted to happen. "*Didi.*"

She looked at him, feigning innocence. "Yes, my darling?"

"Did you invite—"

Hugh pushed the library doors wide. "Hello, brother. I hear you have some news to share."

18

Desi watched with great interest as two very handsome men and two very beautiful women (one with a baby on her hip) streamed into the room. They all exchanged greetings with Alice and Elenora, who took the baby and cooed at him like she'd lost her mind. It was funny, really, to see the woman who'd been so stiff and formal suddenly chattering on in baby talk and making silly faces.

It humanized her, an odd thing to think about a vampire, but with that small change, Desi didn't feel nearly so intimidated by the matriarch.

Now the others who'd come in…that was a different story.

The two male vampires were in a deep and slightly contentious conversation with Jules that included sideways glances at her every so often. His brothers. She could see the resemblance, but she also recognized them from the pictures on Julian's dresser.

But that photo hadn't done the two women justice. They were about as perfect as women could get. The one with the baby was clearly a vampire. The other, a striking blonde, Desi wasn't sure about. Some kind of supernatural for sure, but nothing she could pinpoint.

"Desi?"

She turned to look at Jules and smiled like she hadn't a care in the world. "Yes, love?"

Anger snapped in his eyes. He hadn't said anything about meeting the rest of his family, so this had to be a bit of an ambush. "Come meet my brothers."

"I'd love to." She walked over, mentally getting her game on. Charming men were no big deal. Usually. And if she could do that, maybe it would help defuse the situation. She didn't like that Julian's grandmother had done this to him. Well, if it was some kind of test, Desi intended to pass.

She looped her arm through Julian's, fully prepared to bring the happy wife to this party if that's what it took. Especially since these two in front of her were clearly sizing her up. "Hello, Julian's brothers."

Jules pointed at the men in turn. "This is Hugh. He's married to Delaney there next to our grandmother. And thanks to his procreation skills, he took the burden of grandchildren off the rest of us. That's his son, George, that Elenora is currently Eskimo kissing."

"So nice to meet you, Hugh. Your son is adorable." She shook his hand. "And I've heard tremendous things about you."

"Have you?" Hugh gave Jules an incredulous look.

Julian sighed. "And this is Sebastian, the eldest of us. His fiancée is the pretty but deadly one, Tessa, who's speaking with Alice. Tessa is a valkyrie."

So that's what the blonde was. How interesting. Desi took Sebastian's hand as he reached out. "How great to meet you. Jules says you're an absolute financial genius."

He seemed surprised that she knew that. Or that Jules would refer to him as a genius. Either way, it felt like a victory to throw him off guard. "Well, I don't know about all that…"

She kept it up. "He says you're a whiz with numbers."

The barest hint of a smile appeared on his face. She considered that another win. "Handling the family finances *is* my job."

The two men called the women over and more introductions were made. Thankfully, Tessa and Delaney didn't seem to have an ounce of judgment in their eyes. In fact, they were looking at her with a mix of curiosity and admiration. And maybe the tiniest bit of pity. What exactly did they think about Jules to look at her that way?

Wentworth appeared at the library doors and, with great seriousness, announced, "Dinner is served."

The group moved forward, led by Elenora, who'd yet to let little George go. Tessa and Delaney hung back by Desi as Jules went off with his brothers. He glanced at her, his expression asking if she needed saving, but she waved him on.

Delaney spoke first. "How on earth did you manage it?"

"Manage what?"

"To pin Julian down," Delaney answered. "Sweet crispy crackers! He's the biggest playboy I know. Or was, obviously."

Tessa nodded. "Sebastian could not believe his little brother had settled down. He was convinced you were a witch and you had him under a spell."

Desi laughed. "Nope, just your average neighborhood vampire."

"Hah! You're not average, that much is clear. So come on, how did you do it?" Delaney shook her head. "You must have done something no other woman ever has."

"Well..." Desi thought about it as they walked through the house. She couldn't tell them the truth about how she and Julian came to be married. At least, she was pretty sure that wasn't something he'd want her to share. "He pursued me pretty hard, but other than that, it was a fairly standard courtship."

"He pursued you," Tessa clarified.

"Yes," Desi said. "Took me a while to say yes to going out with him, but he eventually won me over."

"That's it," Delaney said. "You must have been the first woman who didn't fall into his lap with an adoring smile thinking he was everything right with the male species."

Desi's brows lifted. "Is that what usually happens? Actually, never mind. I've seen him at work being the VOD. I know how the women look at him."

"Well," Tessa said. "However it happened, welcome to the family."

"Yes," Delaney said. "It's about time that one settled down." She shook her head. "And don't worry about Elenora. She'll give you a hard time, but she did that to all of us. Just stand up for yourself and you'll be fine."

They walked into the dining room, another utterly impressive space.

"Thanks," Desi said. She liked her new sisters-in-law. Too bad they weren't going to like her very much when they found out about the divorce. Poor Jules. She had a feeling his family was going to come down hard on him when the truth came out.

Place cards marked everyone's seats. Desi found her spot between Jules and Elenora, who was at the head of the table. Sebastian was at the other end, flanked by Alice and Tessa. Next to the valkyrie was Delaney, then Hugh. Little George was squeezed between them in a fancy mahogany high chair.

They all took their seats, then a young woman in a black and white uniform served wine. Desi hadn't been to a dinner party like this in ages. And she'd never been to one with this much strain in the air.

Jules was still fuming about his brothers showing up. Desi couldn't help but be upset by that. Regardless of what the future held, tonight they were a team. She smiled at Elenora. "Jules didn't mention what a large gathering this was going to be."

"Oh?" Elenora said. Her diamond and pearl earrings could have fed a small nation. "It must have slipped my mind."

Julian snorted as he lifted his wine glass and took a substantial drink.

Desi kept her smile on. "I hear ginko biloba is good for that."

Elenora looked over the rim of her glass. "Good for what, dear?"

Desi picked up her own wineglass. The aroma was fruity and gorgeous. "Memory loss."

Someone muffled a laugh at the other end of the table.

Elenora's eyes narrowed ever so slightly.

Hugh lifted his glass. "To Julian and Desdemona. May their love be as immortal as they are."

"Here, here." Sebastian raised his glass and everyone around the table joined him, although Desi noticed that Elenora was slow in doing so.

As everyone drank, Desi swore she could feel the annoyance rolling off Jules. He still wasn't over the family ambush, that was certain. She reached under the table and patted his leg. They'd get through this.

Of course, he'd be the one left behind to deal with the fallout of their breakup. She wondered if there was a way to soften that blow for him.

The girl who'd brought the wine returned along with another woman, and dinner was served. Rack of lamb with mint chutney, roasted fingerling potatoes, spring peas, and honey-glazed carrots. The food was incredible, and thankfully, occupied Julian's family enough so that very few questions got lobbed at Desi.

There was also some talk about a new housing development, Pumpkin Point, but after the family had spent a few minutes on that, the questions turned back to Desi.

"Speaking of real estate…" Sebastian looked at

her. "Do you plan on keeping your place in Las Vegas?"

"I…" She wasn't sure of the right way to answer that.

Julian laughed. "Of course she's keeping it. The Skye Towers is a great investment." He grinned. "And speaking of things that get better with time, how is my darling nephew, Delaney? I can't believe how much he's grown."

As Delaney and her husband launched into a full report on the child, Desi smiled to herself. Apparently, asking new parents about their child was a sure way to change the course of any conversation.

It wasn't until coffee and dessert, a gorgeous coconut cake from Delaney's shop, that the focus shifted back to Desi again.

Sebastian led things off. "Now that we know why Julian has been spending so much time in Las Vegas, I must ask what it is you do out there, Desdemona."

She sliced into her cake with the edge of her fork. "I have my own show, called Vamp. It's a standard Vegas show in that there's lots of magic, pretty dancing girls, a few exotic animals, and some great special effects."

"Vamp?" His brows pulled together. "As in a femme fatale or…"

"Yes, a femme fatale. Who also happens to be a

vampire." She smiled. "It's very Nocturne Falls in that way."

Julian put his fork down. "She's a vampire pretending to be a human pretending to be a vampire. It's exactly what we do here."

"Clever," Delaney said. "Maybe you could move your show here? Or are you thinking about moving to Vegas, Julian?"

"We, uh…" Jules looked at her.

"We're working all that out," Desi said. She forked up a big bite of cake. "This cake is amazing, by the way. I love coconut. And the hint of lime is perfect."

Tessa nodded. "I agree. This might be my new favorite."

"Thanks." Delaney smiled. "It's something I'm trying out for summer."

Desi finished the bite she'd just taken, sensing an opening. "Do you sell it at your store?"

"I do."

"I haven't been to your shop yet, but Julian said it's a very popular spot. How did you get into baking? Have you always wanted your own shop?"

Delaney happily answered and once again, the conversation was no longer about Desi. And when Delaney was done, Julian pushed back from the table and tossed his napkin onto the plate. "Thank you for a lovely evening, Grandmamma, but Desdemona and I should be going."

"So soon?" Elenora shook her head.

Julian slanted his eyes at her. "We've been here for nearly three hours. That's not soon. And we have a lot to do."

He stood to help Desi with her chair and his brothers got up as well.

Then George started fussing, and Delaney scooped him up. "Poor thing. It's a little past his feeding time. We should really go too. But it was a perfect dinner, Elenora. And so good to meet you, Desdemona. We must do lunch. You, me, and Tessa. We'll leave the boys at home. Except for George, he doesn't count." She kissed his fat cheek. "You're still sweet enough to join us, aren't you Georgie-boy?"

"Oh, please bring George," Tessa said. "He's my favorite of all the Ellingham men."

Sebastian hmphed, but Tessa ignored him to tickle George's tummy.

Desi frowned. Lunch out meant Delaney must be able to daywalk just like Julian. Could they all? And why had she assumed Desi could do it too? Desi had to know more. "You talk like the sun isn't an issue."

"It isn't," Delaney replied. "Not with one of the Ellingham amulets. Or hasn't Alice made you one yet?" She clucked her tongue. "Elenora, don't be stingy. We can't have Julian's wife stuck inside all by herself."

Desi's mouth came open. She'd seen the amulet that Jules wore. Now she realized Delaney had one on a bracelet at her wrist. And so did Elenora. The men were in suits, so if they had one on too, it was hidden under their clothing.

Then she realized the room had gone very, very quiet.

Julian finally broke the silence. "Hugh, Sebastian, I need to talk to Grandmamma alone."

His brothers answered with a nod and a grunt and by ushering the women out.

As soon as they'd left, Desi found her voice. "I take it the amulet isn't something I'm supposed to know about."

"There is no amulet," Elenora replied. "Delaney doesn't—"

"Oh, come on, Grandmother." Julian sighed in frustration. "Obviously, there's something that allows us to daywalk."

Elenora's eyes sparked with indignation. She put her hands on the table and leaned forward. "This is not open for discussion."

"Really?" He glared at her. "Because two days ago, you said you'd give Desi one. Now you're not?"

"Two days ago, you hadn't filed for a divorce," Elenora snapped back.

He growled. "It would be nice to live in a town where personal business stays personal."

The tension was suffocating. Desi hated being the reason for it. She held up her hands. "Whatever this amulet is, I don't want one."

They both looked at her.

Julian shook his head. "Of course you do. What vampire wouldn't want protection from the sun?"

She glanced at the ring on her finger. "Jules, this is obviously a family thing. And since my position as your wife is about to come to an end just...don't worry about it. I've managed two centuries without the help. I'll get along just fine."

Elenora's brows shot up. "Wise woman."

Julian scowled at his grandmother.

Desi lifted her hands higher. "Please, don't say another word about it. It's not my business and I certainly don't want you two cross at each other over it."

Elenora gave Jules a rather smug look. "It's too bad you couldn't manage to keep her. She's the best one you've brought around in a long time."

Desi rolled her eyes and turned toward the older woman. "Julian has nothing to do with why I'm divorcing him. Nothing. The blame is completely mine, got it? I don't have the capacity to love him in the manner he deserves."

She stabbed a finger on the table. "And he does deserve to be loved. So much. He's the most incredible man I've ever met. He's kind, and funny, and generous, and doesn't take himself too seriously like a lot of vampires I know, plus he's gorgeous and sexy and smart. He's a total package."

She tapped that finger on her own chest. "I, however, am not. I come with more baggage than a Vegas hotel could handle. Not to mention, I'm narcissistic, self-centered, overly ambitious, cold-hearted, and only concerned with what's best for me and my life."

"Des…"

She glanced at Julian. "You know it's true." She pushed her chair in and looked at Elenora again. "It really was nice to meet you, and your home is the most beautiful place I've ever seen. I don't have any hard feelings toward you or any of your family. In fact, I'd love it if Julian and I are able to remain friends when this is all said and done, but even if we can't, you won't have a thing to worry about from me. Your daywalking secret, whatever it is? Totally safe with me."

Elenora didn't have an instant response for that, and Desi didn't care. She smiled at Julian. "I'm ready to go home."

"That was…very you." Julian laughed softly as he turned out of Elenora's drive. "By which I mean perfect and amazing. You might have actually convinced her that your knowledge of the amulet isn't a threat."

"It isn't. I don't care a thing about it." Then Desi put her hand up. "Don't say anything about it, either because I don't want to know."

"Not another word."

She sighed. "I probably shouldn't have talked to her quite that boldly. I'm sorry if my outburst is going to make things difficult for you."

"It won't. She respects those who stand up for themselves." Then he shook his head. "I really was trying to get you one. You would have had to give it back after the divorce, but I thought it would keep you safe until we could figure out who was after you at least."

She reached over and gave his leg a squeeze, sending a sharp jolt of desire through him that he instantly tamped down. "That was kind of you. But like I said, I've been fine this long. I'll continue to be fine."

They both went silent for a few minutes, giving him time to wonder what had taken over her thoughts. Maybe now would be the right time to tell her that Alonso was dead. Or maybe as soon as they got home. Then she could go to her room and be alone if that's what she needed. That was the plan. He'd tell her as soon as they were back in the penthouse.

She spoke suddenly. "Must be nice, though. Not having to hide from the sun, I mean."

"It is." He shrugged. "Comes with some strings attached, though. Not as much as it used to, but…it's always a possibility with my grandmother."

Desi nodded. "I'm sure. Explains a lot. About how you haven't turned to ash yet, I mean. Anyway, seriously, I don't want to talk about it. The less I know, the better."

He couldn't argue with her about that. Elenora was probably freaking out that a soon-to-be non-family member knew about their amulets, but she'd mellow in a few days. He hoped. Otherwise…he wasn't sure what. Maybe she'd come up with some non-disclosure statement for Desi to sign.

With Elenora, you really never knew.

Happily, he changed the subject. "You want to go straight home or do something else?"

"Home is good."

"Have you gotten that email from ticketing yet?"

She sat up a little. "You know, in the flurry of getting ready, I never checked." She pulled out her phone and opened up her email. "Yep, it's there. We can look at the attachment on my tablet as soon as we get in."

"Excellent. I have an idea about what to do with the names when we narrow it down."

"Good."

He looked over at her. "Because you're ready for this threat to be handled or you're ready to go home?"

She glanced back at him. "Because I'm ready for the threat to be handled. As far as going home...you might not believe me, but this crazy little town is growing on me."

"Even with my grandmother here?"

She smiled. "Even with her here. It's a great place to live for people like us." She put her phone away, but her gaze stayed on her lap. "Your family is really nice too. All of them. They love you."

She seemed wistful. Or maybe a little sad. That made him hurt for her. He knew she didn't have a lot of friends and he'd never once heard her talk about family, but he'd always assumed those were deliberate choices she'd made. "You can come back and visit any time you like."

She laughed. "Yeah, thanks."

"No, I mean it."

"I'm sure you do, but at some point, there will be a new woman in your life and I have a feeling she won't be on the same page as you with that invite."

He didn't answer right away. He couldn't imagine having another woman in his life. After Desi left, he planned to spend a long time alone. Just recovering from the loss of her was going to take some doing, but to get to the place where he could be in a relationship again? That seemed unfathomable.

He pulled into the Excelsior's parking lot. "Once we deal with that list of names, we could watch a movie. I think that new Tom Hiddleston movie is playing On Demand now."

"Which one?"

He parked and turned the car off. "Marty Poppins."

She laughed. "You really want to see a remake about a magical nanny who sings and dances his way through life?"

"With Anna Faris as Bernice, the chimney sweep?" He nodded. "Yeah, I'm up for that."

She shot him a look. "I guess you are if you know the story that well."

He palmed the key fob. "Do you not like musicals? I'd think you of all people would, I mean, you make your living on stage. Plus, Mary Poppins is a classic, so aren't you at least a little interested to see the remake?"

"I am." She shook her head, her grin sheepish. "And actually, I love musicals. But I never thought you would."

"I love a shoot 'em up action flick as much as the next guy, but there's something about a good song and dance movie every once in a while." They got out and walked toward the lobby together. He itched to hold her hand, but didn't, finally reaching for the door instead. "Not sure what that says about me, but it is what it is."

She trailed a finger on his chest as she passed him, leaving a wake of heat on his skin. "It's because you have a lot of kid in you. Like that pantry full of candy."

"You think that's a bad thing?" He followed after her, doing his best to control the desire she'd brought to life with her touch.

"Evening, folks," Lou called out.

Julian gave the man a wave. "Evening, Lou."

Desi waved at him too before continuing her thought. "It's not a bad thing at all. In fact, I think it's amazing that you can be nearly four hundred years old and still tap into your inner child. It's one of the things that made me fall in—"

Her eyes widened and her mouth closed.

Love. She was going to say love. She loved him? She loved him. He stood there staring at her, willing her to continue.

"Hope you had a nice night," Lou said. "There's a delivery for you."

And just like that, the spell was broken. Julian grimaced as Desi turned toward Lou. He looked at the man. "What is it?"

"Not for you, Mr. Ellingham. It's for Miss Clarke." He smiled oddly. "Actually, it's for Desdemona Valentine, but I searched that name on the Internet and your picture came up, Miss Desi."

"That is my stage name, but it's my real name too. Clarke was another of my names. You know how it is for most vampires." She walked over to his desk.

"Yes, ma'am." He reached underneath and pulled out a long white florist's box. "Here you go."

She took it, but turned to squint at Julian. "Did you send me flowers?"

"No, I would have just given them to you. It's possible Delaney or Tessa did."

"That fast?"

"They're thoughtful woman." He went closer to look at the box. "Delaney loves a big gesture and she'd definitely think it was her duty to welcome you to the family properly since she married into it first."

"Well, if she did, that's above and beyond."

He looked at Lou. "Do you know who delivered these?"

Lou nodded. "Joe. He's the regular delivery guy from the Enchanted Garden."

"Marigold Williams's shop." Julian looked at his watch. "Closed now. When did these arrive?"

"Right after you left."

An uneasy feeling came over Julian. "Then Delaney didn't send these. I don't like this. No one's supposed to know you're here." He took the box from Desi and put it on Lou's desk, then he held out his hand. "Box cutter?"

Lou took one out of a drawer and handed it over.

Desi chewed on her lower lip. "You think this is from my stalker?"

"We'll know soon enough." He slit the tape on the sides of the box and pulled the top off.

Nestled inside a swath of white tissue paper was a bundle of long-stemmed black roses.

Desi sucked in a breath. "Just like Sam got."

A note lay on top. Julian snatched it up, opened it, and read it out loud. "Enjoying your visit?"

He swore softly.

Desi backed away, shaking her head. "They know I'm here. How?"

He grabbed her hand. "I don't know, but we're going to figure this out." Then he looked at Lou.

"Have you seen anyone odd around here lately? Anyone come in looking for Miss Clarke?"

"No, sir."

He gestured with the note that was still in his hand. "No one gets up to that penthouse without my permission."

"No, sir."

That was already standard operating procedure, but Julian felt better saying it. He tucked the note into his pocket, then shoved the roses toward Lou. "Get rid of those. Or take them home for Rella, if you think she'd like them. I don't care either way, I just don't want to see them again."

Lou pulled the box off the counter and tucked it under the desk again. "You got it, Mr. Ellingham."

Julian turned his attention to Desi. "You okay with that?"

"Absolutely."

"Good. Let's get upstairs. We have work to do."

Desi paced the expanse of Julian's living room while he looked at the list of names she'd forwarded to him. They'd both changed out of their dinner clothes and into more comfortable ones, meaning he was back in his black tee and drawstring pants.

It was fast becoming one of her favorite looks on him. She'd opted for leggings and a slouchy tee. Nothing fancy, but they were in for the night.

Julian let out a soft grunt. He stared at the laptop screen, the soft glow lighting his handsome face and giving his focused expression extra seriousness. He was so concerned about her that her heart almost couldn't bear the sweetness of it. But that was Julian. Earnest, sincere, and loyal. How amazing that this man was on her side, despite her rejecting his love. She didn't deserve him. But here he was anyway.

He glanced up. "You okay?"

No. She was a conflicted mess, but she nodded anyway. "Any idea how they found me here?"

"No, but I'd like to know that too. And we can assume they know Sam's not you. Which doesn't mean she's not still in danger, so I'm keeping Harlan up to date and making sure he's still being vigilant." His fingers flew over the keyboard. "There. I dumped the list into an Excel spreadsheet and ran a search for duplicates. Found a lot."

"What's a lot? How many?"

"Since your show started, you've had over three hundred repeat attendees."

She sighed. "That's both awesome and completely unhelpful."

"I'm not done yet." He typed some more, his eyes narrowing in concentration. "I'm searching for the names that show up the most."

She stopped pacing. "And?"

"Fifteen names, all of whom have seen the show more than five times. We can eliminate me, that makes fourteen." He looked up as he shrugged. "It's a start."

She nodded. "It is. Still feels like a big number."

"We'll get there. I need to make a few calls." He glanced at her again, studying her. "You need something? I know you said you're okay, but you don't look it exactly."

She sat on the couch across from him. "I'm fine.

I don't know. I just feel unsettled."

"I bet you do. This is very unsettling." He moved his gaze toward the kitchen. "Hang on, I have just the thing."

"I'm not going anywhere." She stared at the flickering television. He'd put a movie channel on for a diversion. Neither of them had paid attention to it. The volume was low, too, but vampires had excellent hearing. And she didn't need to hear it to know that the movie was The Princess Bride.

He went into the kitchen and came back a few minutes later with a large, glass appetizer platter. Except instead of conventional snacks, all the little compartments were filled with different gummy candies.

She laughed and shook her head.

"See?" he said. "You feel better already, don't you?"

She snagged a Swedish Fish and popped it in her mouth. "I do."

"Good." He set the tray on the table in front of her. "I'm going to make a few phone calls, then I'll be back."

"Where are you going to make them?"

"In my office. I won't be long."

"Why not make them here? They are about me, right?"

He nodded. "That's why I was going to go in the other room. I didn't want to upset you further."

She took another fish. "You won't. I can handle it." And she wanted him here, next to her.

"Okay." He reached for his cell phone and dialed. He didn't have to wait long for an answer. "Good evening, Birdie. Sorry to bother you so late." He smiled and nodded. "You might say that. I need some help." More smiling. "Thank you, but you don't know what I'm going to ask you to do yet."

Whoever Birdie was, she seemed pretty agreeable to Julian's request. Or maybe it was just Julian.

He continued. "I'm going to email you a list of names. I need you to find out everything you can about those people, and then more specifically, if any of them might currently be in Nocturne Falls. I'm also going to include a list of dates on which these people should have been in Las Vegas. I'd love to know if they were or not. Is that too much?"

He smiled. "Great."

Apparently, it wasn't too much. Birdie must be a real pro at whatever it was she did.

"You're the best," Julian said. "And feel free to let the sheriff in on this. He knows what it's about. And he has my permission to fill you in."

Desi raised her eyes. This Birdie person just got even more interesting if she was connected to the sheriff. Also, Julian wasn't fooling around.

"Thank you very much. Call me anytime if something worth mentioning turns up, otherwise

I'll come see you in the morning. With doughnuts." He smiled. "You too. Good night."

He hung up. "That went well."

"Details?"

"Birdie Caruthers is the sheriff's aunt and works the reception desk at the department. She's also exceptional at digging up dirt on people. And she's a werewolf. And a bit of a busy body, but in the best possible way."

Birdie sounded like someone Desi needed to meet. "All right, some inter-species cooperation. I like that. Who's next?"

He scrolled through his contacts, then tapped one. "Marigold Williams, owner of the shop that delivered those roses."

Desi sat back. It was good to have a husband, however temporary, who was well connected.

"Hey, Marigold, it's Julian Ellingham. I'm sorry to call you this late. Did I wake you?" He grimaced. "I am truly sorry about that, but I wouldn't have called if it wasn't an emergency."

Desi felt bad. People's lives were being disrupted because of her.

"That delivery from your shop that showed up at my building tonight, that was for a friend of mine who's staying with me. I need to know who sent those roses."

He listened for a bit, and did some more nodding. "Okay, that's fine. First thing is perfect.

Thanks. Sorry again about waking you."

He hung up. "She's home and can't check her system until she opens up in the morning."

"Fair enough."

"Now we wait." He tossed a couple gummy cola bottles in his mouth and chewed. "There's not much else we can do. You want to watch Marty Poppins and work our way through this pile of sugar?"

"I thought you'd never ask."

It was the perfect distraction. Candy, a fun movie, and most of all, Julian at her side. They sat in the dark, the tray of sweets half on his lap and half on hers. Occasionally, their hands would touch when they reached for the same thing. Sometimes, when Desi timed it right, it happened on purpose.

She snuck glances at him throughout the movie. He looked happy. Mostly. She hoped he was. She wanted nothing but good things for him. Even if the idea of another woman in his life made her sick with envy.

She shoved that thought aside, because she had no right to it. If she was purposely removing herself from his life, she had no say in what he did with it. She knew that. But it still stung.

His brothers were so happy. No doubt Jules wanted that same life for himself. Why wouldn't he?

She sighed, causing him to glance over.

His brows bent in concern. "You okay?"

She smiled and nodded as she made something up. "Just wishing we weren't out of licorice of all sorts."

He winked. "I can fix that."

"No. Stay." She grabbed his hand. "You'll miss the movie."

"Okay, but just say the word and I will."

"I know."

They went back to watching and snacking. It was so comfortable with him, she felt like they'd known each other forever. And yet, she still hadn't shared the whole truth of her life with him.

He deserved that much before she left. But not now. It would destroy this peaceful, happy moment, and this was something she wanted to hold on to to help her remember how good life could be. She felt safe, and although she had no right to it, she felt loved.

She tipped her head onto his shoulder, just for a moment. Just to test out what it felt like to be someone in love. Someone who could love.

Then he bent his head and kissed her temple.

Her eyes stung with tears at the simple gesture. For all of Alonso's awfulness, leaving Julian behind might hurt her even more. How was she going to walk away from this man? How could she not love him?

She did. She knew that. It was the terrible truth

she'd been trying to deny, but what was the point of lying to herself that way?

What it came down to was she was a coward. She was afraid to be hurt again. Afraid that something would make Julian snap the way Alonso had and she'd bear the brunt of it again. Afraid that this time, she wouldn't survive.

But Julian wasn't Alonso. And just because they were both men and both vampires didn't mean they'd make the same kinds of decisions.

Did it?

"No," she whispered.

"What was that?" Julian whispered back.

She wiped at her eyes and picked her head up. "Nothing." She stared at him as the credits began to roll. "No, that was a lie. It wasn't nothing. I…" She had to tell him something and it couldn't be that she loved him. "I was just caught up in memories."

He didn't seem like he quite understood.

She blinked a few times, trying to keep the tears from spilling. What she wanted to tell him was that she'd tried and tried not to, but she'd fallen in love with him anyway.

"Bad memories?"

She sighed. This was headed in a direction she hadn't been ready to take, but there were only so many times she could put off telling him the truth. He deserved to know. "Yes."

He moved the tray of candy to the table, then twisted to face her. "Memories that have to do with Alonso."

She tucked one leg under the other and turned toward him. "Yes."

"I'm sorry it affects you so much." His eyes held compassion. "Listen, I need to tell you something. I've put it off a few times, because I wasn't sure when the right moment was, but you need to know this. Alonso is dead. Remy asked his grandfather about it and the man confessed to putting a stake through Alonso's heart. In part because Alonso was stealing from him, but in part because of what he'd done to you."

"Really?" Alonso was dead. She'd always wondered how that news would make her feel. She was surprised to find herself a little numb to it. Maybe because she'd wished it to be true for so long that it had already become a reality in her mind.

"Yes. Really."

"I owe Remy an apology. And a thank you to his grandfather."

"I can get you his number."

"Good. I owe you an explanation, too." With her elbow resting on the back of the sofa, she dropped her head into her hand. "It's just not an easy thing for me to talk about."

"You don't need to explain anything to me."

"Yes, I do." She had to tell him, even if it would ruin the nice evening they'd been having. Memories of that day were already swirling past like seabirds drafting the ocean's breezes. She closed her eyes and the dank scent of salt water filled her senses. She opened her eyes again, but kept her gaze on the cushion between them. "We had just completed a run for the Lafittes and were on our way back to New Orleans for whatever cargo was next.

"Then Alonso spotted a Spanish galleon off the starboard side. There was no way they saw us. It was night and we were running dark. Having a captain and a few crew members that were vampires gave us some deadly advantages." Her chest constricted as the memories continued to slip through her mind. "She was twice our size and sitting low. Alonso smelled gold.

"He gave the order and we attacked, using the dark to our benefit. We drove the ship aground on a small island."

"This was in the Caribbean?"

She nodded.

"Which island?"

"One of a thousand spits of land that have never been named." She could still picture every inch of it. "It was three thousand five hundred and seventy steps long, and eight hundred and one wide."

His brows lifted in response to her detailed

knowledge, but he didn't ask anything more, although she could see the questions in his eyes.

"When the defeated crew had been dispatched, something Alonso took an unnatural pleasure in, even though I repeatedly asked him to show mercy, we boarded the broken ship. There was gold, just as Alonso had suspected, and a great deal of it. Silver too. Some jewelry, silks, a lot of wine, and a few crates of books. It was a treasure ship and fat with it. He'd never come across anything like it and I doubt he ever did again. It was his greatest conquest."

Julian hung on her words. "What happened then?"

"Taking all that treasure aboard the Night's Mistress had her almost bursting at the seams. It was too much for his ship. But Alonso wasn't about to let any of it go." An uncontrolled sob rose up through her.

Julian grabbed her hand. "You don't have to finish if it's too hard."

She shook her head, using the anger in her belly to fuel her words. "One of the crewmen suggested he leave half the treasure behind on the island, then return for it. Another crewman agreed with that idea. Alonso shot them both dead. They were human so to him, they didn't matter. But he liked the idea well enough that he decided leaving something behind was the way to go."

"What did he decide to leave behind?"

She lifted her head to stare into Julian's eyes, the rage inside of her no doubt brightening her eyes with the fire of intense emotion. "Me."

Julian squinted at her. "So you could watch over the treasure?"

She was shaking with anger. "There was no treasure to watch over. That was all onboard his ship."

Julian refused to understand. "You can't be telling me that he left *you* on a deserted island in the middle of the Caribbean Sea."

"Yes, that is exactly what I'm telling you. My husband of thirteen months leveled his sword at me, and told me to disembark or he would run me through the heart to make room for three chests of doubloons, two casks of wine, and a crate of gold dinnerware."

Julian's mouth hung open. "That can't be possible."

"I wish that was true."

He felt numb with disbelief, but that soon gave

way to pure, unadulterated rage. He pushed to his feet, too distressed to sit. "This man was your husband?"

"Yes."

"How dare he? To even think he'd earned that title. I'm glad he's dead or I'd do it for him. That bloody…" Julian clenched his fists so tightly his knuckles cracked. "No wonder you don't want to be married."

She nodded slowly. The memories were overwhelming her. He could see it in her eyes. She had the same far-away look she'd had the day of the panic attack.

He sat back down. "Tell me the rest. What did you do?"

She shook her head with such a small movement it almost wasn't noticeable. "I got off the ship."

He gasped. "You did? But you're here now. How did you survive?"

"I'm not sure. Sheer determination. Stubbornness. Anger. Being a vampire made it both easier and harder. I had my increased abilities that made some things possible that wouldn't have been otherwise, but when the sun is your worst enemy and you've been stranded on an island…that was problematic, to say the least."

He shook his head. "How did you manage?"

"I lived in the ship. Even though Alonso and the crew stripped it nearly bare, it provided plenty of shelter. I knew it wouldn't last forever, though, so at night, I used what I could salvage to build a passable hut on the island."

"Amazing." But of course she had. She was incredible.

"It was hard, but my strength made it possible. The island had a stand of palms, too, so I used them for added shade."

"How did you feed? Vampires have requirements humans don't."

She grimaced. "Sea creatures. Fish, sharks, whatever I could get my hands on."

"Which explains why you don't eat seafood now."

"Let's just say I've had my fill."

"Did you have fishing supplies?"

"No." She let out a soft, bitter laugh. "Not having to breathe meant I could be underwater for however long I needed to be. On the nights with a full moon, I would wade into the small lagoon on the far side of the island until I was ten or fifteen feet under, then I would just wait."

"How did you get off the island?"

She thought back, remembering that fateful night. "I had this feeling one evening, one of those gut things you can't ignore, that I should light my signal fire. So I did. A few hours later, a fishing boat showed up. I've never discounted that inner voice since that night, I promise you that."

"Amazing." He rubbed at his temple. "I cannot believe you survived such an ordeal. And yet, knowing you, I can. But I hate that you went through it, and I hate that your husband did this to you." He ground his teeth together as the muscles in his jaw tightened. Anger spilled through him like molten metal. "I hate him with a rage I've never felt before. I want to kill him."

She snorted. "I'm okay with that. Revenge fantasies were all that kept me going sometimes."

"How long were you there?"

She took a moment. "Seventeen years."

"Bloody hell." He stared at her, awestruck. "Bloody, bloody hell." Then he closed his eyes for a moment. It was that or snap. The idea that this piece of garbage Alonso had done this to his Desi was horrifying. He'd buy Jean Lafitte dinner next time he was in New Orleans to thank him for ridding the world of such a wicked man.

Julian opened his eyes and took a deep, cleansing breath. "Thank you for sharing that with me. I completely understand how difficult it must be for you to trust or love anyone now. But I hope you know that I would hurt myself before I would hurt you."

"I know you're not him, but…" Her smile was kind, but a little sad. "Alonso made those same kinds of promises to me when we married. He swore his love and protection, his undying loyalty, his life before mine."

"And he was clearly a liar," Julian spat out.

She nodded. "Ultimately, things were more important to him. And I know how important things are to you, too. Not saying you're anything like him, but I've been through too much to risk my heart—or my life—again. I told you because you deserved to know. And so you could understand why no matter what I feel, I won't allow myself to go down this path again."

"Things mean nothing to me. Not compared to you."

She tipped her head, her smile flattening a little. "You're an incredible man, Julian. I wish things could be different between us, but this bell can't be unrung. My wounds run too deep. I'm sorry. I really am. I think if I weren't so broken, we could be very good together."

"We already are good together."

She put a hand on his arm, then leaned forward and kissed his cheek. "Thank you for listening. I've never told anyone that story. I feel a little lighter for it. Especially knowing that Alonso will never be able to hurt me again."

"That's good. I'm glad for that."

"Me, too." She got to her feet. "But I'm drained. I'm going to bed. But if you find anything out about those names before twilight, feel free to wake me up."

He nodded. "Okay. Good night."

"Night."

She left, but he stayed there, staring into the air and thinking through all she'd told him. His anger simmered just below the surface of his understanding. It was impossible to know what had happened to her and not react. Not when he loved her like he did. Because try as he might to deny those feelings, they were there. He knew she'd been about to say she'd fallen in love with him, and knowing she loved him only brought his own feelings closer to the surface.

The need to do something crackled over him like a hot ray of sun, biting and snapping at him until it pushed him to his feet. It also gave him an idea.

He checked on her first. She was asleep, television on like it had been before, but this time he didn't turn it off. Maybe she liked it on because it kept her from feeling alone. Whatever the reason, he just closed her door and went to his room. He changed into jeans, a T-shirt, and his leather jacket.

He dashed off a note and left it on the kitchen counter. *Won't be gone long. Call if you need me. This is for you. Love, J*

Then he did something utterly rare and completely unsettling. He reached up to his throat and unclasped the chain holding his amulet. He slipped it off his neck and held it in his hand, just studying it for a moment. He'd worn it since the day Alice and Elenora had presented them to him and his brothers.

He'd grown so used to being immune to the sun's dangers that at this point, his own forgetfulness was more likely to be the cause of his death. But Desi was more important. And proving to her that he was not Alonso was paramount.

He lay the chain and amulet over the note.

Time, suddenly, was no longer such a luxury. He left, locking the penthouse door behind him. He called the lift, rolling his shoulders impatiently. When it arrived, he stepped on, and punched the button for the lobby.

Lou gave him a nod as he walked out. "Mr. Ellingham."

"No one gets upstairs. No deliveries. No flowers. No packages. Nothing. But if something or someone does show up, you call me immediately. If she needs anything, you call me about that too." The sun would be up soon, so it was unlikely Desi would wake before he got back, but he wanted all bases covered. Especially if he didn't make it back.

"You got it."

Julian exited the building and climbed into his car. Then he turned out of the parking lot and opened it up. Elenora was about to get another unexpected drop-in.

When he arrived at his grandmother's, the sky

had just begun to lighten at the tree line. He left his car in front of the house and pounded on her doors. He hadn't felt this sort of desperation in nearly three hundred and fifty years. The approaching dawn stung his nerves like invisible wasps.

"Grandmamma. Alice. Open up." Then, finally, Elenora herself opened the door. She was wrapped in a silk dressing gown, her jewelry still on, and a pair of satin slippers covering her feet. "What the blazes—Julian, what's wrong?"

He pushed past her into the safety of the house's coverage. "We need to talk."

"What's happened? Tell me." She clutched at her robe, pulling it together at her throat. "You're frightening me, child."

"I need a new amulet."

She let go of her robe and her eyes narrowed. "What have you done?"

"What I should have done a long time ago. I gave mine to my *wife*."

She snorted out a breath. "Giving your amulet to the woman who's about to divorce you is not an emergency that requires such dramatics. Unless she takes off with it and you fail to retrieve it from her, which I will very much expect you to do."

"No."

"Julie!" She shook her head as she pointed toward the door. "Enough of this nonsense. Go back to your wife, such as she is, and explain that you will not be providing her with an amulet. She shouldn't even know about it. And you know the rules. They are for family only. Family who intend to stay family."

"I won't make it."

"What do you mean?"

He pulled down the neck of his T-shirt. "I have no amulet. It's with Desi. I tried to explain that to you."

She paled, an impressive accomplishment considering her already ivory skin. "You did what?"

He let the fabric go. "As I stated, my wife has mine. Now, should I go wake Alice up or would you like to do that?"

The dreams that woke Desi were uncommon. Most vampires didn't dream during daysleep. But these dreams, nightmares really, were so awful that they had forced their way into her subconscious, compelling her to relive her time on the island. They were almost as terrifying as being trapped there again.

She sat up in bed, staring in the dancing light of the television and trying to ground herself in the here and now before the past pulled her under a second time.

It took a few moments, but the dreams receded. It was an unsettling way to wake up. And by the itch on her skin, the sun was bright in the sky.

She fell back onto the bed, throwing her arm over her face. Those dreams had come because of what she'd shared with Jules last night, but they were a small price to pay for letting him in. Now, she no longer had to push him away. He knew and understood there could be nothing between them. And he'd accepted it.

Hadn't he?

Actually, she wasn't sure about that. But it seemed like he had. And maybe they were a little closer to remaining friends. That would be nice.

Daysleep wasn't immediately forthcoming. It happened. Feeding would help. She got up and pulled on her robe, then shuffled out into the hall. The lights were off, but there was enough sun coming through the sheers on the windows to make the place oppressively bright.

No Julian either, from what she could sense. Maybe some info on the names had come through and he was out chasing it down. She blinked a few times to clear her sleepy eyes and checked the clock. Not quite eight a.m. She couldn't have been asleep more than a few hours.

Yawning, she made her way into the kitchen, selected a bottle of O negative, and poured herself a glass. She stood at the counter and drank until something very curious caught her eye.

She put the glass down and pulled the paper and the necklace closer. She recognized the chain and amulet instantly. It was Julian's. Why wasn't he wearing it?

She read the note. Then glanced at the windows. That stupid, wonderful, crazy man. Her heart clenched at the thought of him out in that sun without protection. She ran back to her room and dialed him on his cell.

He answered right away. "Morning, gorgeous."

"Are you hurt? Are you okay? Did you hole up somewhere? What are you doing?" She knew she sounded like a panicky mess, but she didn't care.

"I'm fine. I'm at my grandmother's, but I'm about to head to the police station. What are you doing up so early?"

"Bad dreams. Couldn't sleep. Then I found your note and your amulet and freaked out."

He laughed. Laughed! She wanted to smack him a little. "Sorry about your bad dreams, and for scaring you, but all is well."

"But your amulet is here."

He had the nerve to laugh some more. "I talked my grandmother into providing me with another one."

She shook her head, grinning despite herself. Julian lived a charmed life. "You did, did you?"

"Yes. She wasn't exactly thrilled, but—"

"But you're the baby of the family and you get what you want, don't you?"

He sighed. "Not everything."

She knew he meant her.

"Have you tried it on yet?"

"No. It's not mine. I don't feel like I should."

"I gave it to you. Put it on."

"I don't know." Wearing a chain that had been around Julian's neck for so long felt like such an intimate thing to do.

"C'mon. For me."

She put the phone on speaker, then set it on the counter. "Hang on." She picked the chain up, weighing it in her hands. The amulet was beautiful. Some kind of deep red, polished stone set in a fine, pale silver metal that had the heft of platinum. There was filigree around the edges, but upon closer inspection, it seemed like there were words worked into the design. More markings patterned the back.

She hooked the clasp around her neck and let the chain settle on her skin. The cool metal warmed quickly, but that wasn't the sensation she really noticed. "Wow."

"You put it on?"

"Yes. And the sun doesn't bother me anymore. I mean, I can still feel it, but it's not irritating anymore."

"You definitely have it on."

"I don't feel nearly as sleepy as I did a minute ago, either."

"That's the amulet." His voice was light and happy. "And now that you have it on, why don't you meet me at the police station and we can see what Birdie found out together?"

The thought of going out in the sun sent a new wave of panic through her. "I don't know."

"What's not to know?"

"It just feels…wrong." She laughed nervously. "Okay, I will, but it's going to take some getting used to."

"I know. It goes against the grain of who we are, but I promise it's safe. How long do you need? The station's about ten minutes away from the Excelsior."

"I just got up. Forty-five minutes?"

"Perfect. See you there." He hung up.

Outside. During daylight. Her hands went to the amulet around her neck. Did she trust this? Did she trust Julian?

Yes. After all, the amulet worked for Julian. And she certainly trusted him. She sighed. He was not Alonso. She knew that. And yet, there was a part of her that was still burdened by doubt. After what had been done to her, it was nearly impossible not to have some hesitation.

The universe was testing her. Pushing her to trust. Forcing her to face her fears. And if she did that, if she passed the test…what did that say about her future?

She put her glass in the sink and went to get ready.

Thirty-three minutes later, she had her hand on the penthouse door, when something occurred to her. With a grin, she ran to Julian's closet. She needed sunglasses. She opened the drawer of them and picked out a classic pair of Ray-Bans. They would do nicely.

Then she hurried down to the Excelsior's lobby. Lou wasn't there, but his replacement waved at her. Freddy, she thought the man's name was. She waved back.

"Morning. You're Mr. Ellingham's guest, right?"

She nodded. "Miss Clarke."

"Right, right." He pointed at himself. "I'm Freddy. Can I call you a Ryde?"

"I called one on the way down. It's only a minute away."

"Very good. Have a nice day."

"Thanks. You too." But all she could see were the glass doors in front of her. And the big picture windows. And all that sun.

Every instinct in her vampire body said turn around and run. Faintly, she could hear the call of gulls and the crash of waves. She closed her eyes. This was not the island all over again. She opened her eyes. She could do this. Julian had survived for centuries with this amulet around his neck.

But what if it didn't work on a different person? What if the witch had made the amulets to protect each one of them specifically? Julian would know that, wouldn't he? The salty stench of the sea rose up around her.

She couldn't do this.

Her phone rang. Julian. "Hello?"

"I'm guessing you're on the verge of melting down right now."

She let go of the tension that had been boiling up inside her. "How did you know that?"

"I remember what it was like the first time I walked outside with my amulet on and I didn't have anything close to the history you have. Talk to me. How are you doing?"

"On the verge of melting down about sums it up." She laughed, the sound wavering and full of nerves. "You're sure this thing works, right?"

"Absolutely. You want me to come there? Do this with you?"

"No. I can do it." The Ryde pulled up. "I have to. My car just arrived. Okay, stay with me on the phone."

"You got it."

She took determined steps toward the door. The heat from the morning sun pulsed through the glass. "This is nuts."

"It is. But magic is like that sometimes."

"Right." She put her hand on the warm glass and pushed.

"Hey, how about after the police station we get some breakfast? It might not live up to the pizza, but there's a lot of great food in this town."

"Sure." She hesitated, half in, half out, and inches from the first ray. She closed her eyes and stepped forward.

"Great. I know a place that makes amazing blueberry pancakes and incredible cinnamon buns."

The burst of flame and the searing burns never materialized. She opened her eyes. She was outside. In the sun. "I did it," she whispered.

His smile came through loud and clear. "I'm so proud of you."

"Thank you." She swallowed down the emotions thickening her throat. "Thank you so much."

"You're welcome, Desi. Now get in that car, I'm waiting on you."

The ride to the station felt like something out of a carnival. Seeing things in the sunlight made everything look new. She stared out the window, spellbound by the passing scenery. She wasn't sure Julian understood the gift he'd given her. Or maybe he did.

Then an unhappy thought popped into her head. Was this his attempt to keep her as his wife? It was tempting, but it wasn't going to work. In fact, even if he said otherwise, she was giving the amulet back after the divorce was final. As sad as that made her, it would be the right thing to do. She wouldn't be the reason his family was angry with him.

But was he trying to game this relationship in some way? Why had he decided to go against his grandmother's wishes? This amulet never should have been Desi's and she knew it.

When she got out at the station, he was waiting there, all smiles and looking very pleased with himself, but she had a thousand questions.

She hopped out of the car, still amazed she didn't instantly combust, and approached him, her mind buzzing with all the uncertainties this new wrinkle had created. She pushed the sunglasses onto the top of her head.

"You look beautiful." He met her halfway on the sidewalk. He had a pastry box in one hand. "I'm so glad you came."

"Thanks for making it possible." She sighed. "But we really need to talk."

"Of course," Julian said. He was thrilled she'd joined him, but even more thrilled that Elenora had relented and made it possible. And who knew that Alice had a batch of emergency amulets already made up? The things Didi kept secret sometimes. But then, keeping secrets was very Didi. And very infuriating. Usually. Right now, he was too happy to be mad about anything. "What do you want to talk about?"

"What do you think?" She glanced around. "Not here, though. Not on the street."

"Let's go inside. We can use the conference room. But brace yourself, you're going to have to meet Birdie first. Especially because I promised her these doughnuts."

"No problem. I'm happy to meet and thank anyone who's helping me."

He held the door for her, and they went in. Birdie was at her desk.

She greeted them in her usual fashion. "Oh, Julian, you said she was pretty. You didn't say she was a supermodel."

Desi laughed, a sound that never failed to lighten Julian's soul. He shook his head. "Birdie Caruthers, meet Desdemona Valentine."

Birdie leaned over the counter to shake Desi's hand. "So nice to meet you. Welcome to Nocturne Falls."

"Thank you," Desi said. "And thank you for helping us with that list of names."

Birdie waved the words away. "There's not much I wouldn't do for any of the Ellingham boys, but Julian especially." She winked at him. "I'm ready to share what I found out when you are. I'm waiting on one more query, but I don't think it'll make that much difference."

Julian put the box of doughnuts on the counter. "Excellent. But first, Desdemona and I need a few minutes in your conference room for a conversation of our own."

She opened up the box and studied the contents with great interest. "Go right on in. You know where it is. When you're ready for me, you just give me a holler."

"Thank you, we will." He escorted Desi to the room, then shut the door. "Okay, what's up?"

"We need to talk about this amulet. About what strings are attached to it."

He shook his head slowly. "There are no strings."

Her look said she didn't believe him. "I heard your grandmother at dinner. Clearly there are strings."

"No. It's my gift to you. And whatever happens with my grandmother is on me. I'll deal with her. But I don't ever want you to be in danger from the sun again. If I can do anything for you, I want to erase that worry."

"But…we're getting divorced."

He did his best to keep his expression neutral. "I'm aware."

"You don't want this back when the divorce is final?"

"Wouldn't be much of a gift then, would it?"

"But your grandmother said—"

"And I said leave that to me."

"Julian, I…this is overwhelming." She sat in one of the chairs at the long table. "This amulet is life changing."

He took the seat next to her, turning the chair toward her. "It is. In more ways than one. You have to be careful with it. Don't flaunt it. Don't talk about it. Other vampires will take notice. Our family secret has to become your personal secret as well."

Her hand went to the amulet. "Understood."

Then she frowned. "You're really not doing this as an attempt to sway me into staying?"

He lifted his head, his eyes narrowed. "You've known me for a while now. Is that really how you see me? A game player?"

"Maybe on the outside, but no. You're one of the most genuine people I know."

"Thank you. And I know you well enough to know that you're going to do whatever you want, regardless of outside circumstances."

"True."

He spoke from the depths of his aching heart. "I just want to take care of you, Desi. Even when I'm not around."

"Oh, Jules. This is the most generous gift I've ever gotten." She abruptly leaned forward, bracing her hands on his shoulders, and kissed him. The hard, insistent press of her mouth on his punched him in the gut, instantly crumbling his resolve to feel nothing more for her. He steadied himself, struggling not to react.

Then the kiss continued, growing hungrier. Desi leaned into him, almost climbing onto his lap.

What was left of his resolve vanished. Thunder pounded in his head, brought on by a storm named Desi. He pulled her closer and gave himself over to the urges coursing through him. He raked his fangs over her bottom lip and the metallic taste of blood spilled across his tongue.

The darker side of him roared for more.

He lifted her onto the table, then put his hands on her hips and tugged her closer. His hands slid over her to sink into the back pockets of her jeans and cup her backside.

She gasped at his actions, but made no effort to end the kiss. Instead, her arms went around him, and her hands flattened on his back.

His mouth trailed lower, down her throat. "Wife," he growled against her skin. "If you started this kiss as another attempt to thank me—"

"Take me home," she rasped.

His body tensed at her words, every muscle and sinew as taut as a tightrope. He'd waited an unendurable amount of time to hear such a request from her.

The door opened and Birdie strolled in, paperwork in hand. "Okay, that last query just came through—whoa, there. I thought you two were just talking?"

Desi slid off the table, tugging her shirt down.

Julian stepped in front of her. "We, uh, got carried away."

"I'll say." Birdie snorted, then she shook her head in teasing disapproval. "I'll just come back when it's a little more PG in here."

"No." Julian glanced over his shoulder at Desi. She seemed mostly recovered. "We need to discuss those names."

"You sure?" Birdie asked.

Desi put her hand on his back. "Yes. I'm sorry about what you walked in on. Won't happen again."

"Well, that's disappointing," Birdie said as she took a seat and opened the file in her hands. "Just maybe give a person a warning next time."

"Yes, well, about that…" Julian picked up Desi's chair, which had gotten knocked over during their amorous activities. As much as he'd rather continue with the kissing, they needed to get to the bottom of who was harassing Desi. "Let's focus on the names, shall we?"

"You're the boss, applesauce," Birdie said. She tapped her finger on the printouts in front of her. "Fourteen names but not a lot of info on most of them. One, a woman by the name of Heather Cross, runs a Facebook fan page for you."

"I have a Facebook fan page?"

Birdie nodded. "With over forty thousand likes."

"Wow." Desi looked at Julian. "You think she could be my stalker? Like maybe she's one of those who wants to keep me in her basement and make me put lotion on?"

Birdie snorted. "I don't think Mrs. Cross is about to go full *Silence of the Lambs* on you. She's got three kids, drives a minivan, and has been married for nineteen years to the same guy. Who happens to be a plumber. She doesn't fit the whack-a-do profile. Also, on the dates that Julian gave me, she was nowhere near Vegas. For one, she was at her niece's wedding and the other at a plumbing convention with her husband. She's not your woman."

"Next," Julian said.

One by one, Birdie went through more of the names, explaining why they weren't a possibility. Then she pulled out a new sheet of paper. "Three names left. And three who might be interesting in this case."

"Brian Brennan. Vera Mears. And Abigail Helmsman." Birdie looked over the rims of her reading glasses. "Interesting thing about Miss Helmsman. The deeper I dug, the more it appears that's not her real name. It's actually Helsing."

Julian let out a soft curse.

Desi shook her head. "Isn't that a little obvious? And also, are we really going to go there and say that I'm being stalked by a vampire hunter?"

Birdie held up a finger. "Listen. Abigail Helsing is thirty-six years old, lists her address as Upstate New York, but hasn't received mail there in seven years, carries a membership in the Talisman Club—"

"I don't know what that is," Desi interrupted.

Julian let out a derisive breath. "It's nonsense, is what it is."

"Vampire-hunting nonsense, although they've branched out to include all kinds of supernaturals,"

Birdie said. "Her membership is also a clue to this woman's mind-set."

Julian turned to Desi. "The Talisman Club was formed in the 1800s by a man who claimed to be a descendant of Stoker's Van Helsing."

Desi frowned. "That's a fictional character."

"I said it was nonsense."

"But," Birdie said. "There is some evidence that Stoker based Van Helsing on a real person. A friend of his who claimed to be able to cure vampirism."

Julian rolled his eyes. "With a silver stake through the heart. This group persists today, but in very small numbers. They've become extreme fringe, as opposed to regular fringe."

Desi flattened her hands on the table. "Birdie, why didn't you tell us about this woman first?"

"Because I can't verify her whereabouts on the dates in question. She could have been anywhere."

Julian's phone rang. He pulled it out and checked the screen. "Hang on, this might help us."

He answered. "Good morning, Marigold."

"Morning, Julian. I came in a little early to look up that name you asked me about. The order came in on the florist network so most likely it was placed online. I just filled it because I was the closest shop to the address."

"Understood." He could hear her tapping on a keyboard.

"Payment was registered to a company credit card."

"And the company's name?"

"Harker Enterprises. Does that mean anything to you?"

"Yes." A hot, angry feeling settled into his stomach. "Can you send a copy of that to Birdie at the station?"

"Sure. I'll have it over there in a few minutes."

"Thank you. You've been very helpful."

"You're welcome. Have a nice day."

"You too." He hung up and looked at Birdie. "Harker Enterprises is the name of the company that sent Desi a bouquet of black roses with a threatening note."

"As in Mina Harker?" Birdie asked.

"That's my guess," Julian answered.

Desi grunted. "Another fictional character from Stoker's Dracula. How original."

He glanced at her. "Right? And I'd bet if we could dig deeper, we'd find it's the same company that sent Sam's flowers too."

He turned back to Birdie, who was already typing. "What can you tell me about Harker Enterprises?"

"Give me a few...more...I'm in." She pushed her glasses back on her nose a little. "Would these other flowers have been sent from the Desert Blooms shop?"

Julian nodded. "Yes."

Desi's eyes went wide. "How did you figure that out?"

Birdie grinned. "I do a little hacking in my spare time."

"Isn't that illegal?" Desi held her hands up. "Not that I'm complaining." Then she laughed. "Birdie Caruthers, you're a total badass."

Birdie nodded. "I really am." Then she leaned in and started typing again. "This is interesting." She turned the laptop around. "Look at the logos for the Talisman Club and Harker Enterprises."

Julian and Desi studied them. Both had a silver spiked cross at their centers.

Julian let out a long, slow whistle. "So they're definitely related, but this doesn't exactly connect Abigail Helsing with the threats."

Birdie took her laptop back. "Give me half an hour and I bet I can make that connection. You two go eat or make out some more or something and let me work. If there's a link between them, I'll find it."

With the kiss suddenly front and center in Julian's mind, he slanted his eyes at Desi. "You want to grab some breakfast?"

"Those blueberry pancakes you mentioned?"

He grinned. "I wasn't sure you heard that with everything else going on."

"No, I did." She smiled back. "And I'm game."

"Good," Birdie said. "And since you're going to Mummy's, I'll take a cinnamon bun."

24

The pancakes were everything Julian had promised, but they still weren't quite enough to take Desi's mind off a few things. Her stalker, for one.

That kiss, for another. And what she'd been on the verge of doing because of it.

And thinking about both of those left her at a slight loss for words. Or maybe it was being this close to Julian after they'd almost consummated their marriage in the sheriff's conference room. Whatever the reason, she felt strangely nervous around him for the first time. Like fireworks were going off inside her.

"You okay?" he asked. His quad stack of cheesecake-stuffed blueberry pancakes was almost half gone.

"Thinking," she answered.

He nodded as he devoured another bite. "Lots to think about."

She nodded too and dug into her two plain blueberry pancakes. "Yep."

He swallowed. "Like that kiss."

She almost choked.

The sly look on his face said he knew exactly what he'd done. "You didn't really think we weren't going to talk about that, did you?"

"I…" Why were words suddenly so hard? "I've never been so confused in my life."

His lids lowered along with his voice. "You didn't seem confused when you asked me to take you home. Or should I say demanded?"

Heat washed over her. She stared at her plate for a moment. "I was overcome."

"With what?"

He knew with what. He was baiting her. Awful man. But she could play. "With confusion."

His brows bent. "Confusion?"

"Yes." She leaned in and kept her words soft but distinct. "About you. About us."

"What's so confusing? We're divorcing, and you're going back to Vegas." He sipped his coffee. "Or did jumping my bones in the station mean you changed your mind about part of that?"

"That jumping was mutual."

"I'll accept that. But you started it."

She pursed her lips at him. "You're a little rotten."

"I've heard worse." He shrugged one shoulder.

"Never from someone I was married to and just gave a very special, life-changing gift to, but sure."

The mischievous glint in his eyes made her laugh. For a second. "I have a show to do and responsibilities and a life in Vegas."

He moved his hands up and down like he was weighing her words. "Calling your existence in Vegas a life is being very generous, but I'll give you the other two."

She rolled her eyes.

He smirked. "You like me all of a sudden, don't you? And you don't know what to do about it."

"I've always liked you." But with everything he'd done for her, it had become increasingly difficult not to admit she loved him too.

"Like is good. Like is something. It's not love. But it's something." He held his coffee cup out like he was about to wax poetic. "I must admit, I always hoped for a little more from the woman I plotted my troth to."

"Pretty sure it's plighted. And I'd like to remind you that the plighting happened while I was intoxicated."

He sipped his coffee, then put his cup down and exchanged it for a crispy piece of bacon. "Well, it's moot now anyway."

"Why's that?" She took a bite of her pancakes.

All traces of humor left his gaze. "The lawyer called me this morning. He said the paperwork is

246

done. All that's left is for us to sign it and get it filed. I guess we should put that on the old to-do list, huh?"

She nodded numbly. The divorce was essentially final. That was exactly what she'd wanted. What she'd thought had to happen. But now…it felt like a defeat. Like she'd just lost her best friend.

Maybe because she had.

The pancakes turned to sawdust in her mouth, but somehow she swallowed and held herself together. "Maybe tomorrow? My lack of sleep is catching up with me. I think by the time we're done at the station, I'm going to be dead on my feet."

"Pun intended?"

"What? Oh. Not really." She smiled. "We should order that cinnamon bun."

"Right." He got their server's attention and asked for one to go with the check.

Desi was desperate to keep the subject on something besides the divorce. "You think Birdie's found anything?"

"Like she said, if it's there to be found, she'll do it."

Desi used her fork to push a hunk of pancake around on her plate. "I still don't understand how this woman tracked me here."

"We can ask Birdie about that too." He cleaned his plate, then pushed it away before wiping his mouth. "Maybe it's as simple as you sending those flowers to Sam. Maybe Talisman has a way of monitoring your credit card activity."

"Um, that's completely illegal," Desi said.

"Yes, but considering what they're all about, I don't think they care."

"I'm sure they don't." She shook her head. Real-life vampire hunters. It was so archaic it was hard to take seriously.

The server returned with a small shopping bag and their check. Julian put a generous amount of cash on the table, then looked at Desi. "Ready to go?"

"Yes." The sooner they got to the bottom of this, the better.

Birdie was ready for them when they got back. She was at the front desk again, working on her laptop and munching on a neon pink doughnut. "You're just in time."

Julian handed her the pastry in its bag. "I don't know where you get your appetite, but here's your cinnamon bun as requested."

Her eyes lit up. "That'll be my lunch dessert." She tucked the bag away, then put a piece of paper on the counter between them. "Harker Enterprises was started by Arnold Helsing."

The name spiked Julian's memory. "Arnold Helsing?"

Birdie looked up. "You know the name?"

"Yes. I had a run-in with him outside of a plasmateria in Brussels. It's been over thirty years ago, but the man definitely thought he was a vampire hunter. And that I was a vampire."

Concern filled Desi's eyes. "What happened?"

"He attacked me. Tried to run a silver-tipped spike through my heart. But I overpowered him and that was that."

Her eyes widened. "You killed him?"

"*No.* I knocked him out and left him inside a nearby church. I thought that would be enough to confuse him. Maybe get him to change his ways."

Birdie shook her head. "I'm not sure it worked. At least not enough to convince his daughter not to follow in her father's footsteps. He's Abigail's father." She glanced back at her screen. "Looks like Arnold Helsing died a few years ago, leaving her everything. She's a very wealthy woman."

"Great." Julian rested his arm on the counter. "What else?"

Birdie tapped the paper. "She's the Talisman Club's primary contributor. In fact, she sits on their board."

"They have a board?" Julian found that surprising.

"Oh, they have a board all right." Birdie's brows lifted. "And nearly thirty thousand members. They're much bigger than I realized. Kind of blew me away."

"That makes two of us."

Desi wrapped her arms around herself. "That's not good at all."

Birdie nodded. "It's downright sucky if you ask me." Then she sighed. "Unfortunately, it gets worse."

"Perfect," Desi said. "How?"

"The Harker Enterprises credit card was used two days ago at Salvatore's."

Desi grabbed Julian's arm. "That's where you took me for pizza. She was following us."

"More than that," Julian said. "She must have sat there and watched us the whole time." He swore softly. "This ends now. Birdie, do you know where she's staying in town?"

"Not yet, but I'm working on it. The credit card was probably a slipup. I'm guessing she's paying cash everywhere else. I'll let you know as soon as I figure out where she is."

"Good." Julian thought for a moment. "Do you know what this woman looks like?"

"All I have is her driver's license photo, and it's a few years old. No telling what she looks like now."

"Email it to me."

"I will." She hesitated. "There's one more thing I found, but…" Birdie's shoulders lifted apologetically.

Julian knew that shrug. "It's more bad news, isn't it?"

"It's not good news." She sighed. "The Talisman forum is all abuzz. Abigail has promised that she's hot on the trail of a prominent vampire and plans to turn them to ash publicly. She says it's the only way to prove that vampires really exist."

Desi grimaced. "This woman wants to make a viral video of killing me? What a psycho."

"I agree." He looked at Desi. "Which is why I'm taking you home. And you're staying there."

Desi wasn't thrilled about being under Julian's version of house arrest, but she didn't fight it either. Being stuck in his apartment meant she couldn't go to the lawyer's office and sign the divorce papers.

Julian dropped his keys in the glass bowl on the foyer table. "I know you're not happy about this."

"No, I'm not. But I understand how much danger I'm in with this woman here in town." She shivered.

"Hey, nothing's going to happen to you. I won't let it. Plus, you're safe here." He put his hands on her shoulders. "Do you need anything before I go?"

What she needed was for him to stay. "No, I'll be fine. Can't say the same for your Swedish Fish stash, but if you leave me alone with all that sugar, you really only have yourself to blame."

He grinned. "I'll gladly suffer those consequences." He looked like he was thinking about kissing her. That thought must have passed because he took his hands off her.

"Where are you going when you leave here?"

"Back to the station to see if Birdie's found anything new, then to fill the sheriff in on what's going on. I'll be calling my brothers too. We need to spread the word. There are a fair number of vampires in this town, and they deserve to know we have a hunter in our midst."

Desi nodded. "And it's all my fault."

"I brought you here. If it's anyone's fault, which it isn't, it would be mine. And listen, before you go having a guilt trip over this, if you have to face down a hunter, there's no better town to do it in than Nocturne Falls."

"I'm sure you're right. But I've never come up against anything like this."

He cocked his head. "Des, you've survived far worse."

She sighed. "And look how damaged that made me."

"You know what they say about damaged people."

She shook her head. "No, what?"

"Damaged people are the most dangerous kind, because they already know how to survive." He lifted his hands toward her haltingly, as if he was about to do something he didn't think he should, then he pulled her into his arms. "That hunter ought to be afraid of you, not the other way around."

She smiled up at him. "Thanks."

He kissed her forehead, then let her go. "All right, I'm off. Be back as soon as I can."

"Take your time. I'm not going anywhere."

With a wave, he grabbed his keys and took off. She stared at the closed door until she heard the chimes of the elevator, then she walked to the windows and watched him drive away. When she couldn't see his car anymore, she plopped down on the couch and turned the television on.

Daytime TV was a mishmash of crazy talk shows, old movies and news. She settled on an old Debbie Reynolds movie, then turned the volume down and texted Sam. It was still pretty early in Vegas. *You up?*

Desi wasn't hungry at all after the pancakes, but the talk of Julian's candy had created a craving in her. She went to the pantry to snag some, coming back to the couch with a bowl of Swedish Fish and gummy cola bottles.

Her phone chimed as she sat down.

Yep. Shouldn't you be asleep?

Long story.

How are you?

Desi's thumbs flew over the keyboard. *I'm fine. How are YOU?*

I'm getting there. Going home tomorrow. Taking Harlan with me. ;)

You like him, huh?

He's amazing. Super cute, so sweet, & ultra sexy. I wanna keep him.

Desi snorted. *I think that's up to him.*

Please. Women decide these things. But I think he's willing.

Are you healing?

Pretty well. This cast is no fun.

Desi shook her head. *I can imagine.*

The flowers really are beautiful. Thanks again for those.

You got it. Anything else you need?

Not since the first delivery.

Desi frowned. *First delivery?*

Harlan. :D

She laughed. *Right. Got it. Take care of yourself. See you soon.*

You too. Bye!

Desi tossed her phone onto the seat next to her, then settled in to watch the movie. By the time it was over and the candy was gone, she'd started to drift. She had a feeling if she took the amulet off, she'd probably pass out.

But she didn't want to be asleep when Jules was out there working on her behalf. She grabbed her phone and dialed.

He answered right away. "Everything cool?"

"Yes. Just wondering how it's going."

"Good. I thought you'd be asleep."

"I can't. I mean, I could, but it doesn't seem like the right thing to do with everything else going on."

"Darling, you really should get some rest. At least for a few hours. Now is not the time to get run-down."

She sighed. "I understand. But...it still feels wrong."

He laughed. "Whatever you want to do. Listen, Birdie found a location tag on one of Abigail Helsing's Instagram pics from two days ago. It pinged to Atlanta. She could definitely be in Nocturne Falls by now. Especially if she's the one who used the Harker credit card at Salvatore's."

"Well, who else would it be? We have to assume she's here."

"Unless she's not..." He cut himself off.

"Not what?"

He sighed. "Not working alone."

"There's a cheery thought."

"I know."

"And since when does a vampire hunter have an Instagram account?"

He snorted. "Yeah, social media at its finest."

"I guess that's part of her plans to make my death go viral."

"Hey, let's not talk like that, okay? It's not going to happen."

She took a beat. "No, you're right, I can't think like that."

"No, you can't. And listen, Sheriff Merrow is sending a deputy to hang out with you."

Desi froze. "Not Remy. I'm sure he's a decent guy, but—"

"No. It's daylight, remember? And he doesn't have our extra something. Sheriff Merrow is sending Deputy Jenna Blythe."

"Blythe? That sounds very piratey."

"It's not, I promise. In fact, you've already met her sister, Tessa."

"Sebastian's fiancée?" Now this was interesting. Desi sat up a little. "So is Jenna a Valkyrie too?"

"Yes. And an excellent deputy to boot."

"Okay, sounds good. When will she be here?"

"Not sure. Soon, probably. I'm sure Freddy will call up."

"Has Birdie found anything else new?"

"Nothing yet." He softened his voice. "Everything's going to be okay. I promise."

She smiled at his words, knowing how deeply he meant them. "I know. Call me if anything happens."

"I will. See you later."

"Later." She hung up and went to the windows in time to see a patrol car pulling into the parking lot. Desi snorted at the thought of a valkyrie coming to protect a vampire. If the hunter showed up here, she was going to get more than she bargained for.

A lot more.

On a whim, Julian drove to Pandora's office. He hadn't called so he had no idea if she was out showing a house or not, but he was in the area, so he took a chance.

He walked in, the little bell over the door announcing his entrance.

The receptionist turned around from the whiteboard she was updating and smiled. She was a pretty redhead, which made him wonder if Pandora had a gingers-only employment policy. "Hi there. Welcome to Williams Real Estate. How can I help you?"

"I'm looking for Pandora. Is she around?"

"She should be back to the office in a few minutes."

"Thanks. I'll wait."

"Would you like some coffee or water?"

"No, I'm good."

The receptionist gave him a closer look as she capped the marker in her hand. "Have we met? I feel like I know you."

"I don't think so." He stuck his hand out. "Julian Ellingham."

"Oh, that's why I know you." She shook his hand. "Monalisa Devlin."

"You're Van's girl." He'd heard the name but had yet to meet the woman who'd metaphorically slain the dragon.

She blushed. "That's me."

"Nice to meet you. Van is a good man."

"Yes, he is." She tipped her head. "Hey, is it true that Desdemona Valentine is staying with you?" She suddenly shook her head. "Sorry, that's none of my business."

The fact that Desi's visit was so widely known threw him. "She is. How did you know that?"

"I was there when you called Van about getting someone to do some security work in Vegas. I asked him what it was about and he told me." Monalisa shrugged. "I only asked you if she was staying with you because I grew up in Vegas, and Desdemona's sort of a big deal out there. Anyway, I'm sorry about being nosey. Just ignore."

"It's okay. I haven't really been that secretive about her staying with me." He put his hands in his pockets. "How is it that you thought you knew me?"

Monalisa got an odd little grin on her face. "A couple months ago in Vegas, Van and I were out with Pandora, Willa, and Nick at a restaurant. You and Desdemona were a few tables away. We only figured that out when we looked at the pictures we took and saw you two in the background."

"Huh. I guess Desi and I weren't that much of a secret then either."

She laughed a little. "I'm learning in this town, secrets don't stay hidden long."

"No, they don't." Something that was both bad and good.

The bells over the door jingled, and he turned to see Pandora strolling in.

"Julian, what brings you by? Tired of penthouse living? You know I could get amazing money for that place."

He chuckled. "No, I'm quite happy at the Excelsior, thank you. I was hoping you could help me in a different capacity."

She handed Monalisa a file. "Put this on my desk?"

"Sure thing." Monalisa took it and went behind the half wall to do as Pandora asked.

Pandora looked at Julian. "Do you mean help in a witchy capacity?"

"Maybe."

She nodded. "Let's go into the conference room and talk."

He followed her back. She opened the door, then stepped aside to let him in and turned to Monalisa. "Hold my calls. Hey, did we have any calls?"

"Two about Pumpkin Point. I got their info and directed them to the website."

"Perfect. All right, hold my calls." Pandora came in, closed the door, and took a seat across from Julian. "What can I help you with?"

The room was small, and the table only had four chairs, but the space still managed to feel welcoming and professional. Pandora was exceptional at her job. She was pretty good as a witch, too, and he knew she'd appreciate straight talk. "There's a vampire hunter in town, and I need help finding her."

"Someone's hunting you? And it's a woman?" She shook her head. "Not to make light of the situation, but this isn't that surprising."

"What's that supposed to mean?"

"You have a reputation as a lady killer. Seems like it was only a matter of time before one of them took it personally."

"It's not like that at all." Except for the part about being married, he explained everything that had happened, right up to the flowers being sent and the name of the hunter they'd come up with thanks to Birdie.

Pandora sat back. "Wow. That's serious. And can I just say this woman has some real nerve coming to this town thinking she's going to bag herself a vampire."

"Agreed, but I'm sure she has no clue about the real nature of Nocturne Falls."

"Probably not. She's in for a rude awakening." Pandora tapped her nails on the table top. "Or not. If she comes to town, or if she's here already, won't drinking the water make it impossible for her to tell if someone's a vampire or not? Won't the spell in the water sort of negate this whole thing?"

"Maybe. Maybe not. I've heard Alice say her spell relies heavily on a human's ability to be persuaded. If this woman has her mind made up about Desdemona being a vampire, Alice's magic may not have an effect."

Pandora nodded. "Magic does have its limits at times. I know that firsthand." She straightened. "Where do I come in?"

"I need to find this woman before she makes any kind of attempt at Desi. I'm hoping you can help me with that part of it."

"I'm sure Desi is in a safe place now, right?"

"Right." He nodded. "She's at my penthouse and Deputy Blythe is on her way over to run security."

"You think this hunter would be so bold as to do something in broad daylight?"

"I'm not discounting anything."

"Smart. Okay, do you have anything that belongs to this woman? What's her name?"

"Abigail Helsing."

"This Abigail. Do you have anything of hers? A standard location spell needs something like that to focus on."

"No." He growled in frustration. "Is there any other—wait. What about something she's touched?"

"Hmm. That's a gray area. It could work, but if other people have touched the item too, the spell is just as likely to locate them. It really needs to be a personal item."

"Which I don't have." Julian bounced his fist on the table. "I have to find this woman."

"I'm sorry. You know I'd help in a heartbeat if I could." She thought for a moment. "You said Birdie had hacked her way into the Talisman forum, right?"

"Yes. But trying to contact Abigail that way would take too long."

Pandora leaned forward. "I was thinking about a different approach."

"I'm listening."

"Set yourself up as bait. Use the forum to tell this woman you've found a vampire and need her help. Then you can specify the time and place. She'll come to you."

He shook his head. "I get what you're saying,

but putting that kind of info out there could bring a horde of vampire hunters to Nocturne Falls. This place is supposed to be a haven for supernaturals. Not a mecca for those who think we're trophies to be hunted."

"You don't have to post the information wide. Just PM her."

"PM?"

"Private message. Trust me, Birdie will know how to do it."

"I'm going to call her right now." No point in wasting time. He pulled out his phone and dialed.

Birdie answered after a single ring. "Julian! Are you a psychic vampire? I was just about to call you."

"I hope that means you have some good news."

"I don't know if it's good. I think it is. I mean, sure, it's good."

That wasn't very reassuring.

She kept talking. "What did you call about?"

"What's your news?"

"You first."

He rolled his eyes. "Pandora mentioned something about being able to PM Abigail Helsing through the Talisman forum, but we can discuss the details of that after you tell me your news."

"Huh. Well, maybe Pandora's the psychic one. I sort of already did that."

He straightened. "You did?"

"Yep. My membership finally got approved so I was able to get in and start searching for her posts, and I found one where she offered a one million dollar bounty to anyone who could deliver her a live vampire."

"And?"

"And you have a meeting with her in half an hour."

Every nerve in his body came to life. "That's not much time."

"I know, but she's pushy."

If Birdie thought the woman was pushy, that was saying something. "Where?"

"Pinehurst Inn."

He rolled his eyes. "Naturally." If there was something shady going down near Nocturne Falls, that's where it happened.

"You want backup? I could send Hank. Or I could come."

"No, I appreciate the offer, but I want to draw as little attention to this situation as possible. And a vampire of my years against a human is already an unfair fight." He pushed his chair back and stood. "I'll handle it myself."

"All right. I'll text you the details. Good luck."

"Thanks, but she's the one who's going to need it." He hung up and looked at Pandora. "Gotta run. Birdie knew about that private messaging business already and set something up."

Pandora got to her feet. "You're going to meet with this hunter? What are you going to do, if you don't mind me asking?"

"I don't know yet. But I'll figure it out." Whatever it was, it had to end with Abigail Helsing coming to a very serious understanding. Julian had never taken a human life and he didn't plan to now, but if this hunter insisted on threatening Desdemona, she was going to find herself in a world of hurt.

Desi walked into the lobby and made a beeline for the woman in uniform at the front desk. "Hi. You must be Deputy Blythe."

The woman turned. "Miss Valentine?"

Desi stuck her hand out. "Yes. Pleasure to meet you."

Deputy Blythe had a firm grip. "Likewise. Sorry about your situation, but you won't have anything to worry about while I'm here." She gestured toward the lobby's seating area. "Do you mind if we have a chat? Any information you can give me can be useful."

"Sure, but would you rather do it up in the penthouse?" Desi didn't think Julian would mind having the deputy up there. He'd had Remy up, after all.

"No, I prefer to keep an eye on things from here. First line of defense and all that."

"Fine with me."

They walked over and took their seats. Deputy Blythe chose the one that allowed her a view of the door.

Desi sat and folded her hands. "What would you like to know, Deputy Blythe?"

"Call me Jenna, please."

"Jenna it is, then. And you can call me Desi."

"Great." Jenna pulled out a photo, clearly blown up from the hunter's driver's license. It was a little grainy, but easy enough to make out. "Do you think you've ever seen this woman before?"

Desi stared at the picture. "I know ticket sales say she's been to my show five times, so I guess I've seen her in the audience, but those faces blur together night after night. Unless someone has something really remarkable about them, they don't stick in my head."

Jenna nodded. "Makes sense. And I think we can assume this woman wasn't trying to stand out." She put the photo on the table. "Can you think of any other ways this woman might have crossed your path? Things that happened that you couldn't explain, or didn't understand until all of this came to light?"

Desi stared at the photo and thought. The woman in the picture was as nondescript as a person could be. Caucasian. Brown hair with blunt fringe that reached the top of thick-rimmed glasses, both of which hid her eyebrows. Behind those glasses were brown eyes and a dull stare that did nothing to make the woman appear remotely intelligent. She didn't wear a speck of makeup or attempt a smile. In fact, her lips seemed pressed together in a way that intentionally distorted her mouth. The only thing that stood out about her was how unusually glossy her hair was.

Desi looked closer. "You've got to be kidding me," she whispered. She glanced up at Jenna. "She did all this on purpose."

Jenna looked at the photo. "What do you mean?"

"I mean in that photo, the one she knew she couldn't hide from, she deliberately made herself look different. I bet in real life, she looks nothing like that. I'd swear by it. Why else would she wear a wig in her driver's license photo?"

Jenna squinted at the picture. "You think she's wearing a wig?"

"I know she is. That shine? That's not natural. That's the gleam of cheap wig fresh out of the package. She could have at least shaken it out." She put a finger on the photo. "Trust me. I wear a lot of wigs. I know a bad one when I see it."

"I believe you." She reached for the radio clipped to her shoulder. "I'll let Birdie know about this right away. If anyone can do anything with this new info, it's her."

"Good." But it wasn't good. They had no idea what this woman looked like, meaning she could be anyone, anywhere.

Just when she'd started to feel safe again.

Julian knocked three times on the door of the Pinehurst Inn's number five room. The place wasn't much of an inn. It wasn't much of anything these days but a source of trouble. Unfortunately, it was just outside the town limits of Nocturne Falls and the owners stubbornly refused to sell. At least not for the amounts that the Ellinghams' had offered.

He frowned and knocked again. The place was an eyesore, and the odd combined scent of mildew and bleach seemed to waft toward him on every breeze. Although the mildew was winning. Maybe they should up their offer, but he hated to pay such an exorbitant amount for a property that should rightly be bulldozed.

No one was answering. Maybe the hunter had come to her senses and left. On a whim, he tried the handle. Locked. He glanced down as he started to leave. A postcard leaned against the doorjamb, one corner of the stiff paper crushed as though it had been tucked in the door.

He picked it up.

Had to relocate. Come to 1900 Nutmeg Lane. -A

He sighed. Nutmeg Lane was a street in the new Pumpkin Point development being built at the other end of town, but on a late Saturday afternoon, there'd be very little, if any, construction going on there. For a clandestine meeting, it was a good choice. He wondered if the hunter wasn't just a little smarter than he'd anticipated.

No matter. Being a vampire still meant he had the upper hand. He got back in his car and drove to the address. The houses in this new community were not exactly starter homes, but not exactly McMansions either. They were just the kind of homes a growing family would look for, which was the demographic the Ellinghams hoped to serve.

Especially with Harmswood Academy's enrollments growing. Supernatural families wanted the best for their children just like human parents, so Pumpkin Point was an attempt to provide those families with some much-needed room. And at reasonable prices.

Plus, fresh blood in any town was always a good thing.

He turned onto Nutmeg Lane. This was the

model home street. The seven floorplans that would be available were nearly complete. Number 1900 was the largest at the end of the cul-de-sac and had already been spoken for. There was no car in the driveway. Odd, but then, so was this whole situation.

He got out and walked to the front door. It was open. He went in, listening. He picked up the telltale thump-thump-thump of a human heart. She was definitely here. "Hello? Ms. Helsing?"

He shut the door and walked past the foyer toward the dining room. "Hello? It's DracSlayer4000. From the forum." He rolled his eyes at the name Birdie had chosen. "Ms. Helsing?"

The hiss of sudden air movement preceded a sharp sting on the side of his neck. He swatted at whatever insect had landed on him and found something else instead. He looked at the object in his hand. A small glass vial with a needle tip and fletching on the other end.

The room tilted.

Tranquilizer dart. "Bloody hell."

He spun in the direction the dart had come from, catching a second in the chest. His limbs went leaden, and his feet refused to move.

A slim blonde stepped out from behind the basement door, an odd-looking gun in her hands. "Hello there, vampire."

"I'm…not…" His tongue stuck to the roof of his mouth as his eyes rolled back in his head and everything went black.

As Deputy Blythe drove them to the station, Desdemona was trying very hard not to have a panic attack, but she was on the verge of failing. Sunset had come and gone and only a faint purple line remained at the horizon. And despite the time that had passed, the texts that had been sent, and the voicemails left, Julian had not responded.

Strangely enough, the panic attack threatened not because she felt like she'd been left again, but because she feared for the man she loved.

Because she absolutely did love him.

Allowing herself that realization made things better and worse. There was a vampire hunter in town and her *husband* had not been in contact with her in nearly four hours. Maybe a short span of time for some, but it wasn't Julian's way. He was constantly checking in with her, seeing if she needed anything, making sure she was okay.

Well, she wasn't. And neither, she feared, was he.

Deputy Blythe parked the patrol car. Desi jumped out and ran inside to find Birdie. What she found was a gathering of Julian's friends and family.

Birdie waved her over amid the chaos. "You all right?"

"I'll be fine." The correct answer was no, but she wasn't about to fall apart. Not when Julian needed her to be strong. "Anything new?"

Birdie shook her head and frowned. "No, sweetie, I'm so sorry."

Desi sighed as the noise around them died away and the group's attention shifted. The sheriff had come out of his office.

He held his hands up. "We're going to organize into teams and do a search. We've already got Nick and Van in the air."

Desi shot a questioning look at Birdie.

"Gargoyle and dragon-shifter," she whispered back.

"We'll divide the town into quadrants and each take one. The deputies on duty have their assignments." He glanced over at Deputy Blythe. "I've already radioed Lafitte to take the northeast hills. Cruz will take over for him at sunup. You take the northwest."

"Got it." She headed back to the parking lot.

"Sebastian and Tessa, everything southeast of Main. Hugh, everything southwest. Pandora, Cole, and Willa, your neighborhood and the one adjoining. I already have a team at the Pinehurst Inn, but nothing's turned up there yet, and I don't suspect anything will. I've got Greyson Garrett covering the industrial park as well. Whatever you do, do not approach the subject yourself. This is a human we're dealing with, and certain precautions need to be—"

Desi's hand shot up. "What about me? I know I don't know the town that well, but I can follow GPS."

"Ma'am, seeing as how you were the intended target of this hunter, I would prefer you remain here at the station."

She pursed her lips. "And I would prefer to be out there looking."

"I understand that, but I don't need two missing vampires. You stay."

She let out a frustrated growl.

Birdie grabbed her hand. "C'mon. You can sit at the desk with me and monitor calls."

The sheriff continued. "I'll be patrolling the lake district and Pumpkin Point. There are a couple volunteer firemen going from shop to shop with the hunter's picture, even though we know, thanks to Miss Valentine, that the subject may look different. All right." He clapped his hands. "Let's go find Julian."

As everyone else dispersed, Desi's frustration grew. "I can't just sit here and do nothing. This woman is in town because of me."

Birdie patted her shoulder. "I know how upset you must be."

Desi shook her head. "I can't believe in a town of supernaturals like this that a human could get the upper hand with a vampire."

"Well, we don't know what's happened yet. If anything. Maybe Julian's waylaid for some other reason."

"Then why wouldn't he answer his phone?"

"Dead battery?"

"For four hours?" She shook her head. She understood Birdie was trying to make her feel better, but her gut knew Julian was in trouble, and her gut had not been mistaken yet. "Something's wrong."

Birdie wrung her hands together.

Desi racked her brain for anything that might help. "What about Alice Bishop? The witch that works for the Ellinghams?"

"What about her?" Birdie asked.

"Could she cast some kind of spell to find Julian? Can't witches do that?"

"Speaking of witches, did you know he went to see Pandora right before I told him about the meeting with the hunter?" Birdie's eyes held sympathy. "He'd asked her about the same kind of spell to find Abigail Helsing. Pandora said she cast a spell to attempt to locate Julian before she got here, but it wasn't that helpful. See, Julian's lived here for so long and been all over this town so much, that the spell turned up a thousand different locations for him. Everywhere from the Pinehurst Inn, where he went to meet the hunter, to Pumpkin Point, that new development at the other end of town. And Pandora's a pretty good witch too. Not Alice-powerful, but more than capable. The only good thing that came out of the spell is she's positive he's still in town somewhere."

That was something, but not enough to keep Desi out of the stranglehold of desperation. She clenched her jaw and balled her hands into fists. "I cannot do nothing."

Birdie nodded. "I completely understand. What do you want to do?"

Desi rubbed the throbbing spot between her eyes and tried to think beyond the anger. "What about more human methods? Have you tracked his cell phone? They do it in movies all the time."

"Tried that. No response."

Desi started to pace. "There's no way to find him? I don't accept that. What else did you find out about this hunter? Maybe there's something in her past we could use. Hey, do you have a cell number for her? Maybe we could track that."

"No response from her phone either." Birdie sat down and tapped a few keys on her laptop. "I've been trying to crack her password on her email, but so far nothing there, either." She looked over her shoulder at Desi. "I know you're worried. We all are. But with Van and Nick up there, looking for Julian's car, it's just a matter of time."

"I supposed he owns the only Maserati in town?"

"As far as I know." Birdie went back to her screen.

A thought shook Desi. "His car."

"What's that?" Birdie asked.

"His car. It looks like the cockpit of an airplane inside that thing. It's all computerized. I've seen cars get hacked in movies too. Is that possible or just Hollywood?"

Birdie tipped her head like Desi was on to something. "I'm not sure." She held a finger up. "But I do know that car has SatGuard."

"That's a tracking system, right?"

"Right." Birdie's typing picked up tempo.

"Are you going to hack in and find his car?"

Birdie laughed. "Honey, we're the law. All I have to do is put in my password." She hopped off her seat, flung her lime green purse over her shoulder, then hoisted her still open laptop into her arms. "Well, once we're in the car. Ready for a little road trip?"

"You can't find him on your laptop?"

"I've already activated the silent radio signal, but in order to pick it up we need to be within three to five miles of the car. And clearly, that's not where we are now because nothing is coming in."

The front door of the station opened and two older people came in.

Birdie greeted them immediately. "Stanhill and Corette, your timing is perfect!"

The older man didn't look convinced. "Corette had a flat or we would have been here sooner."

"No," Birdie said. "You're right on time. I need someone to man the front desk."

Corette's eyes widened. "Where are you going? Did you find Julian?"

"Not yet, but we're working a lead. You're in charge!" She headed for the door even as she was nodding at Desi. "Let's go."

Desi didn't need to be told twice. In minutes, they were in Birdie's sleek navy blue Mercedes, tooling through town. Birdie explained who the couple was who'd come into the station. Stanhill worked for Hugh Ellingham, and Corette was his fiancée and Pandora's mother. Then Birdie mapped out the route she and Desi were going to drive. They'd decided to start at the center and make slowly widening circles. Birdie showed Desi what to look for on the screen.

She watched it with great focus, but sadly, it remained blank.

Desi's frustration was increasing faster than their current miles per hour. "What if he's so far out of town that he's beyond range?"

"Pandora was certain that based on the results

of her location spell, he was still within the town limits."

"But you said the Pinehurst Inn was outside of town limits."

"It is, but he's not there, so the consensus is the hunter is holding him somewhere closer." Birdie glanced over. "I know you're worried, but there are a lot of people looking for him."

Desi was beyond worried. "I still think we need to go faster. Cover more ground."

"Maybe I should try more of a grid pattern." Birdie shrugged apologetically. "I don't get to do a lot of field work."

Desi thought about everything she knew about the hunter at this point. "The hunter said she planned to make this prominent vampire's death go viral." A chill swept her. "If she's holding Julian somewhere and hasn't sent a note trying to get me to meet up with her, she might have changed her mind about which prominent vampire she's planning on killing."

Birdie paled. "That's not good."

"No, it's not. Where would you go in this town to hole up and not be disturbed? For as long as it took to make this stupid video and...you know?" She couldn't bring herself to say words that meant Julian was going to die. She refused to put that out into the universe.

Birdie was breathing harder. "Somewhere… empty. Remote. Where being disturbed is unlikely. Let me think. We had a situation in the old funeral home a while back, but that's not vacant anymore." She strummed her fingers on the steering wheel. "Out by the lake? If she's planning on letting the sun…anyway, then that would be a good spot to do it in. You might run into a few fishermen, but it's generally pretty quiet out there when there's not a fair or event happening on the grounds."

"Head that way. Now."

The itch burning up the back of Julian's neck and the cotton filling his head told him all he needed to know. Laudanum. That's what she'd tranquilized him with. Since the opiate had existed, it had been used against vampires, but the drug had faded from fashion with the Victorians.

He hadn't realized it was still available. He did now.

Refusing to respond to the itch, he stayed still and opened one eye just a slit. He had no idea how long he'd been out, or if he was still in the Pumpkin Point house. His vampire senses, muddled as they were, told him the sun was down. But how long had it been that way? How late was it? He had no way of telling.

He blinked and tried to focus on what he could see. Lines. Parallel lines. He opened his one eye a little more. Floor joists. That's what he was looking

282

at. He took a shallow inhale through his nose. The dusty smell of masonry and new lumber was heavy in the air.

His fingertips felt rough wood, and whatever was supporting him was hard, but not cold like the concrete floor would be. He was closer to the ceiling than he would be if he was on the floor, too.

Thinking took a lot of effort, but the picture became a little clearer even while his head remained thick. He was on his back in an unfinished basement. Based on the layout he could see, most likely the Pumpkin Point house. And probably on a sheet of plywood, maybe supported on some saw horses. Plywood was about eight feet long and he couldn't feel that any part of his body was hanging off. He closed his eye and tried to think past the wobbly effects of the laudanum.

All of the houses in the Pumpkin Point development had daylight basements. Including 1900 Nutmeg Lane. Most of the houses in Nocturne Falls had them. People needed storage, and they liked natural light, even in the room below ground level.

Unless they were vampires. Like his brother Hugh. Hugh's basement had no windows and he'd converted the space into a laboratory where he'd been trying for years to perfect a serum that would make vampires immune to the sun, amulet or not.

But he was losing focus. What was he doing?

Something about light. Then thinking about light made him open his eye again. Yes, that was it. He was sussing out his situation. Figuring out where he was being held. And how he could escape.

What light was in the room was artificial. Like the light from a flashlight. Except much dimmer. The light from a cell phone. As his senses cleared a little more, he realized that wasn't the only clue that he had company.

The hunter's pulse thudded dully in his ears like a ticking clock. He inhaled again, allowing himself a deeper intake of air.

Human. Her scent drifted in with the cement and saw dust. It was a mix of laundry detergent, floral shampoo, and the underlying aroma of all humans. Blood.

The scent shot through him, causing his fangs to ache. Not a normal reaction. He had too much discipline for that, but the drug created a weakness in his system. It eroded his control.

Whether or not the hunter understood this side effect of the laudanum, he didn't know, but he was going to have to be extra careful with his natural instincts. He would not allow the hunter to be the reason he took a human's life. Nor would she be that life. No matter how appealing the idea was.

If not for the new awareness that had brought his basest instincts to life, he could have closed his eyes and drifted off again. The drug had worn off

284

some, but a great deal of it still lingered in his system, weighing him down like a lead blanket.

Unfortunately for the hunter, Julian Ellingham was not a quitter. In fact, he responded best to challenges.

Desi was proof of that.

Shifting his gaze to the right, he tried to get his bearings as best he could without alerting his captor that he was awake. Over the bridge of his nose he could just make out the windows near the ceiling. On the opposite side of him were the stairs. He was about in the middle of the room. He quickly counted the joists above him. No, he was closer to the windows than the stairs by about a yard.

And as best he could tell, from the direction of the flickering light, the great hunter was somewhere past his feet on the right side. Maybe in that corner of the basement.

That meant he should be able to move his left hand without notice. He eased his fingers back and forth, feeling what was underneath him. By the texture under his fingertips, it was definitely plywood. Then he bent his wrist a little to test his restraints. He immediately felt a sharp pinch on the back of his hand. He flicked his gaze over his shoulder and saw an IV bag dangling from a wire coat hanger. The hanger was hooked on some of the wires running along the joists. Liquid dripped down through a clear tube that disappeared from his sight. That explained the pain in the back of his hand.

Anger ramped through his system, but not enough to flush the drug. Especially since she had him on a constant supply of it. No wonder he felt as weak as a child.

He tugged carefully on his left wrist, but whatever restraints she was using were too strong for him in this state.

The urge to curse and rage and explode with anger gnawed on him like a feral animal. He considered the action and the consequences and decided against it. If he failed to free himself, she'd know he was awake and too weak to escape.

Better to keep her in the dark about that until he had a more solid plan. The muddled mess of his brain wasn't coming up with anything else immediately, however, which only added to his frustration.

He wanted to laugh. Then he wanted to cry. It was the drug. His emotions didn't swing that wildly. But one clear thought finally came to him. If the hunter had trapped him and planned to make him into her big triumph, that meant Desi was safe.

His precious Desi. His wife. His heart. He knew the laudanum was making him maudlin, but he couldn't help himself. The thought that he might never see Desdemona's beautiful face again or hear her intoxicating laugh or taste her sweet mouth nearly undid him, but at least he'd be able to protect her.

A tear trickled down his temple and into his hair. Then the rage returned. He was *not* going out like this. As the example of some hell-bent human who fancied herself a great hunter. He closed his eyes and dug deeper into his addled mind for some idea. Some way to extricate himself from this awful mess. Some path that would lead him back to Desi.

But the laudanum took every new thought and turned it into mist, or sent it down a rabbit hole of old memories, or darkened it into a nightmare.

The truth was, he was trapped, not by the woman who believed she was a descendant of the fictional Abraham Van Helsing, mythological vampire hunter, but in his own head.

Unable to stand the nonsense swirling through his brain another second, he grunted in frustration, realizing too late that he'd unwittingly let the noise slip from his throat.

He cursed the laudanum. If he got out of this basement alive, he would find out who'd made the wretched drug and sue them into oblivion.

Boots scraped the floor. The footsteps grew closer, then the wiry blonde who'd shot him appeared in his field of vision. She peered down at him with great interest, the satisfied gleam in her eyes making him want to snap. "Enjoy your nap, bloodsucker?"

"How long have I been out?" It was an effort to speak. His tongue was as thick as his head.

She dangled a small black box over him. It had a white barcoded label on it and a few wires hanging loose. "Long enough for me to disable the SatGuard on your car."

The lake proved a dead end. At least so far. They were halfway around it and had yet to see another car of any variety.

Desi's throat constricted. "Nothing. There's nothing here."

"We still have a ways to go." Birdie scanned her side of the road.

"Are there any cabins out here? Any old buildings? Barns? Any place large enough to hide a car in?" Desi's head hurt from thinking so hard. Even with her exceptional senses, the trees had begun to blur. She saw human forms where there were none, a trick of the stress eating away at her. She was doing her best to stay focused but, the truth was, she was panicked and scared and had the most desperate, awful feeling that Julian's chances were slipping away.

"No buildings that I'm aware of, but this isn't

my usual stomping grounds. Come the full moon, we head into the forest north of here for our runs. Up by the falls and into the hills. There are lots of cabins up there, but all that's being searched already."

"But if those people had found anything, wouldn't they have radioed in?"

"Probably."

She sucked in a ragged, gasping breath as her stomach knotted. "I can't lose him."

Birdie pulled over and parked on the shoulder.

"What are you doing?"

"If I was hiding out here, holding a hostage, I'd be off the beaten path. Let's get out and walk a little. Between us, we should be able to pick up some scents or sounds and tell if there's a vampire and a human out here somewhere."

"Okay." Doing something was better than doing nothing, which was what riding around in the car, staring at the SatGuard monitoring screen felt like.

"We'll each take a direction and walk for five minutes, then come back and drive a little farther and repeat. Keep your phone on you. We can text each other if we find something. Here, let's exchange numbers."

They did that, then got out, closing the car doors quietly. Birdie pointed to the right, then pointed at Desi to go left.

Desi nodded, and they each took off. If she'd

been out here for any other reason, it would have been a beautiful night. It was clear and the stars seemed infinite. The soft sounds of small waves lapped the shore, a very different sound than the relentless ocean. A few other noises mingled in. Crickets or frogs or some other nocturnal creatures she wasn't familiar with.

But the sound Desi most wanted to hear was the rhythmic pulse of a human heart. She picked up Birdie's in the distance, but she'd heard it enough now that she could rule it out. Desi stuffed her hands into the pockets of her jeans and trudged on.

Helplessness was a feeling she was far too familiar with. She hated it. Being trapped on that wretched island had been horrifying. But in some ways, this was worse. On the island, she'd had nothing but time. Something Julian was quickly running out of. She knew he was here in this town somewhere. She just had to find him before it was too late.

If it wasn't already. At least he had his amulet to protect him from the sun. What she could not understand, though, was how this hunter had bested him.

She looked at her phone to check the time. Two more minutes before she had to turn back.

If she was a vampire hunter, how would she subdue one? That was unfair, seeing as how Desi had intimate knowledge of her own kind that the hunter, in theory, wouldn't have. She thought about the garlic and the crosses and the UV lights.

The hunter had some myths right, but not all. What other myths and truths were there about vampires? And which one would the hunter think was the most effective in rendering a vampire powerless? Desi knew the hunter needed Julian alive for this video she planned to record, so whatever method the hunter chose, it had to keep Julian subdued, but conscious. At least to some extent.

What could do that?

Desi put those pieces together and gave her mind free rein to spin out the possibilities. There was only one thing she could come up with. The one thing every vampire she'd ever known stayed away from.

Drugs. Not alcohol, which could be consumed in large amounts by the average vampire without much consequence (accidental marriages aside). But real, mind-altering, mood-changing, narcotic, opioid drugs. In the past, it had always been laudanum. The drug was part of every vampire hunter's kit, and every vampire had heard the warnings.

One of the stories told was about a hunter in Victorian times who'd repeatedly filled the veins of unwitting human victims with the drug, then left the victims to stagger the streets of London as bait.

The hunter would follow with a watchful eye, waiting for a vampire to strike and the drug to render them weak. Whether or not the scheme worked, she had no real idea, but the hunter claimed to have sent the bolt of a crossbow into nearly a dozen vampire hearts through use of the method.

Desi shuddered as she turned back toward the car. The night was as still as ever, and the only beating heart she could hear was Birdie's. They were no closer to finding Julian. Unless the drug was a clue.

But did laudanum even exist anymore? She supposed it could be manufactured. Or something similar. And if this woman hunter thought she came from the lineage of Van Helsing himself, maybe an out of date method was exactly the one she'd use. Especially one that came with successful hunting stories.

Desi picked up her pace. In a few seconds, she found Birdie, who was still minutes from the car.

Birdie's eyes went gold and she snarled and bared her teeth as Desi skidded to a stop in front of her, then Birdie laughed and put her hand to her chest. "Oh my, you scared the daylights right out of me. Sorry about that little display. Hard not to react to years and years of instinct."

"No harm, no foul." Then Desi nodded. "And that's exactly what I was thinking. Years of instinct.

293

We've got to get back to the car and the laptop. I have an idea."

"I'm all ears."

They jogged back, Desi explaining on the way. As soon as they were in the car, Birdie took over the laptop and started her search.

A few minutes later, the typing stopped. "No need to look for a substitute. Laudanum is still available in the US, but it's getting harder and harder to acquire because of some of its key ingredients."

"Well, it should be impossible to get. It's a horrible drug."

"It is," Birdie agreed. "It's a mix of morphine, codeine, and opium. No one should be putting that into their bodies. The opium part is what's making it scarce."

"Can you tell if Abigail Helsing has purchased any?"

"I can." The typing started up again. "Just as soon as I hack into her credit card account."

"How long is that going to take?"

Birdie looked up and smiled, the light of the screen giving her a slightly malevolent glow. "I'm in." She laughed. "I was in yesterday."

Desi let out a sigh of relief. Birdie was amazing.

She bent her head again. "Okay, lemme search." Her eyes narrowed in concentration. "Oh, this looks interesting. Brighton Pharmaceuticals." She did a little more typing, then lifted her head again to look at Desi. "Abigail Helsing purchased three dozen vials of tincture of opium six weeks ago. We have our laudanum."

"Six weeks ago." Desi's gut twisted. "That's around the time I got the first bouquet of black roses."

Birdie set the laptop onto the seat between them, then started the engine. "Buckle up."

Desi grabbed her seat belt. "Where are we going?"

"To see a pharmacist I know."

Birdie took off faster than Desi thought she was capable of driving, and while she was driving, she dug her phone out of her purse and made a call. "Pete. It's Birdie. I have an odd but serious request. Y'all have any laudanum at the pharmacy?"

She looked over at Desi and winked. "Perfect. Can you meet me there in ten minutes?" She frowned. "Well, honey, I can't help if you're on a date, this is official police business. One of the Ellinghams is in trouble. No, it's not for them. Just meet me there, or I will call your mother and tell her you obstructed a manhunt."

She grinned. "Good boy. See you in eight minutes." She hung up and tossed the phone back into her purse.

Desi felt sorry for Pete, but super happy that Birdie had the power to get things done. "What's the plan?"

Birdie kept her eyes on the road, but tapped the side of her nose. "We're gonna track that little missy down, and if Julian's not with her, we're gonna scare some sense into her until she tells us. Now hang on. I told Pete eight minutes, but we're eleven minutes out."

"You won't get away with this," Julian scowled at Abigail, but she was busy setting up a tripod and camera and not really paying attention. If only looks could truly kill, he'd be free.

She sighed like she was bored. Or Julian was an idiot. "Yes, I will. You're drugged, untraceable, and restrained. You might think you're the top of the food chain, but that arrogance is about to be your downfall. Stupid bloodsucker."

"Someone will see my car."

"Not in the garage they won't."

He mumbled a curse. The hunter was smarter than he'd imagined. "What are you trying to prove?"

She glanced up, her face screwed into an are-you-an-idiot expression that confirmed Julian's earlier guess. "That vampires exist. And are obviously not the superior creatures everyone thinks they are. Humans need to be warned about your kind. And shown that you bloodsuckers can be defeated." She shook her head and went back to the electronics.

"Wouldn't you get more publicity by parading me around at all your vampire-hunter conventions?" He wasn't sure those actually existed, but they had conventions for everything else, so why not?

She was looking through the camera now, making small adjustments. "Oh, I will, but I'm going to use your girlfriend for that. You look too much like a stereotypical vampire. She's much more interesting visually. But don't worry, you're still very important to me. You're my money shot. My viral video. When that sun hits you and you go poof into a cloud of ash, that's going to be gold right there."

So that was her plan. And why he was closer to the windows. Except when the sun came up, the light would stream through, hit him, and do nothing. He wondered how she'd react to that. Or if she had a backup plan. And how he could protect Desi.

Abigail stood up and walked over to him. Close, but not too close. Her pulse increased a little too. For all her bravado, she was afraid. Good. He might be able to use that. "You are going to make me legitimate. The Helsing name will once again be synonymous with vampire hunter. I really should thank you for the power your death is going to bring me."

"You could let me go. That would be thanks enough."

"Yeah, not happening."

He shifted his gaze toward the ceiling, his brain still not cooperating as much as he would have liked. "You're missing out."

She laughed. "On what? Immortality? No, thanks, I'm not about to fall for that trick."

He frowned and looked at her again. "Not in a hundred years would I offer you the gift I've been given."

"Gift. Right," she scoffed. "Like treating humans as cattle is such a noble and amazing way to live your life."

"We don't treat humans like cattle. We don't kill them either."

"We?" She came a little closer. "Just how many of you are there in this town?"

Bloody hell. The damn drug was making him speak without thinking. He shut his mouth. He wasn't getting anywhere anyway.

She walked around to the other side of the plywood he was laid out on and checked the IV bag. "The laudanum makes you want to talk, doesn't it?"

It did. But he was nearly four hundred years old. Maybe a newly turned vamp would break under the drug's press, but he was stronger than that. He hoped.

She smiled that stupid smile again. "I'm close to getting your girlfriend, too, you know. It's just a matter of time before I capture her too."

"I'm aware. We've known you were targeting her for a while."

"Well, goody for you. Fat lot of good it did you." She leaned against the plywood near his feet, causing it to shift slightly.

"You didn't capture her."

"But I got you. And I'll get her. Eventually. Once this video goes viral, I'll have no shortage of help. That will make things much easier."

He grimaced. Bands of vampire hunters roaming the country would only lead to an all-out war. And humans would not end up on the winning side, regardless of Abigail's small victory capturing him.

But she apparently interpreted his grimace another way. "Unless you want to help me now."

"No idea what you're talking about, but it doesn't matter. I have no interest in helping you."

"Really? Not even if it meant I spared you?"

He refused to take her bait.

Didn't stop her from talking. "Come on, I know you're curious." She leaned in a little. "I'll give you a cell phone, you call her and tell her to meet you here and then she takes your place. Easy as pie."

His lip curled in disgust. The idea that he would trade Desi's life for his own was ludicrous. He needed to keep the hunter's focus on him. "I met your father once."

"What? When?"

"Many, many years ago. In Brussels." He picked his head up to see her better. She was listening with rapt attention, but the motion made the air swim. He put his head back down and continued with his story. "He followed me through the streets one evening. Tried to stake me. I had to physically persuade him of the error of his ways. I thought for sure that was the kind of story that would get passed on."

She leaned over Julian farther, her mouth bent in a sneer that caused the words to come out in a growl. "You. You're the one."

"So he did tell you? And yet here you are, still following in his—"

"I owe you."

"For what?"

Her gaze hardened. "For what you did to my father."

Julian snorted. "You're going to kill me over a beating? Let me remind you that *he* attacked me."

"A beating? Is that all you think it was? The man died trying to escape you. After he managed to take refuge in a church, he had a heart attack. The priests found him in the morning, dead at the foot of the altar."

Julian froze. That couldn't be right. That wasn't

what Birdie had told him. "I thought Arnold Helsing died a few years ago."

"Arnold Helsing died thirty-six years ago. Two weeks before I was born. Arnold Helsing Jr., my step-brother, died three years ago. He spent his life trying to find out who was responsible for our father's death. He'd managed to scrawl the word vampire on a piece of paper before he died, but that and his research was all we had to go on."

Bloody hell.

Her ridiculous grin returned. "At last, his death will finally be avenged. Outstanding."

Her glee only riled his anger up. "Speaking of words on paper, you should leave a note with the name of your next of kin."

Her grin flattened. "Why?"

"So the authorities know where to send your body." He had no plans to kill her, but a few good threats couldn't hurt.

"You know what?" She leaned in as she took something from her pocket. "I don't need you or your mouth awake until show time." She pulled the cap off the syringe in her hand and jabbed it into his thigh.

He opened his mouth to say something, but the fresh wave of laudanum took his words, and his consciousness, away.

Birdie parked in the alley behind the pharmacy, making the whole thing feel like some super clandestine affair, which maybe it sort of was, considering they were here for a drug with such a shady reputation. Birdie turned the car off, then looked at Desi. "Pete's a good guy, but very by the book and a little shy. Also, he's fae. Just telling you so the ears don't throw you."

"I can handle pointy ears. Hey, the guy can be a bridge troll for all I care. If he's willing to help, I'm cool with him regardless."

"Good point."

They got out and went up to the steel back door. The alarm company sticker in the center of it was bright and shiny, like it was new. Or someone was cleaning it on a regular basis. Birdie knocked, and a few moments later, a handsome young man answered the door.

Desi had expected to see him in a white lab coat, but he was in jeans and a button-down.

He glanced past them into the alley like he was looking to see if anyone else was watching. Satisfied, he shifted his focus to them. "Hello, Birdie."

"Hi, Pete. Thanks for meeting us."

"You didn't really give me an option." His eyes narrowed as he looked at Desi. "Who's your friend?"

"I still really appreciate you doing this." Birdie tipped her head toward Desi. "This is Desdemona. She's Julian's girl."

Apparently, Birdie's brief explanation was enough. He nodded. "Come in."

The back of the pharmacy was a labyrinth of shelving, all stocked with bottles and boxes of medicines. One long section was secured behind a floor-to-ceiling gate. Were those the most expensive drugs? The most deadly? Both? She could only guess what that gate was securing.

She looked around, but only about half the lights were turned on, filling the place with strange shadows. None of the lights were on in the front of the store, which added to the clandestine feeling.

If Desi had been wearing a coat, she would have pulled it tighter around her.

While she and Birdie stood there, Pete locked the back door behind them, then went to the gate.

A different key from the same key ring went into that lock. "It'll just take me a second. Can I ask why you need the laudanum? It's not a very safe drug. Highly addictive. And very much out of fashion. We only have it in stock because, well, it's Nocturne Falls and you just never know. There are a few supernaturals that are particularly vulnerable to it."

"So we understand. I just need to sniff it," Birdie said. "There's some in town and I'm going to try to track it down."

He glanced back at her, his wide blue-green gaze suddenly curious. "You can do that?"

"Werewolves have a great sense of smell."

He smiled timidly, giving Desi the sense that he was a little afraid of Birdie. That seemed completely reasonable. The woman was a force of nature. "Of course."

He went back to unlocking the gate.

"How's that cutie from the Christmas shop?" Birdie asked. "You still sweet on her? Hey, is that who you were on the date with?"

And just like that, the tips of his ears went bright red. Desi rolled her lips in to keep from laughing.

"I, uh, yes, we are. I mean, I am. Still sweet on her. And yes, that's where I was. Who I was with." He gave the key a sharp turn and wrenched the gate open so hard it squealed a little. "I'll just get that laudanum."

Desi nudged Birdie and gave a look to say she shouldn't give the poor guy such a hard time. He was helping them, after all.

Birdie grinned and shrugged, unrepentant.

Pete came back out with a small brown bottle bearing several labels, most of which looked like warnings and precautions. He unscrewed the top and held it out to Birdie. "Here you go."

She leaned in, closed her eyes and inhaled. Then her nose wrinkled and she reared back. "Ew, that smells like boozy apple pie made with vomit custard."

Desi snorted. "You have such a way with words, Birdie."

Pete sighed. "It's a tincture. It's made with alcohol. That's why it smells boozy. As for the rest…" He shrugged. "It's very bitter. At least from what the research says. The Victorians used to add a lot of sugar to it."

Birdie waved her hand in front of her face. "Well, you can close it up. I've got the scent. No mistaking that one."

He screwed the top back on. "That all you need?"

"Yep. Thanks a bundle. Go back to your date. Make sure you tell her it was official police business. She'll forgive that." Birdie turned and headed for the car without giving Pete a chance to say much else.

Desi followed Birdie out to the parking lot. "What now?"

Birdie pulled her keys out of her purse and tossed them to Desi. "Now you drive."

"But I don't know the town."

Birdie shrugged and headed for the passenger's side. "Doesn't matter, we're going to follow my nose. We'll go back to driving a grid and just see if I can pick up anything that way. If, scratch that, *when* I do, we'll follow it down."

A few minutes later, Desi was driving slightly under the speed limit through an unknown part of town and having a hard time believing they were ever going to find Julian. "You really think this is going to work?"

"You bet your biscuits." Birdie had the window down and was leaning out of it. The wind pushed her hair back and her eyes were squinted shut, but she leaned nose first into the air with great enthusiasm.

Sure, the woman was a wolf shifter, but this was one of the craziest things Desi had ever seen. Still, if it found Julian, she'd never say another word about it.

But three hours and one gas station stop later, they were no closer. Desi sat in the car, her head on the steering wheel. She was going to melt down and lose it. She was panicked, stressed, angry, and scared. It wasn't a combination she'd felt since she'd been on the island. She'd learned to deal with those things in turn, but this was different.

She had no way of stopping this ticking clock. And it was so loud, she could hear it. She tried to push all those emotions down, but it was hard when Julian needed her. And she was failing.

Birdie finished filling the tank and got back in the car. She glanced at Desi, then looked at her a little closer. "You're freaking out, aren't you?"

Desi swallowed. "Yes."

"Hey, I know you're worried, but we're getting closer. I can feel it in my gut, and sometimes you just have to trust that. Plus, we still have the other half of town to drive through."

Desi turned her head. She knew all about trusting her gut. It just hadn't spoken to her lately. "We were already out to the lake earlier."

"Yes, but we didn't have the laudanum angle figured out then."

Desi turned the car on. "The sun will be up in less than an hour. I feel like we're running out of time."

"It's going to be all right, you'll see." Birdie's words were soft and hopeful, like she was trying to convince herself of them too.

Please be right, Desi thought.

"Ready when you are." Birdie tucked her purse next to her and started to lean out the window again.

A truck rumbled past carrying a load of lumber. Desi watched it go. Something inside her clicked. The small, confident voice she'd been waiting to hear. "You know what you just said about trusting your gut?"

"Yep." Birdie was half out the window.

"Well, mine just spoke to me. What's that new development called? Pumpkin Place?"

"Pumpkin Point."

"Has anyone searched out there?"

Birdie slid out of the window and back into her seat. "I think so, but I can call Hank real quick."

"Please. Which way is that place?"

Birdie pointed. "That way."

"Keep directing me while you talk." Desi turned onto the street as Birdie called her nephew.

"Will do." Birdie put the phone to her ear. "Hank? Honey, has anyone been out to Pumpkin Point? They have? And?" She pursed her mouth. "You're sure? Okay." She sighed. "Don't you worry about where I am. The desk is covered."

She hung up. "He said Pumpkin Point got a drive through and inspection less than an hour ago and there was nothing going on. No cars, no signs of life. They didn't go through the houses, but they looked in windows, that sort of thing."

Desi shook her head. Her gut said keep going. "If this woman truly captured Julian, she's crafty. A search like that would be easy enough to avoid."

"You really think so?"

She nodded. "I do. I don't know why I feel so strongly. It's just a hunch. I might be completely wrong, but I don't think I am and we have nothing else to go on."

"This is what your gut is telling you?"

Desi listened to what her head and heart were saying. They were speaking in the same clear, strong voice that had told her to light the signal fire that fateful night on the island. "Yes."

"Then let's do this." Birdie pointed up ahead. "Make a left at this light."

"How close are we?"

"Seven or eight minutes. It's a straight stretch from here until you turn into the development."

Desi pushed her foot down on the pedal. "Hang on."

Birdie grinned and put her window up. "Now you're driving like you mean it."

The miles slipped away and the Pumpkin Point sign came into view. Desi slowed and Birdie buzzed her window down.

The air rushed in and she opened her mouth and leaned into it.

Desi glanced over. Birdie's eyes glowed gold. "What is it?"

Birdie looked at her. "I smell laudanum."

Coming to was harder this time, but Julian no longer cared about the element of surprise. He was too weak to break free anyway. His head lolled to the side of the basement where the light of the camera was. He unstuck his tongue from the roof of his mouth so he could speak. "Still here?"

She looked up. "Oh good, just in time for your big debut." She laughed. "I think I'll call this video Ashes to Ashes."

"You're going to look like a fool."

"Hero is more like it."

He shrugged. The effort made his head spin. "You'll see."

She walked over to him. "I know you have some kind of sun protection. I've seen you out during the day. It just makes you that much more of a threat, but I'm pretty sure I've eliminated that little issue."

He snorted.

"Don't think I enjoyed patting you down either." She held up his silver chain with the amulet dangling off it. "But other than your wallet, keys, and watch, this was the only other thing I found that might be protecting you."

A chill ran though him. He tried very hard to keep himself from reacting, but the drug made it difficult. Suddenly, he could feel the sun's approach on the other side of the laudanum's numbing effects.

She stuffed the chain into her pocket. "Of course,

if that's just some gaudy vampire jewelry, I have a backup plan."

"Oh?" He did his best to sound nonchalant.

She smiled. "Crossbow bolt. An oldie but a goodie."

He looked behind her. A step ladder and a nasty-looking crossbow sat against the wall behind the camera. The chill froze him completely. He was going to die.

She went back to the camera. "If it makes you feel any better, I think some people were looking for you earlier. They poked around a bit, even shined their flashlights through the windows, but when I heard the car, I covered you with one of those painting tarps and threw some wood scraps on top of you. Fortunately, they seemed to have bought you as part of the construction scenery because they didn't poke around long. Thanks for not waking up then. That would have killed the illusion."

He stared at the floor joists above him. There was some comfort in knowing his disappearance hadn't gone completely unnoticed. He felt bad for whoever had been out here, though. When it came to light that he'd been in the basement the whole time, those people would take some criticism. More victims of the hunter's madness.

"Any last words? I could do a little video on my phone if you want to confess your evil ways before you go poof."

He held his tongue. He had no desire to become kindling for her insane fire.

"Really?" She came closer. "You don't even want to say goodbye to your girlfriend? Or this guy?"

He glanced at her. She was holding up a picture from his wallet. George. Precious darling baby George. Julian's heart ached as his anger soared. He went back to staring at the ceiling. "Came with the wallet."

"I don't think so. It's a real picture. Maybe I should look for him after I'm done with you? Just to make sure vampires can't reproduce. I mean, if I'm not too busy showing off Desdemona to the world. Oh, that will be highly entertaining."

Julian ground his teeth together in an effort to keep his mouth shut. He might kill the hunter after all. She would not touch George or Desi. He just had to get free first. He closed his eyes and implored his brain to work. But the constant flow of laudanum into his system made thinking a Herculean struggle. The one thread of an idea that formed had no real heft to it.

He could probably wrench the sheet of plywood off the platform it was on. Helsing had moved it earlier when she'd leaned against it. If he could knock it to the floor, the fall might potentially snap his restraints and maybe, if he landed right, the effort might also tear the IV loose.

Or he might just look like a dying fish, already pinned to the cutting board.

Either way, it was worth a shot. He had nothing to lose. Except…everything.

"That way." Birdie pointed toward the house at the very end of the street. "Smells like it's coming from there."

It was a gorgeous house with a three-car garage and a welcoming front porch, but there were no signs that it was in any way occupied. Desi wanted to trust Birdie's nose. What else did they have to go on? And any chance was better than none, but there were seven houses on this street and very little breeze that might help point to one of them. She clenched the steering wheel a little tighter. "You're positive it's that one?"

"I'd stake my werewolf reputation on it."

"Okay, we should park here and go on foot the rest of the way. We have to get the jump on this woman. We can't risk her knowing we're on to her and having her do something to Julian before we can get to him."

"Agreed." Birdie pulled out her phone as Desi parked the car at the mouth of the street.

"What are you doing?"

"Texting Hank for backup. Don't worry, I'll tell them to come in silent."

"Good. I don't want this woman getting away because she hears sirens, but I am not waiting for them."

Birdie sent the text, then tucked her phone into her back pocket. "No, no waiting. The sky is already lightening at the horizon. Let's go. You're a vampire and I'm a werewolf. And this woman is human. She can't take us both down."

Desi nodded. "That's right."

They got out, closing the doors quietly, then Desi pulled off her short boots and left them on the pavement. She glanced at Birdie. "Ready?"

"Ready."

Desi broke into a barefoot jog toward the house. Birdie kept pace beside her down the street. They made it to the curb a few seconds later, slowing to a stop.

Birdie lifted her face into the air and inhaled. She kept her voice low when she spoke. "Oh yes, this is definitely it. I smell laudanum, human, *and* vampire."

That was all the reassurance Desi needed. She pointed toward the right side of the house. "Let's do a perimeter check first, see if there's a back way in."

"Good thinking."

Desi led, staying close to the house so they couldn't be seen out of the windows. At the rear corner, she stopped suddenly. "Light," she whispered.

And not a steady light, either. It was weak and flickered occasionally, casting wonky shadows over the backyard. It reminded her of a dim television.

Birdie nodded as she looked around Desi to see for herself. "Cell phone?"

"Maybe. Or a person walking in front of the light." Desi peered farther around the corner to see where the light was coming from. There were windows on the ground, but at this angle it was impossible to see in. She glanced back at Birdie. "This house has a basement?"

Birdie nodded. "They all do here."

Desi squatted down and crawled to the first window to peek in. A half second later, she jerked back, every nerve in her body pinging in alarm. Julian was still alive but in definite danger. She retreated as quickly and quietly as she was able.

"What did you see?" Birdie whispered.

"He's in there." The scene spilled out of Desi as she described what was seared into her brain. "Tied down to a big sheet of wood. There's some kind of IV in him. She's in there too. She's got a camera set up and a cell phone in her hand. Maybe recording on that as well. Both of those are putting off some light. She's getting ready to film the video."

"Then we need to get in there now."

"There's a crossbow against one wall."

"We can handle that."

Desi nodded. "But we have to go around to the other side. She'll see us from here too easily."

"Come on." Birdie started hustling around the house. Desi followed, her anger at what was being done to Julian at war with her joy at finding him, but the emotion that rose above those was the screaming urgency to free him.

They came around the side of the house and Birdie stopped short. "What's our plan?"

"We have to get into the house. But how do we do that without her hearing us?"

"I'm not sure." Birdie sighed and tipped her head back. "I wish we could draw her out. That would be easier."

"If you could get her outside, then I could slip in and free Julian without the risk of her interfering."

"Hmm. I might have an idea on how we could both get in there." Birdie's eyes took on the wolfy gold glow again.

"I'm game. What are you thinking?"

Birdie grinned, showing off her suddenly sharper canines. "No one can resist a poor stray doggie."

The sun's itch had become worse than the laudanum's dull prickliness. Time was running out. Julian had held off doing anything because he'd hoped against hope that some of his strength might return or that the search party might circle back. Neither of those things had happened.

And in his delirium, he'd thought for a moment that he'd smelled Desi's orange blossom perfume, but that was just another cruel trick of the drug.

If he had any chance of getting free, he had to act now. He thought of Desi, and George, and the rest of his family. He wanted to see them all again so badly he could taste it.

This had to work.

He flexed his wrists, gathering his remaining energy for one last burst of—a dull scratching trickled down from the floor above.

The hunter looked up, so she heard it too.

Then a faint, canine whine followed with more scratching. It was a pitiful sound.

Julian had no idea what was going on, but the hunter walked to the bottom of the steps and listened.

More soft whining filtered through. Like a dog in pain.

The hunter went back to the wall and grabbed the crossbow, balancing it on her shoulder. "Stay here," she snorted. "Like you can leave. Hah! I amuse myself."

Then she trotted up the steps.

Julian counted her footfalls until he heard her climb all twelve steps to the top floor. He knew there were twelve. He's approved the blueprints.

He heard the door opening. Then the hunter's voice. "Hey there, pooch. Are you lost? What's wrong with your paw? Is it hurt?"

Gathering his remaining strength, Julian jerked his body sideways, throwing his center of gravity as far to the right as he could. The plywood skidded over the saw horses, teetered for a second, then crashed to the ground.

The fall was enough to rip the IV from his hand and break the restraints on his left wrist and ankle, but the real boost came from the laudanum no longer being renewed in his system. He was wobbly and weak, but it was like a switch had been thrown. New strength rushed through him, fighting the drug's dwindling effects.

"What the hell?" The hunter came rushing back downstairs, crossbow leveled at Julian. "What do you think—"

A large gray wolf smashed into the hunter from behind. The impact shoved her to the bottom of the steps just as a cinder block came flying through one of the transom windows, shattering it into pebbles of safety glass. It rained onto the basement floor as Desi jumped through the opening.

"Desi?" She looked like a superhero goddess.

Wonder Woman had nothing on his wife.

She ran to his side. "Jules, are you okay? She drugged you, didn't she?"

"Yes. And took my amulet." The sky was growing brighter through the windows.

"I'll get it back." She kissed him soundly on the mouth, but a loud yelp turned their heads.

The hunter had cracked the wolf across the head with her crossbow. They were face to face now at the bottom of the stairs, but the hunter was flat on her back. The wolf shook off the blow to snarl and snap some more, but the hunter planted her feet on the bottom step and shoved herself out of the way in time to avoid being bitten. She raised the crossbow as she slid, aiming at the wolf.

The hunter's finger twitched on the trigger.

"No!" Desi flung herself across the room and in front of the wolf.

The bolt went through Desi's right shoulder, knocking her back. She cried out as she hit the stairs, then went limp.

Rage brought Julian all the strength he needed. He ripped free of the last two restraints and surged toward the hunter. She cringed but had no time to react further. He ripped the crossbow from her hands and snapped it in two.

The wolf shifted back into a familiar face. Birdie went to Desi's side, cradling her head. "She's hurt bad."

Desi's eyes blinked open. "I'll be okay," she whispered. Then she reached up toward Birdie. "You're hurt too."

Birdie's cheek had already begun to purple where the crossbow had caught her, and blood trickled from her hairline.

Julian made for Desi, but the hunter started scrambling away.

"No," Desi said. "Deal with her first."

Julian turned.

Sunlight streamed through the windows, illuminating the hunter, who'd reached the safety of the rays just seconds ago.

She shook her head at him and yanked a stake from her boot. "Come at me, vampire."

He couldn't. Not while she sheltered herself in the sun's protective glow.

"Jules." Desi's voice was weak. "Catch."

He turned in time to snatch the flash of silver coming at him. Her amulet. He stuffed it in his pocket and turned toward the hunter.

Watching Julian go after the hunter helped take Desi's mind off the pain of having a crossbow bolt sticking out of her shoulder. It throbbed like she'd grown a new, faulty heart there, but she was a vampire and she'd heal.

The hunter, however, was human.

With every step Julian came closer, the hunter took one back until she came to the edge of the sunbeam she seemed to think was keeping her safe.

He stopped just at the edge of the shaft of light. Dust motes danced through it, making the stream of sun seem alive. Then, without losing eye contact with the hunter, he slowly and deliberately took one step forward.

Her outstretched hand, the one holding the stake she'd pulled from her boot, began to tremble. "Are you going to kill me?"

Heavy footsteps thudded down into the

basement and Sheriff Merrow appeared. "No one's killing anyone." He unhooked the handcuffs from his belt. "We are gonna do some arresting, though."

He pointed at Julian. "Hang on to her."

Julian grabbed the hunter and secured her hands behind her back. The stake clattered to the concrete. She squirmed, mostly trying to put distance between herself and the vampire she'd been so desperate to harm.

The sheriff squeezed the radio at his shoulder while taking in Desi and his aunt. "Dispatch, I need two *local* ambulances at 1900 Nutmeg Lane."

Then he frowned at Birdie. "Who did that to you?"

She glared at the hunter. "Buffy over there. Cocked me with the butt of the crossbow."

The sheriff's eyes glowed for a second, then he seemed to get himself under control. "You okay, Aunt Birdie?"

"I'll be all right. I'm a tough cookie."

The sheriff smiled, his eyes showing a new gleam, but this time it was pride. "Yes, you are."

"You just deal with that awful woman," Birdie said.

"That who put the bolt in Mrs. Ellingham too?"

Desi almost smiled. No one had called her that yet, but she couldn't quite bring herself to nod. The adrenaline was starting to wear off and the pain had come back. "Same."

Deputy Blythe and another officer, Cruz by the name on the badge, tramped down the stairs behind the sheriff. He hooked his cuffs back onto his belt, then gestured to Helsing, now gone limp in Julian's grip. "Cuff her and take her to the station."

"You got it, boss." Blythe unsnapped her cuffs as she walked by.

Cruz surveyed the scene, but said nothing except to start reading Helsing her rights as he and Blythe took the hunter off Julian's hands. Blythe began frisking the woman.

Julian ran to Desi's side immediately. "My darling." He kissed her. "I'm so glad you're okay."

"Me too you. So glad."

The sheriff gave Birdie a hand up. "You okay to bring her to the ambulance, Ellingham?"

"Absolutely." Julian lifted Desi into his arms being very careful of the protruding bolt.

"Hey," she said, as he started kissing the side of her face. "You can't go carrying me out there."

"Why not?"

She lifted her brows. "Um, it's daylight?"

He swore softly.

Just then, Deputy Blythe held out her hands. "Sheriff? I believe these things are Mr. Ellingham's."

The sheriff walked to her. "I'll take them."

Blythe handed the items over.

The sheriff gave his deputies a nod. "All right, out she goes."

As the two deputies marched Helsing up the steps, Sheriff Merrow brought the things to Julian. "This what you're looking for?"

Beside Julian's wallet and keys, the chain and amulet lay on the sheriff's palm, their dull gleam a welcome sight.

Julian nodded. "Yes."

Birdie brushed her hands off. "I've got this." She took the chain and fastened it around Desi's neck, then she looked at Julian. "Will that do the trick?"

"It will. Thank you, Birdie. I'm so sorry you were caught up in all this."

Desi shook her head. "Birdie is the reason we're here. We owe her your life."

"Is that right?"

Birdie shrugged. "It's what we do in Nocturne Falls." Then she squinted at them. "By the way, what was that Mrs. Ellingham bit?"

Desi opened her mouth, but Julian answered first. He glanced at the sheriff. "Nothing. Your nephew was just teasing."

"Oh. Well, you two should think about making things more permanent. You make a great couple." The wails of ambulances sounded overhead. "My ride is here. See you kids up top." She turned and started up the steps with the help of the sheriff.

Desi's heart sank at Julian's words. She'd

thought maybe after all this, he might have changed his mind about letting her go, but clearly that wasn't the case.

He looked at her again. "We need to get that bolt out of you and let you heal."

"Won't the paramedics know something's up when I don't have a pulse?"

"The sheriff called for two *local* ambulances. That's code for supernaturals. You have nothing to worry about."

"Okay." She just sighed and let him carry her up the stairs. She leaned her head against his chest and closed her eyes, tired and hurting in more ways than one.

When they walked out of the house, she felt the sun's warmth on her skin, but it was the sudden explosion of cheering that raised her head.

Half the town was standing in the cul-de-sac, grinning and clapping and whistling.

"You've got to be kidding me."

Julian laughed softly as he nodded at them. "That's just how this place is. People care. We protect our own."

"That's really nice that they came out to see that you were okay." She was touched by the display. Julian was loved by these people. Because he was one of them, not because he was famous. Sure, he was *someone* in this town, but there was genuine concern in their eyes, not obligation.

"This crowd isn't just for me."

"Oh, right. Birdie."

"That's not what I meant." He looked at her then. "They're here for you too."

"But I don't live here." A longing filled her, a heartfelt wish to be part of something this good and wonderful. After choosing the solitary life as a means of self-preservation, she saw now that there was value in putting yourself out there. In letting yourself care. You just had to be willing to take the pain that came with that. "They don't know me."

"No, but they know that I...that you're my friend. Trust me, they're as concerned about you as they are me."

"Actually, I think they're mostly here for Birdie." She pointed.

Birdie's ambulance had the biggest crowd around it, including several older men carrying bouquets of flowers.

Julian laughed. "Looks that way."

He carried Desi to the paramedics and set her gently down on the waiting stretcher. She hung on to his hand. "Ride with me?"

"Sure." He looked at the paramedics. "That okay?"

The younger man answered him. "Absolutely. Just wait until we get her loaded, then you climb on in."

Julian squeezed her hand, then let it go and

moved out of the paramedics' way. They got her onto the vehicle and secured her, then Julian was at her side again.

The paramedics started fussing over her, but she waved them away. "I'll be fine. I just need this bolt out. You ought to look at Julian. That awful creature had him drugged up on laudanum."

That shifted the paramedics' attention enough to let her rest. The hum of the road crept up on her and she felt her eyes closing. She was in pain, worn out, and heartsick, and she had no one but herself to blame for the last one. She'd told Julian how things had to be. And in true Julian fashion, he was giving her exactly what he thought she wanted.

The worst part was that all of this, this place, this marriage, this man, would be going away very soon. And the thought of that opened a dark, desperate place in her that made her want to weep.

Maybe if she confessed her true feelings to Julian, she could get him to change his mind. She let herself drift in that dream for a while, imagining life with him without any of the baggage she carried. Was that even possible? She could try. They could be happy. They'd already proven that. And they could be a family.

Maybe even have children.

A sharp pinch brought her fully awake. "Ow. What was that?"

The young paramedic looked up at her from the

IV needle he'd just inserted into the back of her hand. "Prepping you for surgery, ma'am."

"What? Julian?"

Julian patted her arm. "I'm right here. It's going to be fine. We have the right kind of doctors on staff to take care of you. Locals."

She knew he meant supernatural doctors, which was great, but the thought of surgery suddenly panicked her. "Why can't you just yank the bolt out?"

He smiled gently. "For one thing, it would hurt like a mother."

"I get that, but I'm a vampire. I'll heal."

The older paramedic shook his head. "Ma'am, this bolt is barbed on the end. Pulling it out would do incredible damage to you and cause a considerable amount of pain. Surgery will minimize your healing time which, even with your nature, is going to be at least a week. Maybe more."

She nodded, but she still felt unsure.

Julian took her hand again. "Hey, it's okay. I'll be here when you wake up, I promise, but you need surgery as soon as possible. Your body has already begun to heal around the bolt. It's only going to make getting it out more difficult."

She swallowed. "Okay. But I'm holding you to that promise."

He lifted her hand and kissed her knuckles. "You got it."

The older paramedic reached up and did something to the IV bag. "Ma'am, I just need you to count backwards from ten for me now."

Desi keep her eyes on Julian. "Ten...nine...eight..."

Then everything went black.

Hospital chairs weren't the most comfortable things in the world, but sitting in one as Julian had been for the last few hours was still far better than the sheet of plywood he'd been strapped to.

He glanced at his watch again. Desdemona had been out of surgery for about an hour. Any minute he expected the nurse to come and get him and bring him back to her room.

He'd only left her briefly since the ambulance, and then only long enough to run home, shower and clean himself up. If he was going to be the first thing she saw when she woke up, he wanted to look his best. There were a few things he'd had to pick up from the penthouse too, but he'd gotten back to the hospital as quickly as possible. He was, frankly, desperate to see her.

Even if this whole wonderful, awful accidental marriage was about to come to an end. At least now he knew they'd part friends and, while there wasn't much that would ease his pain over losing her, it might not be quite as soul-destroying if his future still included her. Even if it wasn't as Mrs. Ellingham.

He smiled. What a nice ring that had to it. But hell, he'd become Mr. Valentine if that's what it took to keep her.

"Mr. Ellingham?"

He looked up to see a woman in scrubs. "Dr. Navarro? I wasn't expecting you."

"Well, I just checked on Ms. Valentine myself and she's doing fine. She should be awake in a few minutes. If you'd like to come back—"

He jumped to his feet. "Lead the way."

She smiled and took him to the room. Dr. Navarro put her hand on the door handle but didn't open it. "Ms. Valentine's nurse is Cara Willis. If you need anything, just push that buzzer and she'll be in."

"Thank you."

"You're very welcome." She opened the door and left as he went in.

It was a private corner suite, and the best one Julian had been able to procure. The bouquet he'd ordered from Marigold had already arrived, a huge display of tropical flowers that he hoped would put a smile on Desi's face.

A face that right now, showed no signs of life.

He frowned. That wasn't so unusual for a resting vampire, but she was still coming off the anesthesia, and he knew firsthand what that felt like. Although hers ought to be far more gentle.

Her right arm was in a sling and her bed was propped up at about a forty-five-degree angle. She looked comfortable, but he wanted her awake so he could talk to her and make sure for himself that she was all right. It was selfish really.

But maybe, while she was still out, he would do something even more selfish. He bent and brushed his lips over hers.

The electric spark of that contact sent a shiver through him, racking his body with a mix of pain and pleasure. He'd never kiss her again after today. He knew that. So with that one small act, he'd bought himself a final memory to torture himself with.

He closed his eyes and pinched the bridge of his nose, willing away the burning in his eyes. He was going to be happy and cheerful and bright. For her. He could fall apart on his own time.

A soft sigh was followed by an even quieter, "Jules?"

Her voice was barely a whisper. He opened his eyes and smiled for all he was worth. "Hello, beautiful. How are you feeling?"

"Like I just took a bolt through the shoulder." Her mouth bent in a little lopsided grin, most likely due to the drugs in her system. He'd never seen anything so endearing.

"Your arm is in a sling. I imagine you'll be like that for a few days."

She glanced down. "Huh. Sling. That's a funny word. Sling sling sling."

He snorted. "Yes, I suppose it is a funny word. Do you need anything? A blanket? More pain meds?" Although, clearly, she had plenty of those in her system.

"Champagne."

He snorted. "I don't think they serve that in the hospital. How about some water instead?"

"M'kay." Her eyes were heavy-lidded and she seemed to be drifting in and out.

"Water coming up." He found her tray. There was a cup, straw, and pitcher there, so he fixed her a glass and brought it to her.

Her head wobbled a bit as she sucked half of the liquid down, then she lay back again. "Better. Thank you." She poked his chest with her left pointer finger. "You're a nice man."

"I try."

She blinked a few times and stared at the ceiling. "That was some day, huh?"

"Yes. I've never had one like it before, and I'll be happy never to have one like it again. I can't thank you and Birdie enough."

"Birdie is awesome." Desi smiled and rolled her

head toward him. "You owe me."

He laughed. "Seems reasonable. I'd say Birdie owes you too, seeing as how you took that bolt for her, and when they got that thing out of you, they found silver embedded in the shaft. It would have done serious damage to everyone's favorite werewolf."

"Wow." Desi's eyes widened slowly. "Birdie's a werewolf."

"Yep." He was doing his best not to laugh, but Desi under the influence of anesthesia was highly entertaining.

Desi settled back into her pillow a little more.

"You okay? Comfortable?"

"Yeah." A long second went by. "How's my hair?"

"Crazy, but beautiful." Just like her.

The lopsided smile appeared briefly before being replaced by a more serious expression. "Did you talk to that gargoyle protecting Sam? Tell him everything is okay now?"

"Not yet. With everything going on, it slipped my mind."

"I can text her." She started patting the bed with her free hand. "Where's my phone?"

"I have no idea, but I'll take care of it. I'll call Harlan as soon as I leave here."

"Am I going with you?"

"Not tonight, sorry."

She frowned. "Do I have to spend the night here?"

"Yes. Dr. Navarro just wants to keep you overnight as a precaution."

Her eyes narrowed and she waved her finger at him. "What about you?"

He squinted in confusion. "What about me?"

"You were full of laudanum. She should watch you as a precaution."

"Ah, that. I'm fine."

Desi looked unconvinced. "You sure?"

"Yes, I promise."

Her bottom lip wobbled. "I was so worried about you."

"I never had a doubt someone would find me." Her show of emotion touched him. Maybe it was just the pain meds making her so open with him, but he wanted to grab her hand and kiss her and tell her everything was going to be all right. He couldn't. But he wanted to. Just didn't seem like the thing to do with the divorce papers heavy in his jacket pocket. He made himself laugh. "Okay, that's a lie. I totally thought I was a goner."

"You did?"

He blew out a hard sigh. "I think I have a much better understanding of what you went through on that island."

She nodded slowly, staring at the blanket, her gaze distant and a little sad.

Had he brought up bad memories? He hadn't meant to. Maybe now was the right time to give her what she wanted. Maybe that would help. He reached into his jacket and pulled out the folded paperwork and a pen and laid them on her lap. "Hey, I brought the papers with me. All you have to do is sign and you can be a free woman. That should make you happy, right?"

Her gaze shifted to the documents. "Papers?"

"To finalize our divorce. I've already signed them."

She burst out crying.

Horrified by whatever had just happened, he stepped back. "Are you in pain? Should I call the nurse? I can get the doctor if you—"

"I don't want to get divorced," she sobbed. "I love you, you stupid man."

His mouth opened, and for a moment, his lower jaw just hung there while his brain seemed to process her words with the same operating speed he'd had while on the laudanum. "I…what? But you said you couldn't…and I thought…"

"I know what I said. I can't be married again. I can't be in love. But I am in love. With you." She wiped at her eyes with her free hand. "When I thought I was going to lose you, it felt like my life was ending. For all my can'ts, it still happened. I fell in love with you anyway because you're amazing and kind and wonderful. How could I not?" Another sob shuddered through her. "I'm too late, aren't I? You don't love me anymore, do you?" She groaned like her heart was breaking. "I ruined everything."

He leaned in, slid his hands through her hair and kissed her. Hard. Until the sobbing stopped and a different kind of sound came out of her. Only then did he release her. "Desdemona Valentine, I love you with all my heart. I never stopped loving you. Will you please do me the honor of staying married to me?"

She laughed, the sound soothing every pain he'd ever felt. "Are you serious?"

"As a heart attack. Although I realize we are once again embarking in a nuptial direction while you are under the influence of mood-altering substances. Should I wait until you're off the pain meds?"

"No." Her face went gravely serious. "I am fully aware of what you're doing."

"But what about what *you're* doing?"

"That too."

"I hope so." He kissed her again, just a soft, quick brush of his mouth on hers to seal the deal. But when he backed away, she looked sad again. "What's wrong, darling?"

"Did you sell my ring?"

He dug into his other jacket pocket and pulled out a small velvet box. He'd been planning to see

Willa about that very thing, especially since he'd expected Desi to sign the divorce papers. He popped the box open. "You mean this ring?"

She gasped. "Outside of you, it's the most beautiful thing I've ever seen."

He laughed and took it from the box. "I like you on pain meds. You're very gushy." Then he slipped it on her finger.

She held her hand up. "I am never taking this off again."

He brushed a curl off her forehead. "You know, if we're going to do this, we should do it right. Have another ceremony. Here in town. One where neither one of us is intoxicated until after the vows."

She nodded. "So your family can be there?"

"Yes. And you can invite Sam and whoever else you like. What do you think?"

"Let's do it." She flung her uninjured arm around his neck. "I love you, Jules. Like crazy. I'm sorry I put you through so much hell. Do you forgive me? How on earth did you stick around when I was so awful?"

"I never thought you were awful." He kissed the tip of her beautiful nose. "And let's just say, despite what my family might think about me, I'm no quitter."

She sighed and nuzzled her cheek against his. "I want to have your babies."

He barked out a laugh that was half shock, half desire. "Well now, I'm going to have to get the name of these meds—"

The door opened and Birdie strode in. She had a basket of flowers in one hand. "There's my girl. How are you feeling, Desi?"

Desi shoved her hand toward Birdie. "We're married again!"

Birdie stopped short. "Again? So you *were* married?" Then her eyes widened. "Is that an engagement ring or a skating rink on your hand? Lands, child, that is a boulder."

Desi grinned. "Jules has good taste."

"I'll say." Birdie put the flowers on the window sill, then hitched her purse straps higher up on her shoulder and approached the bed. "All right, you two, tell me everything."

They'd just about finished explaining why they were already married when a second werewolf joined them.

Sheriff Merrow stuck his head into the room. "Up for a visitor?"

Birdie turned toward her nephew. "Hank! Did you know these two were married?"

He glanced at Julian like he was fishing for a clue as to the right answer to that question.

Birdie sighed. "You did. I know that look. That's why you called her Mrs. Ellingham. Did everyone in town know but me?"

"No," Julian assured her. "Just my family and even that was unintentional. I told Hank because he was helping me investigate."

Hank stepped into the room and hooked his thumbs into his utility belt. "About that investigation…"

Julian nodded. "Let's talk outside."

The two men stepped into the hall.

Hank cleared his throat. "We have to do something with the hunter."

"I know. Problem is she's human."

"Uh-huh."

Julian frowned and glance toward Desi's closed door. "I need to talk to my family about this. Can you give me a day?"

"I've got her in holding. You can have all the time you want."

"Thanks. I'll be in touch soon." Right after he called a family meeting. The hunter was too much of a danger to just be turned loose, but charging a human with a crime against a supernatural was sticky business.

She had to be punished, but more importantly, she had to be prevented from doing it again.

After being released from the hospital the following morning, Desi had expected a leisurely day at home with her husband. Instead, she showered, changed, and headed off with him to his grandmother's for a very important family meeting.

She sat on a loveseat next to him and looked around the library, stunned by how things had turned out. It was a little surreal to be back in Elenora Ellingham's mansion, especially since Desi was now a permanent Ellingham. The reality of the pain in her shoulder kept her grounded, but the subtle throbbing meant the wound was healing, which was good, because there was nothing fashionable about the stupid blue sling she was strapped into.

His whole family was gathered, just as they had been for the dinner. A family that she now really and truly belonged to. Getting used to that was going to take some time, but that was just fine. She was deliriously happy, and if she was honest, a little bit scared, about her commitment to Julian, but that was life, wasn't it? Risk and reward were paired for a reason. You didn't get one without the other.

And Julian had proven beyond a shadow of a doubt that he was the right man for her. He and Alonso might share some characteristics, but those were surface traits only. Julian was nothing like the man she'd once considered the destroyer of her life. She still hated Alonso, but she finally had begun to see him as strictly a part of her past.

It was hard to think of him any other way when her future was so stunningly bright. And he was ash in the wind.

"We have a very serious issue to deal with, which is why I've called you all here," Julian began.

Alice Bishop glanced at him, then went back to the needlepoint she was working on. She'd chosen a seat in the far corner of the room. Plenty close to listen, but far enough away that her presence might be forgotten. She was crafty, that one.

"Agreed," Sebastian said. "This business with the hunter is unacceptable. We cannot have her roaming free. Not when she's been exposed to the truth of Nocturne Falls."

Tessa looked at him. "Do you think that's the case?"

"I do," Julian said. "She saw Birdie shift. It was unavoidable. And she knows Desi and I are vampires."

"Yes," Desi added. "But she might not know that the town is a haven for supernaturals."

Hugh shook his head. "We cannot risk it."

"Worse than that..." Julian scowled. "She threatened George."

Delaney's eyes went white hot in anger. "What?"

"How dare she," Elenora cried. "How did she even find out about him?"

He nodded. "She went through my things, found his picture in my wallet."

Delaney inched forward on her seat, her body rigid with rage. "What did she say?"

"Just general threats, really. But enough that we have to find a way to put an end to her hunting days."

Elenora jaw was taut with resolution. "You know what I think."

Sebastian sighed. "We cannot kill a human, Grandmamma. It's not the 1800s anymore. These things aren't so easily hidden. And it breaks the laws of the council."

Hugh nodded. "It would also set a dangerous precedent."

She rolled her eyes. "We are powerful creatures. If we cannot use those powers to protect ourselves, what good are they?"

"And risk starting a war?" Sebastian shook his head. "We are not going to kill the human. There are other ways to use our power."

Elenora's lip curled. "She threatened my grandson. She is not going free."

Alice cleared her throat. "There is a spell we might try."

They all turned to look at her. Elenora waved her forward. "Speak up, woman. Explain."

Alice put her handiwork aside, and joined them. "The sanguim vocat. It's a complicated spell and comes with its own dangers, but if it worked…" She shrugged.

Elenora's perfect brows lifted. "In the king's English, please, Alice."

"Supernatural bloodlines aren't as pure as they used to be. A lot of humans carry DNA they know nothing about. Strands of the fae, a trace of nymph, a little remnant of a shifter who once picked a leaf from the family tree. All they're aware of is the full moon gives them energy, or they can tell when a storm is coming, or they know someone's about to call before the phone rings. They don't know the why or the how of it."

Elenora's squint seemed like a lessening of her patience. "And where does this spell come in?"

Alice stuck her hands into the pockets of her cardigan. "Sanguim vocat roughly means blood calls to blood. And it is, in fact, blood magic. A gray area by most coven standards, but this is a special situation."

"I'll say." Delaney crossed her arms. "What does this spell do exactly?"

Alice continued. "It pulls out the supernatural threads in a human's DNA, finds the strongest one, and strengthens it until it's no longer a shadow in the background."

Julian let out a small exhale. "You mean to turn her into a supernatural."

Alice nodded. "If the spell works, yes."

"No," Desi said. "That only gives her more power to fight with. I can't fathom how this could be a good thing."

A slow, understanding smile broke across Elenora's face. "Because, my darling daughter-in-law, if the hunter becomes a supernatural and then raises her hand to another vampire, she does so under a new set of laws. Being human will no longer protect her from the consequences."

Julian took Desi's hand, his eyes on Alice. "What do you need to make this spell happen and how quickly can it begin?"

If Desi had any doubts about the power the Ellingham family wielded in Nocturne Falls, they were banished a few hours later as she stood with

Julian in front of a heavy steel door in an alley in the center of town. They'd parked in a nearby lot. "Where are we going again?"

He swiped a card through a reader. A small click announced access had been granted. "The Basement."

"I feel like we've spent enough time in one of those to last us a while."

"It's not that kind of basement." He winked at her. "C'mon."

She followed him onto the dim landing, then he turned and closed the door behind them. Running lights along the stair treads blinked on. They headed down. At the bottom, the passageway opened onto a bright white hall that felt vaguely industrial.

"What is this place?" There were lines on the floor like a road might have. Granted, the space was big enough to drive a vehicle in.

"This is the Basement. It's an employees-only area of Nocturne Falls. We use it to allow workers safe passage, for storage, for access to things like the gargoyle fountain, and in case of zombie apocalypse."

She whipped around. "What?"

He laughed. "Just seeing if you were listening. We also have some holding cells down here for cases that are beyond what the sheriff's department can handle."

"Is the hunter down here?"

"She is, but it's more about performing the spell in a safe space than being able to hold her. She's human, the station can handle that no problem, but Alice wanted to use one of the secure rooms in case the spell doesn't go as smoothly as it should."

Desi nodded. "I see. I hope that's not the case."

"Me too, but I appreciate her being cautious." He tipped his head to the left side of the passage before them. "We have a little farther to go."

Three minutes later, Julian unlocked yet another door and they walked into a large, nearly empty space. Nearly empty because despite there being almost no furniture in the room, there were plenty of people. Including Alice and the hunter, who was restrained in a chair that seemed made for that purpose. All the rest in the room, save Julian's brothers, were female supernaturals from town, something Desi knew because of Alice's explanation of the spell. The witch had told them that female contributions would be the most effective.

It was impressive that each one in the room had answered the call for help without hesitation.

Julian nodded to Alice. "Is this everyone?"

"Now that you're here, yes."

The hunter was blindfolded and her hands were secured to the arms of the chair, but her chin was raised defiantly. "I demand to see my lawyer."

Julian walked over to her and pushed the blindfold up. Then he leaned down so they were eye to eye. "Doesn't work like that, sweetheart. You wanted to be a vampire hunter, well, welcome to vampire justice."

"Get away from me, bloodsucker. Touch me and I'll—"

"You'll what? Without your tranquilizers and crossbow, you're at my mercy." He laughed. "You should be very thankful the vampire council has strict rules that govern dealing with humans, or you'd be in a world of hurt right now."

She sneered and looked past him at Desi. "I see your girlfriend survived. Too bad. I thought that shot had gone straight through your heart."

Desi opened her mouth to tell the hunter where the next bolt could go, but Julian moved into the hunter's path, blocking her line of sight. "That's my *wife* you're talking about murdering."

"So?" she snarled.

He straightened. "Take a good look around you."

She did, glancing left and right at the semicircle of women gathered. "Yeah?"

He raised his brows. "You're the only human in this room."

Her sneer melted away, and her breathing got a little shallower. "I don't believe you."

He shrugged. "You don't have to."

He walked back to Desi and kissed her cheek before giving Alice a nod. "Your show now."

"Thank you, Julian."

He squeezed Desi's hand, then went to join his brothers near the wall.

Alice stepped forward, holding a wooden bowl and a long, thin wooden needle. "We are gathered here to cast the sanguim vocat. If you are not here voluntarily, or have changed your mind about participating, I ask that you leave. There will be no ill will."

No one moved.

"I'm not here voluntarily," the hunter spat out.

Alice raised her hand at the woman. "Silence, human."

The hunter's mouth snapped closed. Judging by the shock in the woman's eyes, Desi guessed Alice had thrown a little magic at her and helped her shut her mouth.

Alice faced the women who'd come to help, her back to the hunter. "A drop of blood will be required from each of you, but you have my word it will be consumed in the casting. None of your blood will be left behind."

The group nodded in understanding.

"I ask that each of you come forward and state who you are and what you are so that the subject of this spell might better understand the world she lives in and those she threatens."

Desi didn't hesitate. She walked up to Alice and held out her right hand. "I am Desdemona Valentine Ellingham and I am a vampire."

Alice pricked her finger with the wooden needle, then squeezed Desi's fingertip and a single bright red bead fell into the bowl.

Desi went back to her place in the semicircle, and the rest of the women lined up to follow.

"I'm Willa Iscove, fae."

"Jayne Frost, winter elf."

"And princess," Birdie added.

Jayne looked back and shook her head.

"Ramona Mabine, and I'm a brownie."

"I'm Norma Turnbuckle, and proud to say I'm a hobbit."

"I am Monalisa Devlin, and I am a will o' the wisp."

"Birdie Caruthers." Birdie looked around Alice at the hunter. "I'm the werewolf you tried to kill, you silly girl."

"Imari Zephara. Jinn. Retired."

At that one, Desi turned to glance at Julian. She raised her brows. He nodded back as if to say, *Yes, really.*

The women kept coming.

"Pandora Williams. Realtor and witch."

"I'm Undrea Seely and I'm a mermaid."

The hunter's eyes were wide, her mouth agape. Desi understood. The range of supernaturals in this town was staggering. And for them to all be so comfortable with each other and willing to help on such short notice…it almost made her weep to think of how incredible living here could be.

She might finally have some friends, as sad as that statement sounded even in her own head.

"I am Tessa Blythe, librarian, valkyrie and soon to be sister-in-law to Desdemona." She, too, peered past Alice to address the hunter. "You need to understand that we protect our own."

Tessa came back to stand beside Desdemona as the last few women gave their contributions. Tessa gave Desi a small, reassuring smile.

Desi smiled back and mouthed the words *thank you*.

A thought that had been slowly forming began to solidify even further. Regardless of what happened in the next few minutes, she wanted to be with Julian. Physically be with him. As in live in the same time zone.

Vegas, Desi realized, no longer felt like home.

Julian stood between his brothers, watching Alice with great curiosity. The witch had never used her skills in front of any of them before, so this was quite the occasion. It also felt like a huge gift from Alice. She wasn't one to do much publicly, preferring the quiet life of being Elenora's assistant and confidant.

To see her now in such full command of things was unusual. It also softened his attitude toward her. He made himself promise to be nicer to her from here on out.

Alice lifted the bowl as the last woman took her place in the semicircle. "The blood has been gathered. Your involvement here will not be forgotten. Thank you all. I wish you a good day. You are free to return to your day."

The women left quietly, most with a nod to Desi or quick pat on her good arm. A minute later, only

Desi, Tessa, Alice, Hugh and Sebastian remained in the room with Julian.

Alice addressed them. "This could take some time."

Julian walked forward to stand beside Desi, putting his arm around her waist. "We've got lots of that."

Sebastian and Hugh nodded as they came forward as well.

Alice turned toward the hunter and whispered words over the bowl, then held it at arm's length.

Flames danced up from the wooden vessel, then disappeared to be replaced by a fat coil of red smoke. Alice blew the coil toward the hunter.

The woman twisted and turned, but the smoke enveloped her like a veil. She grunted, still struggling.

Alice waved her hand at the hunter, and the woman's mouth came open. She gasped, inhaling the smoke.

"Now," Alice said, straightening. "We wait."

Abigail choked and spat like she was trying to get the smoke out, but Julian knew that wasn't going to happen. Alice's magic was strong.

But fifteen minutes later, they were still waiting, still watching, and Julian was now wondering if the magic would work at all.

A few questioning glances were exchanged, but they stayed as they were. Every breath the hunter took was scrutinized for some sign of supernatural emerging.

Finally, with an hour gone, Alice motioned for them to follow her out of the room. In the hall, with the door shut, she shook her head. "There is no supernatural in her, or the spell would have drawn it out by now."

Julian let out a few choice words.

"I told Delaney I'd call as soon as I knew something," Hugh said. "But this isn't the news I wanted to share. Delaney might kill the woman herself."

Sebastian's eyes narrowed. "Or Grandmamma will."

Tessa planted her hands on her hips. "I could pull my sword now and do the job."

"Wait." Desi put her hands up. "If you kill this woman, which I totally understand wanting to, you run the risk of bringing the wrath of the Talisman Club down on Nocturne Falls. I can't stand to think of this incredible place ruined by fear and fighting."

Julian took her hand, lacing his fingers through hers. "I agree, my love, but I will not have you or George or anyone else I care about in danger. We have to deal with this hunter in a way that puts an end to her awful ways."

"Especially now that so many in our town have revealed themselves to her," Sebastian added.

"I agree." Desi smiled. "And I think I know just how to do that." She looked at Alice. "I know you are a very powerful witch."

Alice nodded. "I am."

Desi continued. "One of the techs in my show is a witch. She casts the main illusions we use, mostly the pyrotechnical stuff, but also a few others. Can you cast illusions too? I don't mean to imply you can't, I just don't know enough about witches to know if you can all do that or not."

Alice took the question in stride. "No, not all witches can. Illusions aren't a problem for me, however. In fact, I have a book I can consult."

Desi's smile brightened. "In that case, I have an idea…"

It took them twenty-seven minutes to assemble everything they needed and get it set up. The process, which had required Sebastian to go to Elenora's for Alice's book and for Julian to run to the sheriff's department, had also resulted in one more audience member, namely Birdie. Fortunately, she was happy to act as the electronics manager once she was brought up to speed.

She was bent over Helsing's camera and tripod setup. Finally, she straightened and gave them a thumbs-up. "All right, we're good to go here."

"You're sure it's connected to the laptop as well?" Desi asked. "I mean, I see the cable, but it'll record to the laptop?"

"Yes," Birdie reassured her. "And it'll instantly be saved to a folder in my cloud, which I've already shared with the Ellinghams and the sheriff's department. There will be plenty of backups." She looked at the hunter. "This isn't something that is ever going to disappear, understand?"

The hunter's eyes narrowed. "I don't know what you freaks think you're doing, but nothing is going to stop me. As soon as I get free, I'm coming back here and I'm bringing a whole crew of hunters with me."

Desi sighed and shook her head. "Anytime you want to start, Alice."

The witch looked up from a small spell book she'd had Sebastian retrieve from Elenora's. "Oh, are we recording?"

Birdie pressed a button. "We are now. I can edit it down into smaller videos once it's all done."

"All right, then," Alice said. "Almost ready. Just need to finish this page. Must get this right." She muttered a few words under her breath, like she was practicing them.

Julian nodded. "Take your time." Desi's idea was a good one, but it had to be convincing or they'd be no better off than they were.

Birdie bent to look through the camera's viewfinder again. "Oh, wow, Alice. That is very convincing."

They all turned to look at Helsing. Her head was back and the muscles in her neck were straining with the effort of what appeared to be a shift of some kind. Small gray hairs sprouted along her jawline and forehead as her face elongated into a muzzle. She growled and the sound was eerily inhuman, but dead-on for a werewolf.

"Hell's bells, Bishop," Sebastian whispered. "You did it."

Alice shook her head as the hunter's transformation continued. "I haven't started the spell yet."

Julian began to laugh, because his life was too good not to. "So she's actually a werewolf?"

Alice nodded. "I believe so. The threads must have been so buried or so thin, the calling spell just took longer to work than it should have."

"This is perfect." He clapped his hands. "You're a shifter, Helsing. A real, live supernatural. How does that feel? You are now one of the creatures you've dedicated your life to eradicating. You're going to need a new profession, because if I get the slightest whiff you're still at it, not only will we release this video showing what you really are, but you will have a host of supernaturals hunting you down in turn."

He leaned in. "And human law no longer applies to you."

She snapped and growled at him.

He couldn't stop smiling. "Oh, and better avoid silver from here on out, or you're going to give yourself some nasty burns."

She leaned toward him, stressing the restraints holding her to the chair.

Sebastian and Hugh went to her sides and each took an arm before looking at Julian. He instantly understood. "The holding cells. Immediately."

"It's really over." Desi looked at Julian as they walked hand in hand into the lobby of the Excelsior. A wave of love and admiration washed through her, almost too much to bear. This amazing man was her husband.

"It really is," he answered. "Tomorrow, she'll be sent packing with info on how to contact the pack in Upstate New York. If she doesn't check in with the alpha in three days, she knows there will be an APB sent out to every supernatural organization in the US, and a week after that, the video will be uploaded to the Talisman Club forum."

They gave Freddy a wave as they walked to the elevator.

Desi pushed the button. "She has no choice but to toe the line."

The doors opened and they got on.

"It's actually a huge gift," Julian said. "And not

one she deserved. When she figures out how amazing her new life is, she'll probably understand how generous we were."

"You really think she'll get to that point?"

"I do. Maybe not immediately, but someday. You can't be a supernatural and not have a greater appreciation for how wonderful and precious life is."

She smiled at him as the elevator slowed to a stop. "I don't think I felt that way until I met you."

He grinned as they walked through the open doors and into the penthouse foyer. "Is that so?"

"It is. I owe you. For centuries, I blamed Alonso for destroying my life. And he did. But what I didn't realize was that someday I'd get that life back. I have you to thank for that." She kissed him. "Thank you for not giving up on me."

He kissed her back. "So we're even, then. You saved my life and I saved yours. What do you think?"

"I think that sounds about right. There's just one little problem we have yet to address."

He punched in the key code and let them into the penthouse. "What's that?"

She gave him her slyest, sultriest smile, which wasn't easy for a woman with one arm in a sling. "We haven't really had a proper wedding night yet."

His jaw went slack. "No, uh, no, we haven't. But

you're injured and all, so I thought…" He ran a hand through his hair. "I can be very careful."

She snickered and started backing toward the hall that led to the bedroom. "Darling, we're vampires. We mend."

He followed, unbuttoning his shirt and stumbling over the shoes he was stepping out of. "I love being a vampire."

She raked an appreciative gaze over him, designed to incite him further. "Oh, you're about to love a whole lot of things."

EPILOGUE

ONE WEEK LATER

"Do you, Julian Fitzwalter Ellingham, take this woman again to be your lawfully wedded wife?"

Julian smiled at Desi. She looked like an angel in her beautiful white gown, and it was great to see her out of her sling, her shoulder nearly healed. But to think he was already married to her felt like more than he deserved. "I do."

The officiant turned to Desi. "And do you, Desdemona Clarke Valentine, take this man again to be your lawfully wedded husband?"

She blinked back tears. "I do," she whispered.

"Then by the power vested in me by the great state of Georgia, I hereby proclaim you husband and wife. You may kiss the bride."

The small crowd cheered as Julian did just that. He did his best to keep it PG, but there wasn't a part of him that didn't want to whisk this woman back to their penthouse for very un-PG activities. Which, as it turned out, they were very good at. But his grandmother had gone to a lot of effort and expense to make this renewal and reception happen, so he restrained himself as best he could.

At last, he released Desi from the kiss, and they turned to face their audience of family and friends. Julian hugged his bride close, the scent of her familiar orange blossom perfume wrapping him in joy. He addressed the small crowd. "Thank you all for coming. And for being a part of this day. While it's true that we've been married for a little over eight months, I think I speak for Desi and me when I say our life together has only just started. And we're so very glad you could join us in that new start."

He glanced at her, and she nodded, eyes shining bright.

He kissed her cheek before looking at the crowd again, then he raised their clasped hands over his head. "Let's party!"

Music swelled through the great hall and servers streamed in with trays of champagne and finger foods for the cocktail hour Elenora had planned. There would be dinner and dancing into the wee hours to follow, because when Elenora did something, she did it in grand style. This occasion was certainly no exception.

Speaking of his grandmother, Julian saw her in

the crowd and nudged Desi. "Do you see what you've done? You made my grandmother cry."

"Maybe she just saw the bill for the catering."

He snickered. "She has only herself to blame for telling you there was no budget."

"True." Desi flattened her lips down like she was trying to stifle a grin. "And I hate to tell you this, but I'm sure it won't be the last time I give her a reason to be weepy."

"I'm okay with that." He laughed. "I love you."

"I love you, too. And I have a little gift for you." She reached into the bodice of her wedding dress and pulled out a key.

He took it, trying to figure out what it was for. "It's not to any car I recognize."

"Because it's not to a car. It's to my place in the Skye Towers. And that's only half of the gift."

"Oh? Thank you very much." He tucked the key into his jacket pocket. "What's the other half?"

"In about a month, when Sam's capable of being back at work, I'm turning the show over to her. She's perfectly capable of taking the lead, and frankly, she's earned it."

A spark lit within him, but he wasn't sure he understood enough to let it fully combust. "Are you saying…what *are* you saying?"

"I want to live here with you. In Nocturne Falls." Her brows suddenly pulled together. "That's all right, isn't it?"

"All right?" He let out a whoop that turned heads. "Yes, it's all right. It's better than all right." He stilled for a moment. "Wait. Are you sure? That's a lot to give up. You've put so much time and effort into that show and—"

She pressed a finger to his lips. "And I'd have to take a hiatus anyway to film the TV show."

"Only for a few weeks. You're talking about giving it up entirely."

"Not exactly. See, you're going to build me a theater as part of the new lakefront retail space. I'll do a show or two a week until..." She shrugged and laughed.

"Until what?"

"Until the first baby. Then we'll reassess. Deal?"

"Deal." Babies. His head spun. "I'll call the surveyor right now and we'll get that thing started."

She laughed and patted his chest. "How about we concentrate on our wedding reception and you call tomorrow?"

Happiness bubbled up in him. It was overwhelming and magical and the most alive he'd felt since he'd been turned. "Yep, much better plan."

"Good. Let's go dance." She grabbed his hand and they started down the dais toward the rest of the swaying crowd.

"Sad that you have to be both brains and beauty

in this relationship." He sighed with great drama. "I shall endeavor to do better, my darling."

"You're doing just fine."

He pulled her into his arms, turning them into the rhythm of the waltz with a few easy steps. "I appreciate your support. We make an excellent team."

She nodded. "Yes, we do. Marrying you was the best drunken accident that's ever happened to me."

He wiggled his brows, letting go of her to snag two glasses of champagne from a passing server. He held one out to her. "Well, now, drink up. The night's still young. And I do love a challenge."

Want to be up to date on new books, new audiobooks and other fun stuff from me? Sign-up for my newsletter on my website, www.kristenpainter.com. No spam, just news (sales, freebies, releases, you know, all that jazz.)

If you loved the book and want to help the series grow, tell a friend about the book and take time to leave a review!

Other Books by Kristen Painter

PARANORMAL ROMANCE

Nocturne Falls series
The Vampire's Mail Order Bride
The Werewolf Meets His Match
The Gargoyle Gets His Girl
The Professor Woos The Witch
The Witch's Halloween Hero – short story
The Werewolf's Christmas Wish – short story
The Vampire's Fake Fiancée
The Vampire's Valentine Surprise – short story
The Shifter Romances the Writer
The Vampire's True Love Trials – short story
The Dragon Finds Forever
The Vampire's Accidental Wife

Can't get enough Nocturne Falls?
Try the Nocturne Falls Universe books.
http://kristenpainter.com/nocturne-falls-universe/
New stories, new authors, same Nocturne Falls world!

Sin City Collectors series
Queen of Hearts
Dead Man's Hand
Double or Nothing
Box set

STANDALONE PARANORMAL ROMANCE

Dark Kiss of the Reaper
Heart of Fire
Recipe for Magic
Miss Bramble and the Leviathan

COZY PARANORMAL MYSTERY

Miss Frost Solves a Cold Case – A Nocturne Falls Mystery
Miss Frost Ices the Imp – A Nocturne Falls Mystery
Miss Frost Saves the Sandman – A Nocturne Falls Mystery

URBAN FANTASY

The House of Comarré series:
Forbidden Blood
Blood Rights
Flesh and Blood
Bad Blood
Out For Blood
Last Blood

Crescent City series:
House of the Rising Sun
City of Eternal Night
Garden of Dreams and Desires

Nothing is completed without an amazing team.

Many thanks to:

Cover design: Janet Holmes
Interior formatting: Author E.M.S
Editor: Joyce Lamb
Copyedits/proofs: Marlene Engel

About the Author

Kristen Painter is a little obsessed with cats, books, chocolate, and shoes. It's a healthy mix. She loves to entertain her readers with interesting twists, entertaining stories and unforgettable characters. She currently writes the best-selling paranormal romance series, Nocturne Falls. The former college English teacher can often be found all over social media where she loves to interact with readers. Visit her web site to learn more.

www.kristenpainter.com

Printed in Great Britain
by Amazon